An Unattractive Vampire

An Unattractive Vampire

Jim McDoniel

Sword & Laser

Published by Inkshares Inc., San Francisco, California, as part of the Sword & Laser Collection
www.inkshares.com

Edited and designed by Girl Friday Productions
www.girlfridayproductions.com

Cover design by David Drummond

ISBN-13: 9781941758649
ISBN-10: 1941758649
e-ISBN: 9781941758632

Library of Congress Control Number: 2015944401

First edition

Printed in the United States of America

To George and Margaret McDoniel, who thankfully weren't too freaked out by a three-year-old whose favorite color was black.

Chapter 1

The rising full moon cast its sensual yellow glow through the balcony window of the oldest, tallest, and most obnoxiously pink house in the town of Shepherd's Crook. If moonlight could express surprise, it would have done so at this most unnatural occurrence. The curtains of this particular window were, as a rule, always kept closed to thwart the Peeping Toms the room's occupant assumed would be trying to catch her changing. Tonight, though, the hangings remained parted, allowing light and shadow to dance merrily over a sight the neighborhood boys—who usually *did* try to catch her changing—would kick themselves for missing.

A woman lay on a bed in the middle of the room. To say she slept would demean both her beauty and the act she was engaged in. To merely sleep would be to lie down and rest, perhaps drooling on a pillow and mussing one's hair. However, in this bed, with this girl, not a hair was out of place and no saliva was to be found. Her wavy blond locks fell about her head and shoulders in a perfect cascade, being buoyed rather than crushed by the pure white pillows around her. Her closed eyes were just the lightest shade of purple, her eyelashes long and dark, and her lips a welcoming, moist crimson. One pale arm rested neatly over the sheet that covered her; the other stretched leisurely above her head. Her comely figure was pleasantly curved, outlined beneath the white silk sheet. The whole effect was topped off by the faintest hint of cinnamon in the air and the haunting sensuality of the moonlight glow.

This girl did not sleep; she slumbered.

There was movement outside the old pink house. The doors to a long-disused storm cellar creaked open, seemingly by themselves. A single cloud passed before the moon, and when it had gone, a new shadow loomed blacker and more substantial than the gloom around it. With fingers spread, two arms lengthened out of the darkness, more tangled and bent than the silhouettes of the tree branches they crossed. The spectre stretched across the lawn, past the windows, the sides, the door . . . and stopped.

A sign hung on the door. The shadow read it, following each word with one crooked finger. When it had reached the end, the figure looked up at the second-floor window, beyond which lay the beautiful young woman, and then reread the notice more carefully. A smile spread across pale lips, only slightly ahead of a dry black tongue. Bony hands with sharp-nailed claws rubbed against each other in greedy anticipation. Dead gray eyes directed their gaze upward again.

Inside the room, the moonlight dulled slightly as a cold mist drifted up from below. All manner of horrifying shapes wisped in and out of existence in this eldritch fog as it swirled and funneled its way toward the window. Drifting over the balcony railing, it crashed against the glass and began to seep into the room beyond. Silence dropped over the entire house.

Creaky floorboards fell silent. Ticking clocks froze. The omnipresent hum of electronic appliances retreated. Even the girl's breathing softened, growing shallower, almost as if held.

The last bit of vapor trickled in, quickly rising to form the tall dark shadow from outside. With a certain air of relish, it languidly made its way across the room. At its approach, the girl stirred. Her body stretched ever so slightly, exposing her neck a bit more. Her heart pounded in her chest. Her lips, so red and luscious, puckered slightly.

Gray lips, as far from luscious as it is possible to be, parted once more, revealing a grin of jagged, broken teeth. Its ears filled with the beat of her heart and the rush of her blood. Now was the moment it had waited so long for. It leaned down, ready to feed.

The young woman's eyes flickered, then parted, then stared up at the monstrous sight before them. She screamed and reached for her pillow. The shadow lunged for her neck, laughing as it did so. And just before its vision went black, it thought: *Everything is going according to plan.*

Chapter 2

Some three hundred years earlier, in the newest, tallest, and not-at-all pink house near the village of Shepherd's Crook, Yulric Bile—The Curséd One, the Devil's Apprentice, He Who Worships the Slumbering Horrors—stood by a familiar balcony window, letting his gaze wander across the landscape toward the approaching lights.

"Ah. They've formed a mob."

A silence spread among his minions, slowly growing in strength until he could all but hear the panicked shrieks echoing in their minds. Bile smiled; their fear amused him. With an absentminded wave of his hand, he gave the nine cloaked figures leave to make a terrified dash for the window. From the other side of the room, Yulric had the perfect view of lumpy bodies in gaudy black robes, shoving and jostling for a view of their impending doom.

For the record, their rather garish attire had not been his idea. Puritans were very specific on what constituted true evil. Black robes with arcane symbols for a start. Spectres that pinched people in their sleep. Naked dancing. Lots of naked dancing. Yulric didn't pretend to understand where this notion had come from, but they were insistent, so every new moon, he took them to dance bare-assed under the stars. The know-it-all Pastor Collins—third from the right, wringing his hands, and crying—insisted they should be dancing during the *full* moon, but Yulric had put his foot down. After all, he had to watch the pathetic, sagging display.

And for what? He had spent months working on this little cabal—corrupting them, teaching them the ways of madness and brutality, binding them to his will—and yet he doubted any were enthralled enough to even slow his enemy down. He suspected they would simply flee and hope no one noticed them. This was hindsight, though. At the time, he had had little choice in minions, as the native tribespeople knew enough to run screaming anytime he approached.

Ah well, there is always the other option, Yulric thought, soaking in the ever more frantic hysteria of his followers. *I wonder who will ask.*

"Master?"

Of course.

"Master, what shall we do?"

Yulric opened his cloudy, dead eyes, with their pin-sharp, narrow pupils, and turned his gaze to the eight hooded figures still huddled by the window. Mostly old, mostly fat, and all scared. Of course they had sent the sole woman in the group to ask the question they were all screaming at the top of their minds. They hoped her gentle voice would soothe him, or failing that, they hoped he would kill only her.

Yulric strode to the window, parting his followers as he went. Moonlight poured in behind him, casting his features into shadow. Except his eyes. They glowed eerily out of the darkness. "My followers," he began, "the time has come for me to die, as it has time and time again. From the ashes of my death"—sin and damnation! He hoped there wouldn't be ashes this time—"the dark lord shall resurrect me to new life."

He paused briefly to see if they were buying it. They weren't, but they faked it well, nodding and prostrating themselves before him. Only the woman refused to make an absurd display of devotion. Good for her.

He continued, "You, my faithful, need not follow me directly. You are free to go."

"Oh, thank God," cried one of the hooded figures, likely the inept Daniel Cartwright.

"Satan," another whispered to correct him. That was Pastor Collins.

"Right. I mean, oh, thank Satan," said the admonished cultist.

"Never fear, Master," bellowed a bombastic acolyte who could only be Jeremiah Phillips. "We shall patiently await your return. Right, Samuel?"

"Yes," answered the man's brother as he moved toward the exit. "And we shall spread your message of evil, decadence, and"—he was groping for the door handle now—"corruption."

"To the Master!" called Jeremiah Phillips.

"To the Master!" the others replied. They all turned to leave as Yulric spoke again.

"However . . ."

The most dreaded word in the English language washed over Yulric's followers.

Their hope dead, a silence fell over the room, one so thick you could scoop it out of the air and serve it for dessert. Trying to mask the horror on their faces, they turned back to him.

"I do . . . require a small service," he said. Eyes widened. Breathing halted. Two or three looked past their leader toward the approaching mob. Time was running short.

"To serve as a conduit for the power of darkness, to open the door for my eventual resurrection, I require the aid of a faithful servant. One of you must remain."

Thoughts sped through the robed Puritans in waves. The horrifying news that one of them had to stay began the swell, quickly replaced by the realization that *one* of them had to stay. Eyes darted left and right, picking out possible candidates while shielding themselves from candidacy. Then, almost in unison, an idea hit them, and they all turned to . . . her.

Anne Stevens. The girl with "opinions." Stubborn, head-strong, clever. She had joined not out of a desire to do evil but out of a desire to make at least a few decisions for herself. The men had always intended to blame her in the end. It was her fault, after all. Really, they had joined only to see her naked.

Anne looked straight ahead as their eyes bore into her. She wasn't happy about the situation, though she'd known it was coming. She was always the chosen to try new potions. To question the Master. To remove her robes first. Hands reached out, intending to push her forward, but she had had enough. No one was going to volunteer her. If she stayed behind, it was going to be her own choice, goddamn it. She gave herself extra points for blasphemy and stepped up. Several pairs of outstretched hands missed, and the men behind them toppled over.

"I shall stay," she said.

Behind her, the men applauded.

"Such courage, such devotion," proclaimed Jeremiah Phillips as he picked himself up off the ground. "Of course, as your most loyal servant, my place is naturally at your side. However, I cannot bring myself to deny young Mistress Stevens the chance to prove her commitment to your cause, and so I cede my place to her."

"Likewise," followed Pastor Collins. "Though, as your second in spiritual authority and natural successor, I find myself moved, and so step aside to let Mistress Stevens provide for your needs in this, your death and eventual resurrection."

The others followed suit, protesting that it was their right to remain behind while simultaneously renouncing said right so they wouldn't have to. Yulric only smiled, having known how this would all play out from the beginning. As one of his "advanced" age had seen many times, events had a way of repeating themselves. Rather than be bored by their reactions, however, Yulric found them quite enjoyable. Like hearing a favorite joke.

He took Anne by the shoulder and guided her to the door.

"Wait for me in the cellar," he told her. "I shall be there shortly."

With an air of determined resignation, she gave him a bow and stubbornly marched off to her fate. The men all watched her go, remembering better days when her naked body had brushed against theirs.

A door slammed shut, a key turned in a lock, and the men returned from their Anne-filled reminiscence.

"Now, where was I?" said Yulric Bile, slowly moving toward them. "Ah yes, I was about to release you."

◆　◆

In the cellar, Anne waited patiently, completely undisturbed by the bloodcurdling screams far above her. They had it coming, after all, the groping old bastards. She gave herself another point for vulgarity.

Eventually, the Master did appear, his face still blood-stained in places, despite obvious attempts to clean himself.

"You will want to change," he said, handing over her clothes. She took them and disrobed. She was not shy about it; though, even had she been, it would not have mattered. It had always surprised Anne how little attention the Master paid her naked form, which really was quite exquisite. It was *lithe, nubile, perky*—all sorts of words that Puritans disapproved of. Yet her body held no interest for Master Bile. She would have wondered about him, only he wasn't exactly chasing after the strapping young men of the village, either. It was almost as if such considerations were beneath him. Anne didn't understand, but then again, she was a Puritan: her entire existence revolved around sex, if only to condemn it.

She was just lacing her boot when the sound of breaking glass upstairs announced the arrival of the village mob.

"It is time," the Master whispered close to her ear.

A desperate little gasp escaped her lips. Her breath quickened. Her heart raced. Her very soul begged her to flee, but she refused. She had made her choice months ago, when she had followed the wolf into the woods and knelt, prostrate before this hellish creature.

Anne braced herself and summoned the remainder of her courage. "Whatever you wish, Master. My life is yours."

A moment passed.

"What are you talking about, silly girl?"

She opened her eyes to find her undead lord staring at her with a quizzical brow. The sound of the front door crashing down could be heard above them.

"Well, out with it," he pressed, in no apparent hurry. "What do you mean?"

"My life," she explained slowly, trying very hard not to condescend. "I give you my life, to aid in your resurrection."

"Oh. That," he scoffed. "That is nonsense."

"It is not nonsense. I am ready," she assured him, offended by his dismissal of her willing sacrifice.

He waved her off. "No, no. Not that. The resurrection. The resurrection is nonsense."

Anne opened her mouth. Anne closed her mouth. This news just didn't make any sense. It couldn't be true. It wasn't true. The deaths, the spells, the naked dancing—what had it all been for if not for the resurrection of the Master? Why all the games? Why all the lies? Why was he jumping into a hole in the cellar floor?

Anne didn't know what to say, and so, naturally, continued to argue her point. "But—"

Before being cut off. "I am immortal, silly girl. What need I with resurrection?"

"But the villagers. The—the witchfinder?" Anne shuddered merely at the mention. That man scared her, and she was not easily intimidated. The weak-willed men of the coven, God rest their souls—Anne deducted points for sentimentality—had been terrified of him.

Even the Master winced slightly. "Yes, I am aware of Master Martin's . . . thoroughness when it comes to his work. It is fortunate, therefore, that you got to me first." He turned to where Anne knelt beside the hole and removed a long wooden stake from beneath his robes. "It was you who drove this stake through my heart." He slowly plunged the spike into his chest, feeling his way around so it brushed just past the muscle in question. When that was done, he took a long, curved finger-nail and ran it deep across his throat. He then tore away the flesh from his neck with both hands, until much of it had been removed. He spoke again, his voice now a low, chittering rasp that somehow vibrated its way out of his skull. "And it was you who cut off my head."

Subterfuge did not come naturally to the Puritans. Even Anne, who was as clever as they came, sometimes had to have deceit spelled out for her. He stared at her pointedly until awareness dawned. "Ooooh," she sighed.

The Master smiled, patting her hands and face tenderly in order to get his blood on her. "Go. Bring them to my 'corpse.'"

Anne nodded and rose to leave. Something was still bothering her, though. A question she needed answered. The Master smiled and waved his hand, giving her leave to speak.

"Why me?" she asked. "You killed the others. Why spare my life?"

The Master considered this for a moment before shrugging. "The others were driven by lust. You yearned for power. That pleases me."

"I wanted freedom," she corrected.

He gave a dismissive wave. "As I said."

She was about to argue the point when a cheer went up outside.

"Go now," he commanded, "before they set fire to the house."

Anne curtsied and left to fetch the mob.

Yulric lay down in his grave, resting his head at such an angle, with the back against the wall and his chin on his chest, so as to make it appear disconnected. It would have been a strain were any of the muscles in his neck intact. As it was, only the still-connected spinal cord could give the game away, and that was easily hidden with a flimsy piece of skin. Done arranging himself, he folded his hands, affected a dead stare, and waited.

In his mind, Yulric smiled. Everything was going according to plan.

Chapter 3

Thunder. Fire. Pain. And then . . .

Yulric Bile, the thousand-year-old vampire, lay on his back surrounded by pink carpet. He was not entirely certain how he had found his way to the floor, only that it had hurt and he was not eager to repeat the experience. For now, he was content to remain where he was and stare up at the ceiling while he tried to remember the past few seconds. He'd misted his way through the window, glided across the floor, gone in for the kill, and then . . .

Somewhere beyond his feet, there was stirring. Despite a collapsed lung, Yulric sighed. He had to move. Lying in one convenient place was an invitation to his own demise. Without the use of muscle or gravity, Yulric floated up, turned toward the bed, and then . . .

A soft shag broke a surprising amount of his fall. Carpeting certainly had come quite a ways.

He lifted his head ever so slightly and received a glimpse of a scantily clad young woman, kneeling on her bed, holding silver in her hands. And then . . .

At least this time, the pain came at an angle. The force of whatever struck him managed to knock him onto his stomach. It also caused his jaw to fly off and bounce away beneath the bureau. No longer fettered by the confines of a traditional mouth, Yulric's tongue detected a dusty tang in the air; one he associated with sieges and sea battles.

"Is that a pistol?" The question came out as an incoherent garble of vowels. He had forgotten he currently did not have a jaw.

"Why won't you die?" came the reply as another shot rang out. This time Yulric was prepared, dissolving into a black mist. The bullet passed through him, shattering the window and lodging itself in the railing. Triumphant laughter erupted from the disembodied fog in the middle of the room, though a lack of pain wasn't really something worth celebrating.

Now what? thought the fog as it coalesced just this side of human form. On the one hand, Yulric did not want to be shot again. It wouldn't kill him, but it still hurt like hell. On the other, he was loath to pass up his first meal in ages.

A little prudence, perhaps? he concluded, disappointed. He had hoped to enjoy some primal gluttony before rational forethought took hold.

In an instant, the girl on the bed was engulfed in tendrils of smoke. They wrapped around her, not quite solid but more than air. She let out a gasp of desperation as she tried to bring her gun to bear. Darkness filled her vision. She prepared for the worst. And then . . .

◆ ◆

Amanda opened her eyes. The fog had once more taken form, a form that was absentmindedly clicking its reattached jaw into place and examining something smooth and silver. She looked down at her now-empty hands and gulped. Carefully, she moved from the edge of the bed, back toward the pillows. Without taking her eyes off the creature, she felt beneath them and came back rearmed with a spritzer bottle and butter knife.

"Get out of my room!" she demanded, her voice filled with a confidence she didn't much feel. The figure stopped looking down the barrel of the gun and focused on her, the strong, independent woman ready to make him damp and butter his toast. Old World politeness kept it from laughing outright in her face, but the patronizing smile sunk her self-assurance lower.

"I mean it," she said. She let out a spray of mist and turned the knife so it glinted in the moonlight.

He stared at her and sniffed, the air now filled with perfume of a very specific buttercup. He looked at the knife, finely polished and ready to spread, then at the weapon in his hand. He fumbled with it for a moment, pressing things at random until he managed to eject the clip. It clattered to the floor, and the figure knelt to examine the gun's death-filled payload. Its *silver* death-filled payload.

"You believe me a werewolf?" Yulric asked.

"Yes," Amanda answered.

The two of them stared at each other in silence.

"A werewolf?" he said again.

"Yes," she repeated.

"Me?" he asked incredulously.

"What do *you* think you are?" Amanda said.

"A vampyr," Yulric answered.

Amanda giggled. "I don't think so."

"'Tis true," he growled.

"Okay . . . ," she agreed condescendingly.

"I am!" he barked.

This time it was her turn to display the smug, patronizing smile. Amanda enjoyed the irony. Yulric failed to see it, since the situation was not particularly ironic.

"The sign downstairs gave a vampyr leave to enter this room. Why would a werewolf respond to an invitation so clearly meant for a vampyr?" asked the supposed vampire.

"Because werewolves hate vampires. Everybody knows that."

This was news to Yulric. He had always gotten on quite well with werewolves. They were good for a laugh, knew the latest drinking songs, and made for very convenient scapegoats.

"What makes you think I am a werewolf?" he inquired.

Spritzer bottle at the ready, she rattled off her list, "It's a full moon. Your clothes are in tatters. Your appearance is grotesque. Big claws, big ears, big teeth. *All the better to eat you with, my dear.*"

Amanda gave herself points for quipping under pressure. Her satisfaction, however, was short-lived under the unresponsive gaze of her assailant.

"All the better to eat you with?" she repeated. Nothing. "'Little Red Riding Hood'?"

"What does riding wear have to do with eating?" asked Yulric.

Now it was Amanda's turn to stare. Her hands dropped to her sides, the potential danger having been overcome by surprise. Not that it mattered. In Amanda's mind, nothing this stupid could possibly be dangerous.

"You don't know 'Little Red Riding Hood'?" she said in disbelief. *"Grimm's Fairy Tales?"*

Yulric did not respond.

"'Snow White'? 'Hansel and Gretel'? Violent tales watered down to make animated musicals?"

"Are we still discussing the red hood?" asked Yulric.

Amanda let out a huge sigh. "'Little Red Riding Hood,'" she quickly summarized, "a story of a little girl in the woods. She talks to a wolf. The wolf goes, eats her grandmother, and dresses in the old woman's clothing. The girl arrives. *What big teeth you have. The better to eat you with.* He eats her, too. Sometimes they escape. Moral, kiddies, don't talk to strangers. Or don't have sex. Depending on your age."

It took a while for the rattled-off story to sink in with Yulric. Even when he'd finished going over it in his mind, he had to ask, "And how is this pertinent?"

"It's a wolf," blurted a frustrated Amanda. "A wolf like a man. A werewolf. It's a werewolf story."

Amanda received no reply. Deep inside Yulric's mind, a heated debate raged. One side logical; the other side less so. One side pleased; the other outraged.

This is perfect, said the logical Yulric. *She thinks us a werewolf. Kill her and be done.*

We are not a werewolf, said the less logical Yulric.

I know we are not a werewolf, and you know we are not a werewolf, but this stupid girl does not know we are not a werewolf, so . . .

We are not *a werewolf,* said illogic.

But we could be, argued logic. *We could be a werewolf. Others will come and try to slay us, as she has, with these silver musket balls, which, while painful, yes, will not kill us. And so we continue.*

The less logical side did not have a response, so logic went on.

All those centuries, the escapes, the elaborately faked deaths, convincing entire continents that a stake through the heart was all anyone needed to do to kill a vampire. What was it for if not this?

"What, indeed?" Yulric mumbled to himself. The entire debate had taken but a moment, which was good, because the girl was already looking at him funny.

He tossed her the ammo clip.

"The silver musket balls did not kill me."

Musket balls? Amanda rolled a set of internal eyes in mockery. Determined to win this argument, she retorted, "They're probably fake."

He rushed her with such speed that she let out an involuntary squeak. His hand closed on hers and the spritzer bottle sprayed him full in the face. "The wolfsbane potion does not keep me at bay."

"I bought it at a Renaissance fair," she said, as if this explained everything.

"I transformed into mist."

She was far too stubborn to give in. "It could happen."

"Indeed. And this also could happen."

The light remained the same, yet shadows passed over him. His form contorted and twisted. Shoulders buckled. Hips sucked in. His entire body collapsed in on itself until finally, where once stood a six-foot-tall corpse, now flew a three-foot-long bat. It hovered in the air for a moment before soaring out the broken windows and into the night. Amanda ran after it, onto the balcony,[1] where she pondered the odds of a werewolf also being a werebat.

Yulric, meanwhile, flew through the night. Finally free after so long underground, he could not help but indulge himself, wheeling high through the air before diving low to the ground.

---

1. Making the evening of one twelve-year-old boy who'd gotten up for a glass of water.

He was the master of his domain. All the blood in all the veins from here to the horizon was his for the taking. He had the power. He had the will. Nothing could stop him.

And then . . .

Light. Screeching. Pain.

◆   ◆

Amanda found him early the next morning crawling back into the six-foot hole in her cellar, from which he'd emerged. Both his legs broken.

"What happened?" she asked.

He looked at her in wide-eyed terror. "There are . . . *things* out there."

He passed out. Amanda looked down at his tattered remains. This was definitely not going according to her plan.

Chapter 4

The mob of Shepherd's Crook, 1680 edition, stormed the home of the demon, sorcerer, and suspected vampyr Yulric Bile. As mobs went, it was a pretty good one. No elder went without a torch. No young man went pitchfork-less. Women wept and gnashed their teeth. John Farthing brought his new gun. John Cross had forged some chains. Benjamin Moss broke down the door to his one hundredth citadel of sin, with some assistance from his son, John. Cider was drunk, hymns were sung, and a fine time was had by all. The only blemish on the otherwise superb revelries of condemnation was the man who had arranged it all: the witchfinder, Erasmus Martin.

Little was, is, or will likely ever be known about one Master Erasmus Martin. It was said that he had traveled to the Far East to learn ancient secrets in ancient temples before burning them to the ground for heathen practices. It was said he'd made a deal with the devil and now sought redemption for his damned soul. It was said he was a milliner's son. Whatever the truth, it cannot be denied that he was very good at his job.

The villagers of Shepherd's Crook didn't know where (England), how (a ship), or why (to hunt the vampyr) Martin had come. He had simply appeared as a passing traveler one dark, dreary day a year ago, before the house—not yet pink— had been completed. He had asked a few questions, inspected the construction, and generally milled about, much to the chagrin of everyone who found him far too competent. It wasn't until he had the gall to seek advice from the native savages that the elders asked him to leave. He had done as they requested, and everyone had tried to forget about him.

That was six months ago. Before children went missing and old people died. Before the blood plague, the animal attacks in the far woods, and the peculiar neck wounds that appeared overnight. Before some women's husbands came home looking altogether too pleased with themselves.

Before Yulric Bile.

Letters had been sent to nearby churches in Salem, Arkham, and even that den of sin and iniquity, Boston. They spoke of the evils faced and pleaded for aid in vanquishing the devil's servants. The hope, ultimately, was to attract the famed preacher Increase Mather to town. He could sign copies of his books, give sermons, condemn a few local ne'er-do-wells of gross negligence, and, if there was time, also rid them of the vampyr.

That was what they had hoped. What they had received was Erasmus Martin riding back into town.

Wherever the witchfinder walked, the mood of the crowd sobered. Conversations hushed. Children stopped playing. Cider was sipped more quietly. That season, the Puritans invented their own word for *buzzkill* and it was Erasmus Martin.

Still, there was no reason *they* couldn't have a good time. So the Puritans continued with their grand displays of piousness and let Master Martin get down to the business at hand, which, in the opinion of the gathered crowd, he was slow to do.

Martin stood before the maw of the house's doorway, weighing his options. Inside, his quarry waited. Based on its history, the witchfinder assumed whatever followers the creature had acquired were already dead. You never could count on this, though, and he had no desire to face a room full of fanatics wielding axes.

Again.

Then, there was the house. Who knew what traps lay in wait for those not privy to its secrets? Rush headlong inside and you would not have a head for long. Martin chided himself for the joke and pledged to flagellate himself later.

The house, the followers, and the creature itself—all dangers to be considered. All reasons for Erasmus Martin to pause. He hadn't lived into witchfinder old age[2] by being reckless. Nor, though, had he earned his reputation by simply setting everything ablaze and hoping for the best.

He took a step forward. The crowd cheered. He looked at them and they stopped. Cheering was not the Puritan way. Contentment was not the Puritan way. Unnecessary hardship, unwavering resolve, and a detailed condemnation of any sexual act, *that* was the Puritan way, and if Martin was going to do this, by God, he was going to do this as a proper Puritan.

Into the darkness, across the threshold, alone but for God.

Once inside, he exchanged his Bible for a stake. He may have been a man of faith, but he did feel better with a weapon in hand. The inside of the house was much like any other lair or den of unspeakable evil. It was dark, dimly lit by a few candles

---

2. Thirty.

here and there to accommodate the eyes of mortal followers. There was very little furniture, a chair or two, but no paintings, no accoutrements. Nothing to show that anyone *lived* there, except perhaps a bookcase covered in worm-eaten, leather-bound volumes. Martin approached with trepidation and flipped through a few tomes. The *Pseudomonarchia Daemonum*, the *Vermis Mysteriis*, Pnakotic fragments, *The Book of Flies*, these were darkest, most vile of grimoires— further proving the absence of life in this rotting edifice. He moved on, making a note to burn those hideous texts once his work was done.

On the second floor, he found the vampyr's followers, or what was left of them. He knew now where the pastor had disappeared to and why the magistrate and his brother had been absent from their homes. Inevitably they would go down as mere victims of the creature. Those with influence were always cleared of wrongdoing when the official records were written, regardless of the truth. Martin didn't like it, but then, liking it wasn't his job. His job was to vanquish this abomination, and with the death of its minions, that had become one step easier.

From outside, a noise rose up that was not righteous: self- or otherwise. Martin stepped over the schoolteacher's body and onto the balcony. Outside, a crowd had gathered around a pair of figures.

"John Starling, what goes there?" Martin called down.

"Master Martin, we caught Anne Stevens coming out of the cellar," answered the young man, holding her closer than was strictly necessary. "She says she has killed the vampyr."

"Indeed," replied a skeptical Martin. "I will be right down."

It was only then, as he turned away from the window, that the witchfinder saw what he had missed during his initial scan of the room: a piece of paper pinned to the far wall. It may have been yellowed and worn with age, but for all that, its subject matter was no less clear. Seared upon this leaf was the image of some unknown, tentacled monstrosity, its great mass undulating with evil as its glowing red eye peered out from beneath a throng of slimy feelers. It sat atop a mountain of human skulls, and, on either side, a pair of angels were depicted descending into gibbering madness. So horrible, so lasting, so utterly indelible was the image that Martin wondered why he had not noticed it before. He could suppose only that it was because then, unlike now, the picture had not been oozing toward him.

Tendrils of ink and ectoplasm climbed their way out of the paper, as if it were a tiny window, and fell to the floor with as much squish as thud. The great red eye blinked and dilated, its gaze spinning frantically around the room before settling on Martin with what was, at best, malice and, at worst, hunger. What passed for ropy arms writhed across the floor as the rest of the beast's great bulk unfurled from the drawing. When the appendages came in contact with the remains of the Puritan cultists, they convulsed excitedly, engulfed their food, then moved on, with the corpses clearly visible through its translucent skin.

When, finally, the last part of this ancient and unkillable creature—its sanguine eye—released itself from the paper prison, a shriek that had very little to do with vocal cords or ear canals roared inside the minds of every living thing within sixty miles. Only then, as the quivering, gelatinous horror from beyond slunk forward to envelop him, did the witchfinder notice the message written in blood *above* the paper.

You did not think I was going to make this easy, did you?

◆ ◆

Several minutes later, Erasmus Martin strode across the grass, covered in a putrid slime and surreptitiously stowing a small hatchet up his sleeve. The crowd backed away, partially because of the horrible sounds they had heard, partially because of the smell, but mostly because he was the witchfinder, and they didn't like him very much. In this way, Martin found himself with an unimpeded view of the girl who'd been caught.

The young woman stood—proud, defiant, and miraculously free from harm, considering she was covered in the creature's black ichor. There were no visible injuries to her person: no gashes, no scratches, no evidence of living blood anywhere. The witchfinder's eyes narrowed suspiciously, and he clutched his side. Nobody came away unscathed from an encounter such as this.

He also noted, in some forgotten chasm in the depths of his mind, that the girl was uncommonly pretty. The face beneath the miasmic ooze was fetching, and the figure beneath the unflattering dress quite full. Puritans had long become masters at gleaning the full human form from within wrappings of pious modesty. Even Martin, who was more resistant than most to such thoughts, could not help but trace the lines of bosom and bottom, if only momentarily.

For her part, Anne's observations of the approaching witchfinder were best summed up by the phrase *manfully ugly*. Despite being of average height, he carried himself as if he were ten feet tall, helped along by his dark broad-brimmed hat and dramatically billowing cape. He was not excessively muscled, yet she could tell what lay underneath the jacket and trousers was taut and strong.[3] What's more, everything about him, from his stride to his eyes, shouted at a single-minded determination and confidence.

If only it hadn't been for the face. The pox had long ago left its mark—or rather, marks—on Erasmus Martin. Not that

---

3. Puritan men weren't the only ones who gleaned curves and bulges.

this was uncommon. Johnathan Carter had been happily married these ten years despite a face full of pox, as had Jon May and John Gables. Unlike Martin, however, they had not spent their time since adding more gruesome scars to their already marred features. In his defense, the witchfinder wore them well, like badges of honor, as much symbols of his office as his hat, cloak, and Bible.

"Here's the girl," boasted John Starling, wrenching her forward for display.

"Yes, I see." That was not all Erasmus Martin could see. One of the boy's hands had lingered too long in a place it had no business being, and now the full might of the witchfinder's judgment fell upon John Starling. Eyes wide with horror, the young man removed his hand, but the damage had been done. Martin looked on, accusing and silent, as John Starling melted away, disgraced, into the crowd.

When the young man, who would forever after be known in the community as John Starling the Lech, was out of sight, the witchfinder turned his attention back to Anne Stevens. There was a brief moment between the two in which her eyes expressed thanks and his head bowed slightly to acknowledge her gratitude, but before anyone saw, it was over. Their faces reset to their respective defaults: his, of conviction, hers, of abstinence. The gathered crowd fell silent to listen.

"You say you have slain the vampyr?" he said.

"Yes," she replied.

"Where?" he questioned.

"In its grave, beneath the house," she answered. "It came for me at twilight. Stole me from my bed on its devilish wings. Imprisoned me and prepared to drink of my life's blood. But noises above distracted it, calls and fearful mewls. Upstairs, it journeyed, from whence it returned sated and covered in blood. Full from its meal and fearing little from a woman, it lay down to sleep. After it, I climbed, taking with me a sharpened piece of wood and an ax. I drove the wooden shard into its heart and removed its head with the ax. Out of the grave and out of the cellar I fled, whereupon I was found, and like this, brought before you. Thus ends my tale."

It was the most a woman had ever been allowed to speak publicly in the village of Shepherd's Crook. The Puritans erupted into their own version of applause—prayer.

Though not entirely convinced, Martin conceded, "Very well. Lead me to the creature's grave."

Anne gave herself so many points.

◆　◆

A pair of lanterns cast light into what was a much-changed cellar. When Anne had left it minutes before, it had been clean and dry, sparsely populated with wine barrels and a few odds and ends. Most notably, you hadn't needed two lanterns to navigate it. Now, though . . . Darkness clung to the walls like tar, only reluctantly revealing the basement's secrets to the flames. Cobwebs had grown with incredible speed, some stretching from ceiling to floor. Shards of shattered barrels littered the ground, making it all the more difficult to walk in the gloom. And deep within the shadows, the innumerable eyes of rats and spiders glowed with unnatural intelligence.

This was a cellar no more; it was a lair.

Into the darkness carefully crept a group of four: the witch-finder, Erasmus Martin; the so-called innocent, Anne Stevens; the door buster, Benjamin Moss; and the dutiful "Yes, Mom, I'll keep an eye on Dad" son, Jonathan Moss. Martin and the younger Moss held the lanterns while the elder Moss held Anne, regaling her with tales of his door-breaking exploits.

"By the time I was John's age, I'd already racked up thirty-five, not including Ol' Goody Blythe, who lived in a cave and blocked the entrance with a boulder. And this was all before '68 when the Massachusetts commissioner ruled that multiple doors in the same lair should count separately. Blasphemy, I say. He just wants to pad his own numbers. I, however, got my hundred honestly—one door at a time."

Anne listened to this patiently, not that she had a choice. She was, after all, just an ordinary Puritan woman, guilty of absolutely nothing other than being born female. She would never dream of telling the old man to shut his damn mouth (points) or mentioning that his last dozen doors fell only because his son had climbed through a window and taken them off their hinges. Absolutely not. She was merely terrified and walking back into a cellar she had been in just once, a feat made easier by the new debris.

"Hold here," Martin ordered. The others stopped and waited as he alone climbed over a wagon wheel, which definitely had not been there before, and disappeared from sight. Seconds passed, then minutes. Somewhere in the basement, there was a deep growl followed by a soft thud. The two Mosses shifted uncomfortably. Anne was sure that one more unidentifiable sound and the pair would bolt. Fortunately or, from Anne's perspective, unfortunately, the witchfinder emerged from the darkness. "Bring the girl."

"Master Martin, you're bleeding," the elder Moss pointed out.

The witchfinder took a handkerchief from his pocket and covered the small cut that had mysteriously appeared under his eye. "So I am. This way."

The three of them clambered over the wagon wheel, slid across a carriage door, and fell right next to the looming Martin. From there, lanterns were raised and the four Puritans looked down into the grave of the vampyr. In the flickering light, Bile looked even deader than usual. His blood shone black, splattered across his white chest. His head had shifted position and now tilted forward and to one side, making it nearly impossible to believe it could still be connected. Even his eyes, which were gray and lifeless to begin with, had clouded over, extinguishing the fire given them by those dark pupils. The effect was so convincing that Anne worried her master might have actually gone too far.

"Heaven protect us," gasped Jonathan Moss, crossing himself.

"Good God," croaked Benjamin Moss, his eyes wide with terror.

"The creature is dead. Let us go" did not say Erasmus Martin. He should have. The illusion was flawless, her performance convincing, and when three people all see such a ghastly sight, it is only right that all three exclaim.

Yet Martin remained silent. The four of them stood in his silence and continued to gaze down upon the body.

Anne's mind began to panic. *What is he thinking? Why doesn't he say anything? What does he know? Does he know? He knows! He must know. If he didn't know, he would ask, he would question, or he would leave. He hasn't asked, he hasn't questioned, and we're still here. So. He. Must. Know.*

These thoughts expressed themselves on the outside in the form of a shudder. Erasmus Martin took note. Fortunately for Anne, so did Benjamin Moss.

"Be at ease, my girl. The creature is dead," he said, putting a comforting hand on her shoulder. "Well done. Well done, indeed. Wouldn't you say it was well done, Master Martin?"

Erasmus Martin, who had been eyeing Mistress Stevens intently, found his cold, hard suspicions crashing into the optimistic certainty of Benjamin Moss.

"I"—Martin searched for a word that would appease the elder Moss, without betraying his reservations—"suppose."

"Oh, he's just disappointed," continued Moss. "He wanted to kill the beast himself. Came all this way, and you do his job for him. And so neatly, too. Even cut off the head. Not many folk nowadays know about that. They'd just stick a stake in it and leave it for dead. But not you. You did the thing right. Why, I doubt Master Martin himself could have done as well, could you, Master Martin?"

"Hmm . . ." Martin grunted noncommittally.

"Don't mind him, dear. He's just jealous. Envy is a sin, Master Martin. You shouldn't let the green-eyed monster have you just because this gray-eyed monster didn't. And it's a most fitting end, don't you think? The monstrous creature done in by a pious woman. Beauty killing the beast. There's something in that, methinks. A parable perhaps. And, anyway, it's not like she's going to take your job. Come now, tell her she's done well."

The old man pushed Anne toward the witchfinder to receive his praises, placing her in that awkward too-close zone, which is good for kissing and little else. Not even Erasmus Martin, as hardened and pious as he was, could ignore the discomfort that came from standing chest to heaving bosom with a woman, her chin tilted up.

"Yes, well . . . ," Martin stammered, suddenly very hot as he peered into Anne's innocent-looking large blue eyes. He stepped to the side, away from the threat of intimate contact, before continuing, "It does appear the creature is destroyed."

"You see, my boy, that wasn't so hard," chortled Old Moss, who was an expert chortler. "I know it doesn't seem like much, girl, but that was high praise from the likes of him. Truth be told, not being set on fire is high praise from the likes of him. Now, what say we leave this dreary den and see if there's any cider left?"

The old man offered his arm. With a smile, she took it. Jonathan Moss followed behind as they started to leave, wondering why he hadn't inherited his father's obvious skill at talking to pretty girls.

"However . . ."

The dreaded word worked its magic. Anne and the Mosses spun around, slowly and in unison.

Martin stretched his arm out over the vampyr's grave. "Appearances can be deceiving."

And with that, he let go of his lantern.

They say great minds think alike, whoever *they* might be. While this may be true, it usually happens only when those great minds are separated by an equally great distance. Two great minds in the same room are far more likely to argue and bicker about differences than unite in a single idea. This is important to note, because on this occasion, when the witch-finder's lantern began to fall, Anne Stevens, Erasmus Martin, and Yulric Bile were all united in a single thought: *Damn it to hell!*

In good time, Anne and the Mosses slowly moved forward to witness the aftermath. They found a smoldering but empty grave.

"Not so dead after all," said Martin with a certain amount of satisfaction. Only he had been on the precipice. Only he had seen.

The lantern had shattered, covering the creature quickly in oil and flame. The beast had managed to maintain the illusion until then but, faced with annihilation, had finally broken. It had writhed. It had screamed. It had hit its fail-safe.

Naturally, Yulric had foreseen this possibility. Erasmus Martin had a reputation for being thorough, after all, and there was nothing quite as thorough as fire. And so the grave Yulric had so carefully constructed was designed to cave in when struck from the bottom, burying him completely and dousing the flames.

Anne turned from the collapsed hole to find the witch-finder watching her, his eyes aglow with accusation. She had staked the beast to the ground. She had cut off its head. She had lied. He had her. He knew it. She knew it. He knew that she knew it, which made it all the more sweet. He savored his moment of victory.

It did not last long.

"Well, it was a bloody good attempt, girl," said Benjamin Moss, once more coming to her rescue. "You have to admit that, Master Martin. It did look dead. Must have missed the heart, though. Not cut off the head, too. Head has to come all the way off, my dear. I expect your arms were tired, all that hacking away. Figured halfway through was good enough. Ah well, can't expect more from a girl, eh, Master Martin?"

Both Martin and Anne looked from the old man to each other. He had just given her the perfect excuse, one every Puritan would readily accept. It may have been a crime to be a witch, but it wasn't a crime to be stupid and weak. The ignorant-woman defense would work. Martin couldn't touch her. She knew it. He knew it. She knew that he knew it, which made it all the more sweet when she said, "I suppose so."

Martin's eyes narrowed. *I know it was you,* they seemed to say.

Anne's eyes widened in response. *Who, me? I'm just a simple Puritan girl. I have no thought or opinion of my own. I leave the thinking to God and men.*

Martin's eyes rolled as he turned away. *Oh, shut up.*

The Mosses caught none of this.

"Not like a woman to miss a man's heart, is it, my boy?" chuckled the elder. The younger, who had recently been unsuccessfully engaged, did not find this so funny.

"What now, Master Martin? Should we dig the creature out?" asked Jonathan Moss while his father explained the joke to Anne. She had already heard about it, of course; the village wasn't that big. Still, his hand gestures were quite amusing.

Martin, meanwhile, considered the younger Moss's proposal. Digging was the simplest solution. Get a few lads with strong backs and shovels. Dig until you find the beast. Finish the job. Simple. Of course, you would have to ignore the fact that all the while you were digging, a creature of terrible power lurked beneath you, waiting to drag you into the earth. How many lives would it take to extinguish this evil forever? How many was he ready to sacrifice? He could practically feel the vampyr's grin emanating from the dirt below.

The witchfinder removed a large silver cross from his jacket. *A stalemate, then.*

"Master Martin?" Jonathan inquired cautiously of the silent witchfinder, who seemed very intent on his cross. It could be that he was thinking or talking to God, but it could also be that he wasn't all there. Jonathan tried again. "Master Martin, should I get a shovel?"

"No," said the witchfinder at last, "we do not need one." He dropped the cross into the grave. It landed flat and began to sink into the mud. As it disappeared from sight, something beneath the ground shifted and then grew still.

The Mosses looked very confused.

"Masters Moss, fetch all the skilled tradesmen in the village. I need two dozen heavy stone slabs with crosses engraved on them, as soon as possible."

The Mosses nodded and hurried off to carry out the instructions. Martin had no doubt that by evening's end, the stones would be delivered. Puritans may not be the brightest, nor the nicest, nor the most civil, nor the least hypocritical of people, but they could certainly work.

Erasmus Martin, too, made his way toward the cellar steps, reaching them at the same time as Anne Stevens. He eyed her warily. "After you," he said, determined not to turn his back on her. She gave him a mocking curtsey and bounced up the stairs in a very un-Puritan way. He followed her, disapproving.

The pair reached the gathered village just as the Mosses were leaving with several of the larger men to gather appropriate stones.

"What's this about not digging out the creature?" asked Goody Cross. "Are you here to slay the creature or not?"

Martin turned to her. "And how many sons are you willing to sacrifice to see me kill the beast?" The woman sputtered and stepped in front of her son to shield him from the witchfinder.

"The vampyr cannot be killed without heavy bloodshed," he declared. "So we trap it underground, entomb it for all time."

"How?" came an unidentified voice from the crowd.

Erasmus removed a silver flask from his cloak. "We consecrate the land surrounding the house. He won't be able to pass through holy ground."

A discontented murmur spread among the assemblage.

"That sounds a bit like popery, Master Martin," accused John Fryer.

"It is popery, Master Fryer," Martin replied. This brought angry shouts from the Puritans. Vampyrs were one thing, but Catholics . . .

"I'm not sure we can condone this idolatry," Fryer jeered. "Why, if Pastor Collins was here—"

"Pastor Collins is dead," the witchfinder said. This quieted the crowd considerably. "I do not ask you to be privy to what I do. Go on your way and I will take care of it."

"And when you're done?" posed Goody Cross.

"I shall go," he said.

The Puritans nodded their agreement and turned to leave. There was just one last thing.

"I do require someone to assist me," he called out. "Young Mistress Stevens, perhaps."

Anne, who had managed to invisibly assimilate into the townspeople's ranks, now found the crowd's attention thrust upon her.

"If she helped you," remarked John Fryer, "if she were a part of this papist ritual of yours, she would not be able to return to the village."

Which means she won't be able to free the creature later, thought Martin. "I'm afraid I cannot conduct the ritual alone. And without it, the vampyr will be free to escape . . . and feed."

That little extra emphasis in his lie is what did it. Anne once more found herself about to be volunteered by a group of panicking cowards. And just as before, she decided to take matters into her own hands first.

"Master Martin," she declared, walking up to the witch-finder. "For the good of the village, I shall assist you."

Again, the Puritans burst into applause-like prayer. The women of the town were a bit too happy to see the back of Anne, probably because their husbands had always been a bit too eager to see the back of Anne. Then, after one last stirring rendition of the Lord's Prayer, they turned and started back to their homes, declaring the evening's festivities a resounding success. Anne and Erasmus were now alone.

"Well," Anne said, impressed that he had gotten the better of her. "What now?"

He handed her a small snuffbox. "You hold the incense," he told her, using a flint to set it smoldering. "Make sure it doesn't go out."

The ritual took most of the night. Every hour or so, Anne would pretend that she hadn't noticed the fire go out and

Erasmus would pretend that the incense was actually necessary and would relight it. By the time they made their way all around the house, the Mosses had returned with the stone slabs. Erasmus oversaw the installation, which required one or two to be recarved, due to Anne "accidentally" scratching off the engraved crosses. By dawn, however, all was set, and the new day saw a town free from evil.

"So, where are we going?" Anne asked as the witchfinder hitched his belongings to his horse.

"You are free to go where you will," he replied, pulling on the leather strap keeping his books in place. "I hear the Quakers are about to have their own colony. No doubt they would take you in."

"And what about you?" she inquired.

"I move on. There are reports a devil has taken up residence in the woods of New Jersey."

She smiled. "Sounds delightful. I think I'll join you." And with that, she took the reins of his horse and led it away, taking her place at the side of the only person who respected her enough to fear her.

Before following his horse and new companion, Erasmus Martin gave one last glance toward the house beneath which his most indefatigable foe now slumbered, then uttered what was to become a most fitting eulogy.

"Until next time."

Chapter 5

Vampires don't sleep. When arriving back at their crypts and coffins before the break of day, they return to their natural state of death.[4] The vampire's consciousness, their being, remains within the husk of its body, aware and waiting for night. In the meantime, it plots, summons visions, reads omens, replays events, and, in general, thinks. One might ask how this is any different from sleeping, at which point, the vampire would rub its neck, mutter something incoherent, and then rip your throat out.

Yulric Bile's not-sleep was filled with not-dreams: memories of the past, visions of the future, and the glowing yellow eyes of a great metal beast speeding toward him. Also, knocking. It had begun faintly but, over the course of his rest,

---

4. Until, of course, you try to kill them; then, they prove themselves to be very much alive, and you prove yourself to be not so much so anymore.

grew louder and louder. Bang. Bang. Bang. *Bang. Bang. Bang.* BANG!

Yulric Bile awoke from death to find an eight-year-old boy shooting him in the head.

"That's not supposed to happen," remarked the child, reloading.

Yulric shook with surprise and rage. If his outrage bothered the freckle-faced child, it didn't show. The boy merely climbed out of his grave on a small stepladder and walked away. How could. A child. Do that. To *him*? The enraged vampire leapt out of the hole in the cellar, letting out a fierce and terrible shriek.

"*Mmmmmmmmmmm! Mmmmmmm . . . mmmmmm?*"

His lips had been sown together. He raised a finger to his mouth and carefully cut the thin metal wire. He spun to face the child as it was rummaging through a bag.

"Ytheh oo ee oy . . . ?"

Salt poured from his mouth. Yulric froze in confusion. There were many herbs, weeds, and random objects to which his kind had an aversion. Some were common, others downright peculiar.[5] Salt, however, had never been one of them.

The child turned back to face the puzzled vampire. In one hand, it held a magical dagger, which moved on its own, and wrapped around the other was a small green serpent. Yulric smiled and matched the child's aggressive posture, letting his nails grow to clawlike lengths. The boy yelled, the vampire hissed, and they both leapt into battle.

◆   ◆

---

5. Yulric had once known a vampire who was repelled by the smell of peppermint. She would also stop to count any mustard seeds she came across. She had problems.

"Simon!"

The combatants froze as they turned toward Amanda. Amanda, who was filled with fear and rage and about to commit bloody, vicious murder. Amanda, who had just found her eight-year-old brother trying to kill the creature from last night with an electric turkey carver and a rubber snake.

"Put him down!" she ordered.

Yulric was halfway through a defiant roar when his gaze fell to her neckline and the searing pain in his head forced him to hiss and retreat.

Amanda, unused to that particular response when a man caught sight of her breasts, looked down to where her mother's gold cross hung around her neck. "Fine," she hissed.

Pulling the necklace over her head, she advanced. Yulric dodged and flailed as best he could in the contained space, but she eventually trapped him in a corner.

"I *said*. Put. Him. Down," growled Amanda. Reluctantly, he lowered the boy to the ground while giving Amanda a glare that was known to wilt flowers, a glare that was mirrored in the younger face two feet beneath his and several inches to his left. Neither the vampire's nor the eight-year-old's gaze fazed Amanda. She was immune. She was a caregiver.

"Over here. *Now!*" she commanded. They both started forward. "Not you. Him."

The boy marched to where his sister waited, leaving the vampire standing alone among the knickknacks, bicycles, and boxed-up Christmas ornaments.

"What did I say about this place?" she asked, reciting lines from the parents' handbook chapter entitled "When Your Child Breaks the Rules."

Simon's young mind paused. It had recently discovered sarcasm, and several cheeky answers were considered before he decided to stick to the script.

"Don't go into the cellar," he intoned.

"Why?" she continued.

Simon nodded toward the recently dug hole in the floor. "Because you didn't want me to know what you were doing."

Amanda's eyes narrowed. She wasn't about to let him undermine her authority with the truth. "Because it was dangerous. And, knowing this, what exactly did you do?"

"I went into the cellar."

"No," she said. "You went into the cellar with a knife. What have I told you about knives?"

"Technically, it's a turkey carver," he pointed out.

"What was that?" Amanda's voice hit a pitch normally reserved for dogs and bats. Yulric, who could become both, checked his ears for blood.

"Don't play with knives," replied the returning dutiful child within Simon.

"Right. Don't play with knives. What if you had tripped and fallen down the stairs? You could have impaled yourself, and then where would you be?"

The vampire envisioned exactly where the child would have been. And where Yulric would have been. And what condiments he would have used. He was very hungry.

"What did you think you were doing?" asked the adult.

Simon mumbled his reply, pulling from the eight-year-olds' handbook a chapter entitled "When You Are Caught."

"I'm sorry?" replied his sister, not having any of it.

"Vanquishing a zombie," he reluctantly repeated in full voice.

"Excuse me?"

Both humans turned to the eldritch voice in the middle of the basement.

"A what?" it asked.

"A zombie," Amanda told it.

"A what bee?" it asked again.

"A zombie. He thinks you're a zombie," blurted Amanda, who was growing ever more frustrated with this thing. Bad enough that it had ruined last night's planned rendezvous by turning out to be a hideous monster, but now it was throwing her off her disciplinary stride.

"And what exactly is a zom-bie?" it inquired, unabated by her rising anger.

"How can you not know what a zombie is?" Amanda barked.

"A zombie smart enough to know it is a zombie would not be a zombie," Simon whispered to his sister. He stepped toward the creature, who had been ready to rend him limb from limb, and explained, "A zombie is an undead creature who rises from the grave to feast on the flesh of the living."

"Like a ghoul?" it replied.

"No," said Simon.

"Ah, a revenant then."

"No."

"A fext?"

"No, listen. An undead creature—"

"—which feasts on the flesh of the living," interrupted Yulric. "The definition does not narrow it down."

"Indeed," said Simon. Zombies of any kind weren't known for making reasoned arguments. Kicking himself over his misidentification, he turned to his sister. "I deserve to be punished."

"For . . . ?" she prompted.

"Going into the cellar when I was expressly forbidden and the wielding of knives outside of mealtimes," he said with a suspicious lack of hesitation. "I'll be off to my room then to think about what I've done."

"Oh no, you don't," Amanda stopped him. "Outside."

Simon stomped his feet and made the scrunched-up face of children everywhere. "But why?"

"Because you're grounded, you little snot," Amanda gloated. "I want you to go . . . play."

"Play?" whined the boy.

"Play." She smiled. "With children."

"Mom and Dad never would have made me play."

A pall fell over the room. Yulric was intrigued by the sensation. Usually, he was the pall that fell over a room.

"Library card," Amanda said coldly.

"I'm sorry," Simon said sheepishly. He knew he'd gone too far.

"Library card," she repeated, her hand outstretched.

"Amanda, I'm sorry," he moaned.

"Give it," she demanded.

Head bowed, the boy reached into his pocket and, with reverence, pulled out a little laminated card. He placed it into her palm, where it was quickly and without ceremony enfolded.

"You're right," she continued. "I'm not Mom and Dad. Mom and Dad pretended not to notice that you liked being sent to your room. They did it because they loved you. But I'm your sister—your big sister—and it's my job to call you out on your crap. So I want you to go outside. I want you to play. And when I come out in ten minutes, I expect to see you engaged in some sort of team sport or imaginary adventure, because if I don't, it'll be all TV for a week. Do you understand me?"

"Yes," muttered a low voice somewhere in the vicinity of the child.

"All right then. Go."

Simon rushed past her up the stairs. She listened carefully to his footsteps and, when she was reasonably sure he had left, turned back to the remaining combatant.

"You!" she spat. "What do you think you're doing, fighting a second grader?"

No one talked to Yulric Bile this way, and because no one talked to him this way, he found it difficult to respond. "He started it."

"Oh, and how exactly does a little kid start a fight with a werewolf?" she asked, her arms folded across her chest. She was baiting him. She had spent the night coming up with all manner of argument to prove he was a werewolf. All he had to do was rise to her challenge.

He didn't.

"By shooting it repeatedly in the head with your firearm," he said.

"Impossible! He doesn't know where I keep—" Amanda's voice cut off as the silver gleam of the Beretta, lying where Simon had left it, caught her eye. Her eyes grew wide, first with shock, then with anger.

"*Simon!*" she didn't yell so much as simply raise her voice. But the tone hit the key of trouble major, which amplifies the sound to the intended listener—in this case, the small boy who had sneaked back to listen at the top of the stairs. In the silence that followed, both the creature and the girl heard small foot-steps rush through the house, the slam of a door, and a bike with training wheels peel out, if such a thing were possible.[6]

Amanda turned around to face the creature. Normally, she would apologize. That was the polite thing to do when you wrongly accuse someone, not to mention when your brother shoots that somebody in the head. Then again, it didn't exactly seem proper etiquette to apologize to an abomination whose very existence is an insult to nature. She settled for a question-ing tone. "What are you doing here?"

---

6. It's not.

"It is daytime," he said dismissively.

"What does daytime have to do with being a werewolf?" Amanda scoffed. "Oh, right. I forgot. You're a 'vampire.'" She used air quotes on this last word.

"Yes, I 'am,'" Yulric retorted, imitating her hand motion, though he did not know why. He supposed this was how people talked now.

Amanda glared her most effective motherly glare. "You have till nightfall. Then, you're gone."

"I can come or go from this house as I please." Yulric smiled.

"Riiiight." She rolled her eyes. "Because of my invitation."

He chuckled mockingly. "Silly girl. Your invitation merely pointed me in your direction. It had nothing to do with my ability to enter." He walked past her as if she weren't even there. "I need no invitation to enter my own home."

He climbed the stairs and entered the house. The effect would have been more dramatic if it hadn't been midday. As it was, he came hissing back down, somewhat singed, and could not go back up until after Amanda had pulled all the shades. After that, the questions remained, but the mystery had certainly died.

Chapter 6

The history surrounding the Pink House of Shepherd's Crook is long, ominous, and surprisingly well documented, since nothing says "Wouldn't you like to donate to the Shepherd's Crook Historical Society?" quite like a haunted house.

The structure was originally built in 1678 for an unknown English gentleman. He took up residence in 1679 and lived there less than a year before mysterious and violent circumstances led to his disappearance. Modern historians agree that he was likely the victim of persecution on trumped-up charges, based on the presence of infamous witchfinder Erasmus Martin—honorary reverendship given, stripped, given again, stripped again, and now being reconsidered by the Shepherd's Crook Community College (formerly the Mather Institute of Greater Theology, the Northern Massachusetts College of Science and the Arts, the Mather Institute of Revivalist Theology, and the All-Faith Universal University of Greater Enlightenment and Understanding).

After that initial owner, the house was left empty for nearly fifty years by the nearby Puritans, who were quite happy to leave well enough alone, thank you very much. Then, beginning in 1728, a series of poor Bostonians seeking cheap land occupied the building. This period, marked by a 1,000 percent increase in murders, suicides, and ritual cannibalism, lasted until 1734 when a family of Quakers moved in. Locals started calling the place cursed after that.

The house saw action in two wars during the eighteenth century. During the French and Indian War, tragedy befell a small scout force of French soldiers who'd taken refuge there during a battle[7] with Shepherd's Crook's plucky native sons. The siege that followed lasted exactly one hour and mainly consisted of the local militia drinking tea outside while waiting for the screams to end. Just over a decade later, it was chosen by the British during the War of Independence as the site for the most disastrously unsuccessful battlefield hospital in the history of battlefields, hospitals, or staying alive. Doctors and historians still disagree as to why, despite above-average sanitation for the time, every injured soldier who'd been treated there, whether it be for a bullet hole or a dose of the clap, had died of acute anemia.

For most of the next century, the house fell into abandonment and disrepair—which was just fine with the citizenry—with occasional bouts of habitation by Irish, German, and Italian immigrants—which was decidedly not. Fortunately, the stays of these foreigners were brief and punctuated by a night when each family ran screaming into the woods, never to be heard from again. This usually warranted a town-wide day of thanksgiving.

---

7. Historians outside Shepherd's Crook call it a "skirmish" or, more often, a "something happened."

Following the hurried departure of a Norwegian couple in 1855, a group of otherwise well-intentioned abolitionists thought to use the Pink House, at this point a fairly awful shade of ramshackle, as a shelter for runaway slaves. After a single night, the former slaves told the abolitionists exactly what they could do with this particular safe house. When pressed, the escapees spoke of queer dreams in which an old white devil drank from their very souls. The Underground Railroad gave Shepherd's Crook a wide berth in the future. "We may be desperate," said one of its conductors, "but we're not crazy."

In 1891, a visiting Boston architect decided to restore the edifice to its former glory, despite the resounding disapproval of the locals. He would spend the next three years and much of his fortune on the renovation, after which he died drunk, destitute, and alone. Though, strictly speaking, this wasn't the house's fault. The rebuilt residence then fell into the hands of New York railroad magnate Gerard D. Huff, whose family traveled there seasonally well into the next century. With occultism all the rage among the upper crust, Mrs. Stephanie Huff would often host séances and Sabbaths for her friends and famous guests. At this time, however, the spirits were not very forthcoming. Even the notorious occultist Aleister Crowley, who could raise a spirit out of a snuffbox, was unable to find a single solitary soul.[8]

Over the next fifty years, very little of interest occurred in the dwelling, except for a dozen deaths by Spanish flu, the murder of an abusive husband, the last stand of a Boston gangster, a War of the Worlds–incited suicide pact, five dismembered pets, and twenty-seven missing children who had entered on

---

8. Though he had looked rather angry after trying. During the postséance orgy, he was overheard muttering to himself, "Show him I'm not a Puritan."

a dare—the same as any old house. In fact, when the '60s and '70s came around with their own brands of occultism and spiritual interest, the hippies squatting in the building[9] were disappointed that nary a ghostly presence could be found. Never ones to remain disheartened, they did what any reasonable proponents of peace and love would do on a boatload of LSD.

They painted the house pink.[10]

The legend of the Pink House died out after that. When authors and film buffs were falling over themselves to find the next Amityville Horror or Overlook Hotel, they passed through Shepherd's Crook with hardly a second thought beyond "My, what an ugly house." As the town slowly suburbanized, all traces of its unique and colorful history were willfully forgotten by a community longing for uniformity. All that remained was a generic ghost story, used for fund-raising, and the journal of Erasmus Martin, kept by the Shepherd's Crook Historical Society and only ever read by two people: the society's sole eight-year-old member and, after a time, his sister.

This long and rambling history is intended to illustrate that the house—over the centuries lived in, inhabited, commandeered, and otherwise populated by various people—had never been *owned* by any of them, only rented.

The rights to the dwelling were still held in trust by a very old and powerful Swiss bank, in the name of one Master Yulric Dunnwulffe Bile.

---

9. Locals started calling the house cursed again.

10. The Shepherd's Crook Historical Society is still having fits.

Chapter 7

On. Off. On. Off.

Amanda let the revelation of her house's ownership wash over her.

On. Off. On. Off.

It was one thing to appear in her bedroom and call yourself a vampire. Turning up again and attacking her brother was pretty awful, too. But claiming to have owned a suburban house for over three hundred years was insane, stupid, and utterly inconceivable.

On. Off. On.

"Could you stop that?" she said, her patience snapping as she considered impossibilities.

Off.

"With the light on," she clarified.

On.

"How does a tiny switch ignite a glass candle?" asked Yulric, partially to her, partially to himself, but mostly to the universe at large.

"Electricity," she answered. After a minute's thought, she clarified, "Bottled lightning."

"Ah," he said. The intricate workings of various circuits, wires, and fossil-fuel-burning power plants were beyond him, but dominating an awesome power of the natural world and confining it to a jar was something he could easily understand. His respect for the troublesome blond girl grew. "I suppose the jars are kept in the walls, then?"

"Sure," she said patronizingly. He flipped the light switch off and on again, this time imagining how the action moved a jar lid over just enough for slivers of lightning to eke out, which wasn't so far from the truth.

"So, you are my landlord," she reasoned. "All those checks, er"—she paused to think back to what Simon's books would call them—"notes of scrip I paid, they were all going to a man buried under my cellar."

"Though it has been some time since anyone considered me a man, I imagine your notes of scrip went to the bank in whose hands I left the deed in trust. So, in essence, yes, your statement is correct." The vampire picked up a frame off a table. "This is very well done. Who is the artist?"

"It's called a photograph. It's a . . ." She sought an idiot's definition of *photograph*.

"Picture made from light," he interrupted. "*Photo* meaning light, *graph* meaning drawn. Not that difficult."

"I suppose not," she conceded. "So, the bank just kept the house for you all this time?"

Yulric looked up from the picture. He gave a condescending chuckle, which only made Amanda angry. "Brandenberg and Sons, or whatever the bank may be called now."

"La Première Banque du Suisse," Amanda said. She'd seen the name on top of her bills enough to know it by heart.

"Ah yes, well, these moneylenders and I have a very . . . special relationship that comes with my being their oldest"— he chuckled again—"living client."

He glanced back at the light portrait in his hands. It showed a whole smiling family: mother, father, daughter, and oddly placid-looking baby. He wondered how long a light portrait took to make, how one wielded the light, and how much pain it inflicted on the subjects during the process. This last thought made him smile. He would have to look into becoming a photographist.

While Yulric's mind swam with misguided ideas of how photos were made, Amanda was summoning up powers of her own, powers that she possessed in abundance, powers that her brother called "pure undiluted contrariness."

"So, over three hundred years go by, and they just hand your money back like *that*?" she snarked.

Yulric's head snapped around at her words. "Three hundred years?"

Amanda smiled at finally having made a dent in this thing's impenetrable superiority. "*Over* three hundred years."

Yulric stared at her as if the words themselves hung in front of her face. Could it really have been so long? Surely not. Deep beneath the earth, he had been vaguely aware of events: a war or two, some Quakers, that English mystic with his love of orgies, and those long-haired children who giggled and did not bathe.

So, fifty years then, he thought before looking again at the automatic candle in the ceiling and the portrait of light. *Maybe one hundred.*

Utterly bemused, Amanda pressed her victory. "For over three centuries, no one wondered. No one questioned. No one suspected you were even here. How is that possible?"

"Cheap rent."

Amanda's triumph, striding fast and confident, smacked into the easily given answer like a toddler's head into a kitchen table: there was a moment of wonder and confusion before realization set in and the child fell to the floor, crying for its mommy. Meanwhile, Yulric examined the room once more with new eyes. Here and there, his seventeenth-century gaze found twenty-first-century technology. Lights lit by themselves. Machines moved on their own. Missing were familiar trappings of household life, like churns and looms and body odor. Those that remained, like tables and chairs, were composed of strange materials and even stranger designs.

And then there had been the horror from last night. The mechanical metal behemoth that had appeared in a flash and trampled him horribly beneath its wheels. How long had it taken to invent such a weapon?

A hundred and fifty years! he thought. *No more!*

Between her utter defeat and the pathetic old man this creature had suddenly become, Amanda couldn't bring herself to be combative anymore. She left him to his increasingly frantic analysis of his surroundings and got herself a beer.

If there had been any lingering doubts as to the nature of the thing in her living room, those were settled upon her return.

Yep, it's definitely a man, she thought.

Yulric Bile had found the TV.

◆　◆

The vampire moped for a week. Not in the way that one might expect him to—with fire and death, blood running red in the streets, and a dark miasma blotting out the sun. No, the vampire moped pretty much the same way everyone else does—he watched television.

Unlike everyone else, though, his legs didn't get stiff and his butt didn't get sore. He didn't have to get up to grab a beer or order a pizza. He didn't bathe, shave, or excrete any euphemistic number, without which he had absolutely no reason to ever set foot in a bathroom. He didn't even sleep, or at least that's what he told Amanda from his position on the couch. She couldn't help but notice that he did occasionally close his eyes and that he was much crankier when he hadn't.

Day and night, he watched. Even late at night, when the only programs were infomercials and phone-sex ads, he watched. Every so often, he would appear in a doorway or from around a corner to ask such things as why some movies were in black and white while the rest were in color. He kept the remote in hand and returned quickly to the couch, uttering perfunctory death threats as an afterthought.

It wasn't that he was intrigued or mesmerized or entranced. Honestly, he didn't even look very interested. He just seemed . . . empty. The great fire of Yulric Bile, which once had threatened to consume the world, had been doused, and nothing could reignite it.

Except—

"Ow!" yelled Yulric, climbing over the back of the couch and rubbing his head. On the other side, a stoic-faced cherub stood, notebook in hand. At the sight of the small boy, Yulric's eyes flamed, his fangs bared, and even his lungs, which worked selectively, began to creak under the weight of his quickening breath.

"Pestilent, dog-eared offspring of a worm-ridden hag!" he screamed. "I'll stick your head in that infernal box stove[11] till your eyeballs pop. May your hair turn to leeches and the days of your life peter out into . . ." At this point, he became so incensed that he began switching languages, from French to Arabic to some nonsensical, squishing noise, and finally into the most incomprehensible of all, Welsh.

The boy scribbled something in his notebook and walked away. Slowly, Yulric's rage faded. As it did, he slid down the couch and returned to watching a woman talk to women about women. That is, until—

"Ow!"

Up popped the bald, bat-eared head once more. Again, the child stood ready to take notes. This time, the fiery eyes of the beast sought out the objects that had struck it.

"Horseshoes?" cried the creature. "Horseshoes? You interrupted the accounts by survivors of the breast plague to test me with iron?" He took a moment to hurl the offending steel back at the boy. Simon, used to an environment where anyone abnormal was singled out and pelted with welt-inducing objects, adeptly stepped aside, with the reflexes forged in a thousand games of dodgeball.

Amanda watched the scene play out from the safety of the kitchen threshold. Since the creature, Yulric Bile, had taken custody of the living room sofa, Simon had begun a series of identifying experiments. Mostly, they involved lobbing various supernatural deterrents over the back of the couch to gauge the level of outrage they caused. Inevitably, these tests ended in a chase, which Amanda would have to break up before death

---

11. The microwave. Another challenging conversation, and as Yulric didn't yet understand what could and could not be put inside, he wasn't allowed to touch.

or fire ensued. So she would tell Simon to stop disturbing their guest, and she would tell their guest to halt his attempts at murder. Both would mutter under their breath and go to their respective corners until Simon found something else he could easily toss.

Except this time. Amanda had suggested the horseshoes.

It hadn't been a problem, the vampire and the TV, it really hadn't. Amanda was usually asleep or at work, and Simon, well, he didn't really watch TV anyway. And despite the occasional outburst of unbridled wrath when he tried to remember how the telephone worked, Yulric's presence was more than bearable. It was actually kind of comforting. So long as he was lounging around, he couldn't hurt anyone. And as long as he didn't hurt anyone, she had nothing to feel guilty about.

But day followed day, and still the vampire retained his spindly clutch on the remote. The weekend came and went. Monday passed and Tuesday, too, and still no sign that the vampire would voluntarily relent from his channel surfing vigil. Amanda had grown concerned that her haven, her sanctuary, the one bright spot in what had become her tedious existence, would be sacrificed on the altar of this intruder's brooding. Something had to be done. And so, something was.

As the creature and Simon began their grand chase, Amanda stole into the living room. With his fists full of horseshoes, the vampire had left behind the remote, which Amanda took up now. Her fingers moved on their own to press the channel number. With bated breath, she sat through five car-insurance commercials until finally the screen turned black, two silver eyes opened, and a husky voice said, "Last time on *The Phantom Vampire Mysteries . . .*"

"What is this?"

Dread crept into Amanda's body. As last week's recap commenced, she looked up to see the ancient vampire staring at the television, in his right hand a horseshoe, in his left, a struggling eight-year-old held by one foot.

Amanda hadn't a second to lose. In a whirl of blond hair and sweatpants, she was over the couch and advancing on Yulric with her mother's cross. The vampire was forced against the wall, using Simon as a protective shield against the twenty-two-year-old's holy wrath.

"Look," she spat at the vampire, "I've let you stay, despite my better judgment and the fact that you tried to kill me and my brother. For some reason, I feel responsible for you being here,[12] and so I've taken pity on you."

The vampire hissed angrily at the *P* word, but Amanda continued, ". . . and let you spend day after day sitting on *my* couch watching *my* TV. However, Wednesday at eight is my time. And, during the next hour, I control all. The couch, the remote, gravity, if it gets in the way. So get behind me, or begone, or whatever. I don't care. But you will not. Interrupt. My show!"

The cornered vampire and the human shield gave each other The Look, the universal look of one male to another when they realize the world is not actually theirs. Then slowly, Yulric Bile set the small boy down and, raising his hands in submission, said, "I merely wished to know what you were watching."

The furies that had risen up in Amanda packed their bags and left, leaving her feeling kind of silly. She tried not to let it show too much. *"The Phantom Vampire Mysteries."*

There was a twinkle in the vampire's cloudy gray eyes at the program's name, if twinkle is what you call it when such a being shows interest. *Spark* would be a better term. *Ominous foreboding*, better still.

---

12. And well she should, since she was.

"May I join you?" he asked. His tone was formal, polite even. Different from before, when any sense of genuine manners was marred by arrogance. There was also a hunger there. A need.

Need. Amanda knew that feeling all too well. It was need that had got her into this mess. Need that had driven her to her brother's books. Need that had brought them to this house, and, ultimately, to the secret buried deep in its foundations.

In the background of the standoff, the opening credits began to play. Amanda realized that, without meaning to, she had missed the opening scene of the show.

In desperation to save her evening, she relented. "Fine. But no questions. And no bathroom breaks, except during commercials."

"I don't go to the—" he began but stopped once he saw her look. Logic, obviously, had no place here.

◆ ◆

"Who is that?"

The question broke the silent anticipation that followed the commercials. Amanda tried to let the interruption go. She tried to ignore the fact that it had been exactly two minutes since her ostensible guest had promised not to do precisely this. However, she could feel his eyes on her, patiently waiting for a response.

"Phantom," she said tersely without looking away from the television.

"Ah," he said, "the mortal protagonist."

"No," she corrected, "the vampire protagonist."

"Ha!" Yulric let out the hearty laugh of one who thinks they understand sarcasm. Amanda smirked knowingly. He would see soon enough.

He did.

"What are those people doing?" he exclaimed. There was a certain anxiety in his voice that pleased Amanda.

"Why, I think they are drinking blood!" she responded in fake astonishment. As she did, she looked at the old thing on the couch. He was sitting up now, wide-eyed and pointing.

"But why would mortals drink blood?" Yulric asked.

"Because, they aren't mortals." She grinned. "They're vampires."

Yulric stared at her, eyes wide in panic and fury. His mouth opened and closed. His claws raked at his own skin. And then, without a word, he sank back into the couch, eyes fixed on the screen. Amanda was able to enjoy the rest of the episode in peace.

Once it was over, she turned to face her burden. His eyes remained on the television, his arms folded. He was pouting again.

"So, this Phantom is a ghost?" he asked without looking at her.

"The ghost of a vampire," she said kindly. Now that her craving was sated, she found herself far less annoyed at the beast. "He refused to drink blood and so starved himself to death."

"Impossible," he muttered, still not looking at her. He seemed to blame her for the program's existence.

"Maybe," she conceded. "But not in the world of the show. Anyway, this action of sacrifice gives Phantom a special kind of power and allows him to come back to the world of the living as a ghost."

"And then he solves crimes," she added rather lamely.

"And the friend?" asked Yulric.

"A vampire," she answered.

"And the lover?" he continued.

"A human," she told him.

"And the difference?"

Amanda looked at him, an eyebrow raised. "I don't under-stand the question."

"What is the difference between the friend and the lover?"

"Well," began Amanda, "Sasha is the woman Phantom loves and the reason why he died as a vampire. He refused to drink blood, for her. Nora, on the other hand, is Phantom's best friend, confidante, and comrade-in-arms, who secretly loves him and is, in all actuality, a better match, but—"

The creature waved his hand to cut her off. A good thing, too, as it allowed Amanda to retain a semblance of dignity. She had very nearly divulged the hours of message-board dis-cussions and fan fiction she had spent on the Phantom-Nora relationship. Not that he would have known what any of that meant. To Yulric, a *shipper* was someone who hired out boats.

"What I meant," he clarified, "is how can you tell which is the vampyr?"

"Because Nora drinks blood and Sasha doesn't," replied Amanda.

"But did not this Sasha drink the blood of a vampyr"—he said the last word as if a skunk had just sprayed directly into his mouth—"to heal herself?"

"Yes, she did."

"Then how?" The old man was now looking at her again. His eyes were growing in anger, but the muffled, futile anger of one who refuses to believe the sky is blue, gravity works, or people evolved from primates.

"Well, Nora is super strong—"

"Marginally," he interjected.

"Superfast—"

"Barely," he interrupted.

"Immortal."

"If you can starve to death, you are not immortal," he countered.

"And much hotter than Sasha."

"Ha!" Yulric laughed mirthlessly. "Incorrect. Nora was said to be quite cold to the touch."

"I mean that Nora was much more attractive, physically. Sexy. More beautiful."

Yulric said nothing. He just looked at her.

"Sasha," she continued, trying to put it in terms the creature would understand, "is more . . . pretty. Not as beautiful. Therefore, she is human."

Laughter. A shrieking, dry, dead laugh erupted out of the creature on the couch. Yulric Bile flopped back into the cushions. His bones crackled and popped as he clapped his hands appreciatively.

"So, this is what we have become." He cackled, trying to catch his breath . . . or whatever he did instead of breathing. "Millennia of legend and lore, and now we appear to you as mere adolescents at the height of beauty and bloom. Tell me, are all the stories of my kind thus? Are vampyrs always immortal champions with rosy cheeks and marble physiques?"

"Sometimes they're bad," she said.

He laughed even harder. "Indeed, sometimes we are bad. Seducing mortals for nefarious ends. Immortality. Beauty. Power. All rolled into a single drama. A pleasant fiction."

"Mostly," said Amanda.

"Mostly?" mocked the vampire. "Is there a downside to their existence? Is the curse of the Phantom having to choose between locks of gold or tresses of auburn?"

"No, the show is *mostly* fiction," replied Amanda. "Because *The Phantom Vampire Mysteries* is written, produced, and acted by actual vampires."

The vampire stopped laughing.

• ◆

The fact that *The Phantom Vampire Mysteries* was made by vampires turned out to be common knowledge. Of course, the vast majority took this to mean members of a somewhat-creepy subculture who liked to pretend and play dress-up. Only those obsessive enough to pore over every interview and feature, to examine the hidden themes behind each and every episode, to download leaked script drafts, complete with notes from the executive producer, only they gleaned the truth—that they were in fact members of a somewhat-creepy subculture who liked to pretend and play dress-up, and were also vampires.

Yulric Bile spent every hour of every subsequent day poring over episodes of *The Phantom Vampire Mysteries*. He snorted incredulously at their barely above-human abilities. ("Spiders? Rats? Can they not transform into *anything*?") He marveled at their ability to withstand classic vampiric banes. ("So she can cross running water anytime she wants?") He laughed far more than seemed appropriate when the vampires were staked and turned to dust. ("A stake through the heart. Why, of course. What else would you possibly need to do?") But not nearly as loudly as he did at the concept of vampire creation.

"Why on earth would a vampyr make other vampyrs?" Yulric screamed at the screen.

"Fellowship? Companionship?" Amanda suggested from the recliner.

"An army?" Simon added.

"Bah!" Yulric exclaimed. "Pointless. They always fall apart. There!" He snatched up the remote and paused the DVD. A moment later, he was on all fours inspecting the screen. "What is that?"

Amanda sighed. "Lord Dunstan is siring a vampire."

"This siring nonsense again!" cried the vampire.

"So vampires are not sired?" Simon prodded.

"I just told you, boy. Vampyrs do not make vampyrs," Yulric retorted.

Simon clicked his pen and added this to a notebook he'd begun taking with him around the vampire. "Then, how do they come to be?"

Yulric glared at Simon, aware that the child was pumping him for information. "It varies."

"For example?" Simon inquired.

Yulric did not answer. He merely returned to the couch and restarted the episode. "We may continue."

It took him less than a week to make it through all five seasons, including commentary and special features. Of course, *The Phantom Vampire Mysteries* was hardly alone in this genre, and Yulric now turned his attention to other vampire stories. He devoured it all—TV shows, movies, books—from the poem written to impress Lord Byron to the popular teen drama about a pair of vampires in love with the same girl.[13] Unlike Phantom, few featured actual vampires, though every so often, Yulric would detect a brief whiff of vampirism in movements a hair too quick or a stare a bit too predatory.[14] However, there were definitively two common threads through almost all the vampire stories: a steady progress toward attractive respectability and a name, Talby.

After three weeks of nonstop research, Yulric came to a decision, though perhaps not at the most opportune time.

"You will take me to meet the vampyrs," Yulric said.

"Get out!" screamed Amanda, pulling the shower curtain out of his hand and hiding behind it.

---

13. You know, that one. The one that isn't that other one.

14. Especially from the vampire named Legosi. Though, those could also have been werewolf signs. He was definitely something, though.

"Not until you agree—" Yulric was cut off by the most vicious, wrathful stare this side of himself.

"Out! Now!" she barked.

Yulric decided to appease her. He did, after all, still need her assistance. "Very well," he said with a little bow, after which he exited the bathroom.

The vampire was waiting on the other side of the door when Amanda finished her shower.

"You will take me to meet the vampyrs," he repeated.

"We are not having this conversation right now," she snarled.

"And why not?" asked Yulric.

"Because I'm wearing a towel!" she shot back.

"And?"

Amanda fumed. *"Simon!"*

"Yes!" came a voice from downstairs.

"Can you come up here?" she called back. The boy appeared, sweaty and disheveled, wearing a dirty apron, and holding a trowel. She didn't even want to know why. "Watch him," she instructed and disappeared into her room.

The vampire glared at the boy and vice versa.

"So, the shower didn't work, huh?" said Simon, wiping his hands on his apron.

"No." Yulric scowled. "It did not."

"I told you," Simon gloated.

Yulric refused to acknowledge that with a response, true though it may have been.

"I don't suppose you know anything about masonry?" asked Simon.

The door opened, and Amanda appeared in her hospital scrubs. "Thank you, Simon."

"Don't mention it," the boy said, taking up his trowel and hopping down the stairs once more.

"Now you," she said, turning to Yulric.

"You will take me—" the vampire began.

"First of all," she spoke over him, "never, *ever* go into my bathroom again."

"I don't—" Yulric protested.

"Never."

"You can't—" he growled.

"Ever."

The vampire snarled, "Or what?"

"Or . . . I'll throw out the TV," she threatened.

Yulric's eyes went wide. "You wouldn't dare."

Amanda summoned the caregiver's ability to bluff. "Try me."

Yulric fumed, then, through gritted teeth, answered, "Very well. Now—"

"Second," she interrupted him again. The vampire hissed in anger. "Any future conversations we have will be predicated on both parties being fully clothed. Is that understood?"

Cracks were forming in the vampire's teeth. "Yes."

"Good," she spat. Taking a deep, calming breath, she continued. "Now, is there something I can do for you?"

The vampire took some deep, unnecessary breaths. Killing the girl where she stood would not give him what he wanted. And the elaborate tortures that immediately came to mind might put her off cooperating. So, with a tiny bow, he adopted a demeanor previously reserved for the most insufferable of Templars.[15] "Dear lady, I humbly beseech your aid in acquiring an audience with the vampyrs." He ended with a flourish of

---

15. St. Jerome of Aquitaine. Jerome the Devout, though no one called him that. References in the letters of his fellow knights are believed to be the first usages of the word *douche*.

his arms and another bow, which he held, looking down at the ground in a grand display.

"That was overdoing it a bit," she said.

"The French never thought so," Yulric retorted, still with the deceitful charm in his voice.

Amanda thought long and hard before answering. In the end, though, the ancient creature's request lined up with her goals exactly: namely, getting him off her back and getting in with the undead. "Fine," she conceded. "I will take you to see the vampires."

Yulric bowed again, even lower.

"Stop that," Amanda said, embarrassed at the ostentatious display. He stood with that horrible impish smile still etched on his face. She went to leave, and to her horror, he made a move to go with her.

"What are you doing?" she asked.

"You said you would take me to see the vampyrs," he answered in tones both polite and utterly condescending.

"Not now!" she exclaimed.

He bit his tongue. Hard. Black blood dripped down his mouth before he spoke again. "Why not?"

"I'm busy," she pushed past him and descended the staircase.

"Doing what?" he inquired, his politeness was running out, and the anger was rising again.

"Working," she shouted back at him.

"You said—" he began.

"Look." She appeared at the bottom of the staircase. "I said I would take you to see the vampires, and I will. When I have time. But now, I don't. So . . ." She tried to think of something impressive to end with but came up empty. She had to settle for an awkward nod before walking out the door.

The vampire remained at the top of the stairs. A smile—a real, horrible smile—spread across its lips.

"Simon!" he called.

"What?" the boy shouted back from somewhere in the house.

"What is your sister's work?" he asked.

"She's a nurse," replied Simon.

The vampire was fairly certain that the young woman had not recently conceived and so assumed the boy was using the word in a medical context.

"A nurse where?" he shouted.

"Shepherd's Crook Hospital," Simon answered. "Why?"

The eight-year-old received no reply. In fact, for the rest of the evening, Simon could not help but note that the vampire was unusually quiet. Not that he lost too much sleep over it. He was too busy building a forge in the backyard.

Chapter 8

Rusty Olsen rode the bus home at 2:00 a.m., sure that everyone was staring at him. *Everyone* may have included only the bus driver, who was staring at the road, a homeless man, who was staring at the back of his own eyelids, and a waitress, who *was* staring at him and had a good grip on her mace. It didn't matter, though. Rusty was always sure that people were watching him. Sometimes, it was because they were judging him; other times, it was because they were jealous of him. Sometimes, it was his red-orange hair or his acne or his stubble.[16]

In this case, it was because he was wearing purple-and-black velvet robes.

The robes hung off Rusty like a person hangs from a ledge—desperately. Custom-made, the robes gave off the illusion of not fitting, quite possibly because they didn't. They had been tailored twelve years ago for a teenager hoping to grow another

---

16. Calling it a beard would be generous.

six inches and shed a few pounds. This had not happened, and so the middle was too tight, the ends were too long, and the hood, big enough for three heads, fell well past his eyes, making it impossible to see.

Rusty tapped his rings impatiently against the bar in front of him. Each finger had a ring, including clawed ones on both pinkies. While this made getting his bus card out of his wallet a ten-minute ordeal, Rusty refused to do without them. Better to go all-out than be seen as a half-assed poser. And besides, he couldn't get the rings off without large amounts of Vaseline. The only concession he made when traveling among "normal" people lay in a black velvet pouch attached to his waist. The items resting in that sacred space were more valuable than gold to Rusty, and losing them would mean utter disgrace and another couple hundred bucks.

They were his fangs.

To be honest, he would have much preferred to wear them, as well. Fewer people openly gawked at a pair of enlarged, sharpened veneer canines. Fewer still tried to mug him for whatever was in his purse.[17] As a weirdo, he was vulnerable, but as a freak, he was fine.

That being said, there had been an incident, of sorts. It had been an innocent-enough mistake. The little old lady had simply needed help getting on the bus. Rusty, black clothes and fangs aside, was actually a very nice boy. So he'd given her a kindly smile and tried to help her up the stairs. The problem hadn't been that the fangs made him look particularly dangerous or threatening, it was that the little old lady, while little and old, was also a kendo master, one who suffered from bouts of dementia.

---

17. Muggers tended not to see the distinction between purse and pouch.

Following the shame, the police report, and the physical therapy, Rusty now carried his fangs in a pouch while in public.[18]

Rusty pulled the cord to signal his stop. With an awkward amount of effort, he extricated himself from his seat and walked to the door. As he did, he passed the twitchy waitress.

Hiss, his mind hissed, filling her with fear, respect, and just a bit of lustful desire.

Yeah, you keep walking, freak, her mind replied, without any fear, respect, and absolutely zero lustful desire.

Rusty exited the bus and began the long and uncomfortable march home. Sauntering through the city, visiting the bars he did, in the parts of town he did, that was one thing. Taking the bus out of the city, that was another. But walking through a quiet suburban neighborhood, with lawns and gnomes and swing sets, while dressed as a dark lord of vampirism was something else entirely. Plus it was cold, and surprisingly, the velvet robes were not warming.

As he walked, his mind turned back to the night he had had. He considered his fellow role-players and how their petty intrigues were destroying his empire. He reflected upon the assassination attempt he'd survived and how insulting it was to be the target of so feeble a plot. He thought about Torvald Blackmyst, née Donald Quiggly, and how he'd decided to quit their group just because he'd gone and gotten himself a girlfriend, the poser.

"You don't leave the coven just because Nancy Tompkins kisses you at our lame-o high school reunion," he shouted to the wind. "You don't change who you are just to get a girl!"

---

18. In another universe, another Rusty would learn that lesson on this trip when an ill-timed smile in the direction of the waitress was met with a face full of mace.

Several dogs in the neighborhood obviously agreed.

Children of the night, thought Rusty as he continued to walk and talk. "I mean, if she doesn't understand your need to live a life of darkness, blood, and betrayal, then she's not worth dating."

The night agreed in the form of a gust of freezing wind. Rusty thanked it with chattering teeth and a few choice curse words. This, in turn, brought the "You're welcome" of house lights switched on. Rusty metaphorically nodded good-bye by shutting his mouth and running home. Rather, he ran a block, stopped to catch his breath, then continued at the same pace he had started at until he reached his house.

Rusty quietly unlocked the front door and stepped inside. The house was dark and still, a sure sign that his parents had gone to bed. As silently as he could, which, considering a lack of coordination, wasn't very silent, Rusty made his way to the basement. Not because his room was down there, no, that was on the second floor, but to get to it, he would have had to walk up the squeaky steps, across the creaky floorboards, and past his light-sleeping mom and dad. His mother would undoubtedly wake and cry and ask where she had gone wrong, and in the morning, Pastor Dan would be there to have a little chat with him. So, instead, he went to the basement where he had stashed his laptop, a change of clothes, and a futon. Well, he hadn't stashed the futon. The futon was always there; more like he was stashing himself there for the evening.

Rusty had done this often enough to be able to navigate his way around in the dark. He felt his way to the edge of the stairs, stopped, went back to grab a can of soda,[19] and then descended, sans lights.

---

19. Pop.

In the dark, Rusty did not notice the soft ticking sound. Nor did he pay much mind to the click that muffled it. In fact, it wasn't until a voice interrupted him midgulp that he noticed anything was amiss.

"Good evening, Vermillion," greeted the voice.

Soda[20] flew from Rusty's mouth in a fine mist, at least in the movie that played in the young man's mind. In reality, there was a great deal of spitting and choking.

A lamp clicked on, and Rusty saw the violator of his sanctum. The distinguished gentleman who sat revealed by the light was just that, a distinguished gentleman. Everything about him shouted an earlier era: his three-piece suit, his white gloves, his pocket watch. He wore a pencil-thin mustache worthy of William Powell, as well as sideburns somewhere between Elvis Presley and Martin Van Buren. Striking gray eyes peered at Rusty over small rectangular reading glasses. The man's other-timely appearance combined with his dashing good looks made quite the first impression, though Rusty couldn't help but register that the basement normally didn't contain the velvet-cushioned antique chair where the man sat. Or a lamp, for that matter.

Rusty, having spit up on himself, gawked stupidly before attempting to muster some impressive indignation. His stature grew by inches while his girth shifted and sloshed.

"How do you know that name?" he demanded. Being years out of puberty, his voice didn't crack, though age had never stopped his acne.

The man smiled. "What other would I use, Vermillion?"

Rusty's mind focused. Only members of his coven called him Vermillion, no matter how hard he tried to get others to

---

20. Pop.

do so. That meant this was vampire business. Not a job for Rusty, then.

"Who are you?" asked Vermillion, his voice artificially deep and gruff. "Why are you here?"

"A friend," said the man, baring a pair of very real fangs as he did so, "who is here to make you the offer of an unlifetime."

Chapter 9

Catherine Dorset was knitting in her head. She was making a sweater for her sister. She had never actually managed to knit anything except scarves, but that was the beautiful thing about the mind—you didn't have to worry about ability or skill or knowledge. Everything came out exactly the way you wanted it to. Which was ugly, because her sister had given her an ugly sweater three Christmases ago, and revenge was a sweater best served bright and unwearable.

Knitting was just the beginning of Catherine's big night in. Afterward, she intended to replay her favorite versions of Jane Austen's novels. Then, she would do her yoga meditations, maybe sing some karaoke or play her guitar before settling down for a night of sweet dreams. All in all, an impressive evening for a woman in a coma.

Catherine Dorset had been trapped inside her own head for the past four years. She didn't really remember the accident that had put her there, but she had heard it described by the doctors enough to get the gist. A car, an intersection, and a drunk driver—really, that was all she cared to know. The exact number of broken bones and cranial bruises was irrelevant, in her opinion. In fact, that was really the only good part about the coma; she never had to feel her injuries. Then again, that might have been the morphine drip. In which case, there was no good part to being in a coma.

Catherine was halfway through her ugly sweater and considering moving on to watching *Pride and Prejudice* when she sensed a presence in her hospital room. This wasn't such an unusual occasion. Catherine was always aware of nurses and doctors coming and going. Since her family had stopped visiting after the first year, it was the only outside stimulus she had to look forward to. Occasionally, they would talk to her about the world or their lives or hospital gossip. She knew a lot of hospital gossip. If she was really lucky, they might even turn the TV on for a while. It may well have been a sad existence, but she supposed it was better than nothing.

This new visitor, however, didn't make a sound. No talking, no humming. She couldn't even hear the person breathing. If it weren't for the clattering noise of her chart being picked up, she'd have sworn she was imagining the whole thing. Even so, as her mystery guest was obviously not going to give her any stimulus, she decided to put her knitting away and indulge in some Regency-era romance.[21]

"How are you not dead?" said a voice.

It shocked Catherine to hear it, partially because she hadn't expected it, partially because it sounded so gravelly and sick,

---

21. One might wonder, if neither yarn nor needles nor cabinets nor arms nor legs were real, why you would put things away rather than just wish them out of existence. The simple answer is that going through the motions gives you something to do.

but mostly because it was coming from behind her. Since in her real room, she was lying on her back in a bed, it meant that either someone was under her bed or . . .

Catherine turned around to find a tall, hideous stranger in her mind. His head was mostly bald with wispy white hairs coming off in irregular patches. His skin was gray, wrinkled, and peeling. Veins bulged and joints protruded. His eyes were clouded like that of a corpse, except in the center, where they were unbelievably black. It was a personage that Catherine would never imagine on her own. She didn't like those kinds of movies.

He stood there, where he couldn't possibly stand, and took in his surroundings as if unsure what he was seeing. He reached a curious hand toward the teddy bear Catherine had possessed since she was four.

"Can—can I help you?" she blurted out just in time to stop him actually touching Mr. Boysenbeary with his . . . Well, it wasn't often you could use the word *talon* with a human being, but in this case, the term nearly applied.

The man's head jolted back as if he'd just remembered she was there. "How are you not dead?" he repeated quite bluntly.

Catherine was surprised. His accent was clearly English, and yet he did not hem or haw or politely ramble, everything an unexciting lifetime of movies and television had led her to believe about British men. The very least he could have done was introduce himself.

Though, perhaps, he didn't need an introduction. Perhaps she should know exactly who this robed, skeletal figure was.

"Are—are you . . . Death?" she asked. It only seemed right to get confirmation. I mean, if you had to card people for cigarettes and alcohol, one should probably check Death's ID, too.

"Why would you say that?" he asked, crossing his arms defensively. The question seemed to annoy him.

"Robed figure, creepy and skeletal, meeting me on another plane of existence," she explained, now doubting that this could be Death.

"Ah," he said. The answer seemed to mollify him, and he regained a bit of his composure. "I am not he. Not the one who ushers souls on to that which comes after. No, I am the death that man fears most: the death of blood and body, filled with pain and darkness, with no hope of anything after. I am that death. I am . . . a vampyr."

Catherine burst out laughing.

"Stop. Stop that," said a very annoyed mystery man.

"I'm sorry. I'm sorry," she said, trying to regain herself. "It was a very good speech. That ending though . . ."

She started laughing again. It was a bit before she composed herself again. When she did, Catherine noticed that the man looked angry. And taller. And . . . closer. She made a note to herself that it was probably not wise to laugh at shady characters who invaded your thoughts.

"Enough," he said, approaching her quickly.

Catherine tried not to be intimidated. She tried to remember that he could not possibly hurt her in her own head. That didn't stop her from backing against her imaginary cabinet, though.

"Tell me, why are you not dead?"

"I'm—I'm in a coma," she said, working her way behind the dresser. Maybe, if she had some time to think, she could—

"A coma?" he questioned, passing through the cabinet as if it were not there. Ghostlike behavior, if ever she'd seen it. Which meant that he couldn't possibly hurt her, right?

She tried to muster some gusto to throw back at him. "Listen, mister," she began, prodding him in the chest. It made her pause. Ghost or not, if she could touch him, then . . . The same thought seemed to be going through her visitor's mind, as well, so to placate him and back up a bit farther off, she said, "I'm asleep. I had an accident, and I can't wake up."

"Obviously," he snorted, insulted. "*Koma*, from the Greek. But how do you still live?"

"My family," she said. "They must hope that I'll come out of this. Or they've forgotten about me. One or the other."

"The sheet of paper says 'four years,'" he stated incredulously. "You long since should have perished." Strangely, his intent didn't appear malicious. He seemed . . . puzzled, that was all.

For the first time, Catherine began to note certain aspects of the stranger. His manner of speech was familiar, not because she heard it in her everyday life but because she watched so many movies with people speaking that way. His clothes were, too—his long, flowing ebony robe seemed like something one would see at a Renaissance fair, except less comfortable, less colorful, and less well-made. These things combined with his extreme age and his questions as to her survival, and her mind finally slid the last gears into place.

This was a very old ghost.

She took pity on this sad apparition, and in a voice people usually reserve for the dying and her, said, "The machines around my head. The devices?" And then, in case he still didn't get it, "The metal things? They keep my body alive. They feed me and give me medicine and monitor my pulse—my heart— to make sure it continues to pump . . . to beat."

"Your body cannot do these things on its own?" he challenged.

"Well, some of them," she corrected him.

"But without their aid, you would die?"

"Yes," she said. She knew this conversation should annoy her or make her sad, but the truth was, it had been so long since she had been heard by anyone that she was actually enjoying herself, regardless of subject matter.

"Then, your body is dead," he said, working out a problem in his head.

"Some people would say so," she replied.

"But you are here, in the darkness." He added, "Asleep, but aware. Consciously dreaming. Technically alive but apparently dead."

"One might even say, undead," she chimed in, seeing his train of thought to its logical conclusion.

"No," he corrected her. "The opposite. Unalive."

Again, it was not an insult. It wasn't even that mean. For the first time, the old man seemed almost kind. Frankly, it made Catherine more uncomfortable. She had to turn away from him.

"Would you like to die?"

The question echoed around the walls of her mind. She turned back to that sallow face, those sunken eyes suddenly free from malice and filled instead with an earnest seriousness. His gaze no longer searched or prodded. Instead, he waited, simply waited, for an answer.

Would you like to die? When you are stuck in a coma, it's a question you ask yourself at least once a day, and since she had no idea how long her days were, it was probably far more often than that. She often thought about death. She often wished for death. In that first year of being unable to talk or move or even wake, she would scream at the top of her metaphorical lungs for someone, anyone, to please, please kill her. Even now, four years on, after she'd found a kind of rhythm and routine to her eternal daydream, even now, there were bad days when she tried to will herself away. It never worked, though, and after eating some chocolates that she imagined and having a good cry, she would pick herself up and find some mental cobweb to sweep.

This was different. This was someone else asking. Not even asking, really. It was an offer. One that, ghost or not, Death or not, she felt certain this strange man had the power to fulfill— continue to live this half-life, unable to affect anything real or tangible, almost a ghost herself, or shuffle off this mortal coil into (a) heaven or (b) oblivion. There was, of course, that third option, but she was fairly certain she wasn't going there. A priest came by pretty frequently to give last rites, and it was difficult to masturbate without the aid of her arms.

It was time to make a decision, one way or the other.

She was weighing her fear of death against utter boredom when the door to her room opened in the distance. It wasn't all that loud and hardly noticeable, except that it was quickly followed by a maddened scream.

"What do you think you are doing?"

The man spun around, staring up into the darkness and out of her head. He appeared to be a bit scared, or at least alarmed. Catherine recalled the look she had worn in high school when her parents had caught her doing . . . something . . . she ought not to have been doing.[22]

As quickly as it had come, the panic faded, and when the man turned back to her, it was with the dignity of a duke and the face of the duke's long-dead grandfather who had fallen victim to some terribly disfiguring plague.

"If you will excuse me?" he said. With that, he faded into the darkness and Catherine was again alone, unable to do anything but cozy up on an imaginary couch with a bucket of popcorn that did not exist and listen to the argument unfold. Death would have been good, but at least she was entertained.

---

22. . . . with her girlfriend . . . in the shower.

◆ ◆

To say Amanda was surprised was an understatement and did not convey the correct level of anger she felt. Even the word *anger* did not convey the correct level of anger. You had to go to old-school words like *rage* and *wrath* and *smote*. She had merely been going about her business changing a coma-patient's saline bag, when she'd opened a door and found her unwanted houseguest crouched over the woman, staring into her forcibly opened eyes.

"What do you think you are doing?" she yelled. With lightning speed and fury, she jumped forward and knocked the creature's hand away from the woman's eyes, allowing them to close. When that was done, she looked up to find the blinking vampire returning to his upright and locked position.

"Back!" she ordered, taking the gold cross from around her neck and thrusting it toward Yulric. He recoiled as if he had been burned, moving toward the safety of the window, hissing as he went. Amanda didn't care. She wanted him to hurt. If he escaped, well, she knew where he lived.

He didn't escape. He merely continued backing up, and when he reached the wall, he backed up that and onto the ceiling. Once out of reach, he folded his arms and waited for Amanda to calm down. Amanda, heaving with fury,[23] flung her cross at him. Yulric swatted it away, taking in a pained breath as it singed his hand. Then, for good measure, she pitched the saline bag at him. This harmlessly bounced off and fell to the floor.

---

23. That's breath heaving, not hurl heaving. And that's vomit hurl, not caber-toss hurl.

"Are you quite done?" he asked as the bag wobbled to a halt. Amanda was not done, but she had run out of weapons within easy reach.

"You have to come down sometime," she said, searching for another weapon. "Eventually the sun comes up."

"So I have until morning," he reasoned. "How long before someone comes to check on you?"

Logic, Amanda found, was far more annoying when it got in the way of being massively pissed off. A few more huffs and a murderous glare later, she was ready for a reasonable discussion.

"What do you think you are doing?" she asked again in a slightly more controlled tone.

Yulric took a moment to unfurl himself so he could now stand at his full height on the wall in a dramatic fashion, right above her head. "Helping," he said.

"Helping?" she repeated, trying to remain calm. "Helping? How is standing over one of my patients and staring helpful?"

"That was not helping. That was curiosity."

"Curious about what?" she asked skeptically.

He pointed at Catherine's body. "I have seen crippled Viking kings wade into battle and heard decapitated saints speak, but at no time, in all my many centuries, could anyone sleep for years and still live."

"Rip Van Winkle?" Amanda suggested.

"Who?"

"Never mind," she said. "Look, we don't use leeches anymore. We can keep people alive now."

"And yet you cannot wake them up," he said. It wasn't a question.

"In this case, no," she conceded.

"Quite cruel. I approve."

Amanda mumbled under her breath. "Yeah, well, I'm glad. And what does your approval have to do with your creeptastic looming?"

"I wanted to see what was in her mind. To see what she saw and felt." Yulric paused. The two stared awkwardly at each other from different planes, like some horribly dull M.C. Escher drawing.

"And?" Amanda asked after seconds of silent anticipation.

"I believe she would like to die." Again, he said this as fact, very plainly, without malice, which for him was odd.

"Well, that's not my call to make," Amanda explained lamely. She glanced over at the patient. If she was listening, Amanda hoped she understood.

"Is it not her decision?" Yulric asked.

"Yes. I'll just go before a judge and explain that I learned the patient's true desires through vampire telepathy," she said, throwing her arms up in exasperation. "They throw me in jail or an asylum, Simon goes into foster care, and you . . . You never get your stupid answers. Congratulations, you've been a big help."

"This was not helping," Yulric said.

"Right, it was *curiosity*. Well, do me a favor? Go home and be less curious."

She started to leave. Then, a thought hit her. A sickening, awful thought.

"How were you going to help me, exactly?" she asked.

The vampire smiled. "By lessening your workload."

Amanda's eyes went wide, and suddenly, she was sprinting down the halls of the hospital, hoping against all hope.

It didn't take long for her hope to die. Alarms were going off. Heart monitors were flatlining. Shouts of "clear!" came from a half dozen rooms. A line of carts waited for the elevator so they could get down to the OR. Everywhere there was panic and fear and death.

Except in rooms that had a crucifix. Those patients were fine.

Amanda turned to find the creature standing on the threshold of the coma-patient's room, a broad, malicious grin across his face as he admired his handiwork. He gave a curt little nod to her and closed the door.

Over the next several hours, Amanda went to work saving lives. She lost count of the number of chest compressions she did, blood bags she changed, and injections she gave. Needless to say, it was somewhere between several and a shit ton. And every time, there were those strange, jagged puncture marks on arms or wrists or necks that needed bandaging.

"What a night, huh?" a doctor remarked. Amanda muttered her agreement. Doctors don't become doctors to be ignored. "No idea what would make so many patients self-harm like that, clawing at their wrists and necks. Must be the full moon."

"Must be," Amanda responded hollowly. She glanced down the hall where the dance of light from the TV was just visible through the cracked door.

"Oh well. They're out of the woods. That's the important thing. Good work, Amber," he told her, unaware what her name was, and then went off to call his wife.[24]

---

24. Contrary to what TV would have you believe, hospitals are not the breeding grounds of steamy affairs and sultry trysts between young, attractive medical professionals. Young, attractive people generally don't go into medicine, they go into acting. That way, they can play young, attractive medical professionals who have lots of steamy, sultry sex, without bothering with the years of study and risk of blood-borne pathogens. Those that do go into medicine tend to be not so young by the end and would

Amanda slowly made her way toward the coma-patient's room, gathering her rage as she went. Not just for herself but for all those who'd almost died. If anger were electricity, by the time she reached the door, she'd have been a Tesla coil. She inhaled and braced herself to once more face the vampire.

The least he could have been doing was watching something other than reality television.

"Can we go to the vampyrs now?" The fiend grinned from his chair.

Shaking with fury, Amanda barely managed to answer. "No."

"No?" said the confused vampire.

"No," she said again. "I have to work."

"Your work is done. I took care of that. Let us go."

Yulric made to walk past her. Amanda stepped in his way.

"No," she said again.

The vampire, looming, with all his dark power, looked her straight in the neck, her slender, vein-filled neck. "We had an arrangement, little girl. I hope you do not intend on backing out of it, otherwise"—he licked his lips with his black tongue—"you will find my patience, like your blood, is only skin deep."

"I haven't forgotten our *arrangement*, monster," Amanda said with the hint of a smile. "I was merely saying, no, you haven't killed anyone."

Yulric laughed dismissively until he saw the smug, satisfied look on Amanda's face.

"You lie," he said with rather less certainty than he meant to.

"I don't," she replied.

---

rather get on with the business of stitching up gashes and performing triple bypasses than tongue each other in storerooms.

"Impossible. Impossible!" the vampire spat with increasing volume and venom. "I drained them of their life's blood. Took them past the limits their bodies could handle. Believe me, I know exactly how much to take out."

"And we," she bragged, "know how much to put in. And what type. And where to put it."

Yulric looked murderous, quite a feat, considering he was capable of murder when looking utterly bored.

"Now, you listen to me," she said. "You want to meet the vampires? Fine, I've agreed to help you. But from here on out, I'm in charge. You do what I tell you. You do not try to out-wit my orders or undermine them or fulfill their letter and not their meaning. You do not *help* me without being asked. You don't do anything without being asked. What you will do is wait at home, until such time as I come get you and say, 'Dearest Unkie Bile, shall we go play with the vampires?' And you will say, 'Oh yes, Mandy, dear, let's.' Until then, you do nothing. Sit. Sleep. Watch TV, using a reasonable volume and without yelling every twenty minutes. Do you understand?"

The vampire's eyes narrowed. "I could kill you where you stand."

Amanda's grip tightened on her cross. "Try it."

The pair held their standoff for a tense minute, each waiting for the other to give in. Then, at long last, and for only the second time in his thousand-year history, Yulric blinked first.

"Good," Amanda said. She couldn't believe that had actually worked. All that was left was to get him out of there before her legs buckled and she started crying. "Now go home and wait."

Without stepping down off the wall, Yulric made his way to the window, opened it, and with a final, spiteful face, became a bat and fluttered away. This had been a humiliating experience for him, an incident that would only become worse because of the three windshields he would collide with on his way back to the house.

Amanda stumbled backward, her nerves shot, her legs no longer capable of holding her up. She caught herself on the edge of the bed, though not for long, as the nearby heart-rate monitor started to wail.

"Sorry! Sorry!" she cried, reattaching the wires she had knocked loose from Catherine's arm. Once done, she collapsed into a chair and just shook. She checked her watch. It was a bit early in the evening to take her break, but she definitely needed it.

"I hope you don't mind," Amanda said, reaching for the TV's remote. She put on a hospital drama about doctor's tonguing each other in storerooms. Catherine didn't mind in the least. She loved this show.

Chapter 10

Rusty dreamt of cheeseburgers. Double Angus cheeseburgers. And pizza. A large—no, extra-large—sausage with stuffed crust. And milk shakes with whipped cream and nuts and hot fudge and caramel and banana flavoring. Not real banana flavoring but the completely fake banana flavoring, which tasted like banana only inasmuch as candy companies had decided that flavor of sugar was banana.

Rusty dreamt of all that, and he wasn't even asleep. In fact, when Rusty wasn't dreaming of food, he was dreaming of sleep. And resting. Lounging, slacking, hanging, lying about, and all forms of do-nothingness that involved food, a TV, and, if possible, the first three seasons of *The Phantom Vampire Mysteries*, for which he also dreamt of a Blu-ray player.

What Rusty had instead was hours and hours on a treadmill.

Rusty hated running. Part of the reason he hadn't done any for the better part of a decade was because he hated it so much. Growing up, his parents had forced him to "participate." This meant he spent the better part of his grade, junior high, and high school years padding out the B squads and JV teams of various sports he was no good at. However, once college had come along, he'd hung up all attempts at athleticism in favor of Frisbee golf, beanbags, and Halo tourneys, none of which required anything more than a saunter and a beer-free hand.

But now, here he was, in another man's loft, running. He didn't want to and he didn't like it, but he was doing it.

Why? Rusty asked himself as his heavy feet thudded out a rhythm. Of course he already knew the answer. It had been explained to him two weeks earlier in a strong, deep voice that held all the authority of perfectly enunciated Queen's English.

"When did you ever see a fat vampyr?" his host had asked him, about twenty minutes into his first run on the treadmill.

"Well . . ." Rusty rattled off a list of fat vampires he had seen in various TV shows, movies, and graphic novels. Many of them had honorifics or epithets that emphasized their robust size, like The Grand or The Round or The Fat. Vampires chose nicknames a lot like mobsters.

His host looked at his pocket watch and sighed. "And were those shining exemplars of vampirism?"

Rusty had to admit they were not. Anytime you saw a fat vampire in fiction, they were lazy, evil, or comic relief. Usually, they were all three.

"Perhaps, then," continued the voice, "we should aspire to something a bit better. A bit more . . ." He gestured to the TV in front of Rusty, which was currently playing the musical episode of *The Phantom Vampire Mysteries.*

"Phantom!" cried Rusty, completely forgetting to run. This caused him to trip and fall face-first onto the still-moving treadmill. The voice let out another sigh. It seemed frustrated that its dignity had not yet rubbed off. Rusty rolled onto his back and again whispered, "Phantom."

"Yes," said the dignified voice. "*The Phantom Vampire Mysteries.* A television show about vampyrs acted *by* vampyrs. Of course, one as clever as you wouldn't have doubted what that meant. Surely, you of all people knew better than to assume these were mere mortals pretending."

"Of . . . course I didn't," Rusty lied, likely quite obviously. Fortunately, his host didn't seem to care; he had already turned back to the television.

"Tell me," the man asked, "is Phantom fat? Does Nora have acne? Are any of these characters less than the physical embodiment of perfection in any way?"

Rusty shook his head. Then he spit blood. The owner of the voice looked at that blood intensely as he continued. "And do you know why?"

"Be-because they're vampires," Rusty huffed.

The man smirked, condescendingly. "Oh, my dear Vermillion. Beauty is not some innate power of the vampyr. The gift of the vampyr is immortality, pure and simple. And that gift can serve no greater purpose than the preservation of great beauty."

"I see," Rusty lied again. He did see the logic; he just couldn't see how he personally fit into this philosophy.

As if he could read Rusty's mind, the Englishman patted him in a fatherly way. "Rusty, do you really think those of natural beauty could truly appreciate such a gift? *Truly* appreciate it?"

"Um, no?" Rusty guessed.

"Beauty, my dear Vermillion, true beauty does not occur without work. Without transformation. And only such beauty, created through great effort, is worth preserving."

The man crossed to look out upon a nearly panoramic view of the New York skyline. Rusty had the unnerving feeling that he was no longer present in the world. "The pyramids of Egypt.

The Sistine Chapel. Beethoven's Fifth. All required time, work, and sacrifice, not only to create but also to be worthy of the immortality they have achieved. The wonders of nature, mountains and oceans, flora and fauna, only came to be through the violence and change of geology and evolution."

He turned back to Rusty, continuing this seemingly well-rehearsed speech. "A person's beauty is no different. It must be forged, worked on, sacrificed for, and only those who are willing, who give themselves over completely, who pay the highest price are worthy of being preserved for all time."

His host had finished. Rusty wasn't quite sure of what to do or say. He had an urge to start clapping, but that seemed awfully awkward, and pitiful, as he was the only one there. Instead, he got back on the treadmill and started running.

"Very good, Vermillion," said the man. "You do that. I'm going to check your belongings for contraband snacks."

That had been two weeks ago. Since then, Rusty had spent every day in his host's upscale loft working out—running on the treadmill, lifting weights, doing sit-ups, even yoga, though the stretch pants made him feel rather silly. On top of that, he had been put on an all-natural, organic, vegan diet. No meat, no dairy, and no carbs. After all, "If you can't exercise self-control over your natural appetites, what hope have you of controlling supernatural ones?" Rusty had stuck to it—mostly. Okay, so he'd sneaked in a few candy bars and a slice of pizza or two. Man cannot live on soy alone. Hell, man can barely live on soy at all.

Even with these lapses, Rusty was shedding pounds. He had already traded in his old pants and belts. He wouldn't be modeling underwear anytime soon, but you had to start somewhere, right?

"Very good," his host said later that night. Rusty wasn't quite sure how the pair of forceps measured the folds of his stomach, but they obviously did, because the man continued to make encouraging sounds as he poked Rusty with the cold metal. "Very good, indeed."

The forceps were placed in a black leather doctor's bag. In their place came a tailor's measuring tape. This went around his waist, chest, arms, legs, and neck. The numbers were then written on a clipboard, checked, and compared.

"This couldn't be better," commented the host. "Even cheating on your diet hasn't thrown off your schedule."

Rusty shifted uncomfortably. Cheating on his diet might make him unworthy, but lying about it might make him more unworthy.

The man chuckled. "Don't worry. Everyone cheats."

Rusty let out a sigh of relief. As he did so, he was encouraged to lift his arms. It was a moment or two before he realized what was going on.

"Um, why are you drawing on me?" Rusty asked.

The permanent marker in the man's hand stopped somewhere around his kidneys.

"You didn't think we were going to do all of this so slowly?" he said with a smile. "That would take forever and you are not immortal yet. People, like wines, have an ideal time in which they are at their best. Past that, they begin an irrevocable decline. It's important we improve you before you hit yours."

"Um, and when is that?" Rusty asked.

"According to my calculations, we have about six months. Maybe a year. So, we speed up the process where we can," the man explained. "Besides, I am eager to begin working on your face."

Chapter 11

Like an artist at an empty canvas, Amanda stood in front of her wardrobe. Her gaze shifted as her mind threw this dress with those shoes or that blouse with these pants, searching for a look that both fit in and stood out. And it had to be supersexy, as she was about to walk into a nightclub of ultrahot vampires and wannabe vampires alongside a walking cadaver who didn't understand why commenting on her weight was inappropriate.

"I don't see the problem," he had said as Amanda seethed and Simon excused himself from the room. "You can afford to eat. Unlike those poor wretches on TV. Actors being destitute and hungry. Time may have passed, but some things never change."

And so she needed something that would instill enough confidence to offset anything her tagalong might say. The dilemma was really on her choice of top, as that would decide what she wore with it. If she wore a halter style, well then a pair of tight-fitting black leather pants might go nicely. If she went with a proper blouse, then a short miniskirt and glasses would be needed to complete the sexy-librarian look. If she went with a form-fitting black[25] dress, the whole top-and-bottom decision became moot.

Tonight, her eyes kept falling upon the corsets. She didn't get to wear them often and was on her way to one of two places in the modern world where they were acceptable.[26] Plus, a corset would send the right message: "Yes, I do look good, but I'm not going home with you, and if you think any differently, try figuring out how to get this off me." With very little finesse and quite a bit of struggle, she wriggled into the garment, using some practiced flailing and the handle of her closet door to tighten it—not to beauty-is-not-breathing Victorian standards, but enough to give it the proper amount of squish up top.

With this decided, everything else fell into place. A long black skirt that was slit on either side, up to her thighs so her long, silky legs slipped out of them. Full-length black sleeves gave her a bit more coverage and warmth. A collar fit snugly around her neck for a bit of class, without covering her décolletage. After this, it was just a matter of applying jewelry and caking on eyeliner.

Amanda looked at herself in the mirror. With the exception of her hair, she was the very image of a Goth goddess. For a moment, she considered putting on a black-bob wig. It would definitely have helped her status among the hard core, for whom blond hair was decidedly too mainstream. However, when it came to everyone else, blondes still held more sway, so she went without.

---

25. It took a lot of nerve to show up at a vampire club in something other than black.

26. The other being a Renaissance fair.

All that was missing were her knee-high, high-heel boots. Unfortunately, these were not in her bedroom. The last time she'd worn them, she had immediately taken them off. Which meant they were in the hallway closet. Downstairs. Where her brother was.

This was the part of her life that Amanda had the most trouble with: trying to balance her long-term, vampire-based goals while maintaining enough authority to keep her brother in line. Covering up as best she could, which wasn't very much at all, she tiptoed her way to the stairs.

She crept down the three-hundred-plus-year-old creaky staircase, wincing at each prolonged squeak and groan of the wood. At the bottom, she poked her head around the corner to see if her brother was there. He wasn't. Breathing more easily, she opened the closet and rummaged. It had only been a month since her last outing, and yet, as per the law of hallway closets, what she was looking for had managed to wind up in the back underneath fallen jackets, old shoes, and sports equipment she couldn't remember ever buying. Upon extricating her somewhat squished leather footwear, she sat on the third step, worked her feet into them, and zipped them up. Standing carefully, Amanda straightened her skirt and turned to get her purse.

Simon was sitting on the fourth step, waiting for her. How he had managed to get there without making a sound was beyond Amanda.

"Hey . . . Simon," she said awkwardly. She felt like a teenager again.

"You're going out," said Simon, balancing between making a statement and asking a question.

"Yeah," she replied meekly. She tried desperately to cover her cleavage with her arms. Thanks to her choice of corset, though, there was an awful lot of cleavage. "I'm taking Yulric to meet the other vampires."

"Remember your mace," he advised, standing to walk up the stairs.

Trying to regain her adult authority, she changed the subject. "Are you going to be all right here by yourself?"

"I have Sun Tzu to keep me company," he said. He held up a leather-bound book too large for a boy in Batman pajamas.

"Only three chapters and then to bed, understand?" she called after him.

She waited until she heard his door close before climbing the stairs herself to snag her purse and a warm cape. She then awaited her failed plan B to come up from the cellar so they could go see her failed plan A.

◆ ◆

Yulric never liked going into situations blind. That was the easiest way to die. Knowledge was power, and, in this brave new world, he was sorely lacking. He may have been outclassed by those who knew how to play music from a bar on their arm or extract notes of scrip from mechanical devices, but ancient knowledge still applied.

Hence, the dead cat.

Dissecting the feline he had purloined from across the street, he began to examine its entrails. A cat was not best for this type of work, but the area livestock was sorely lacking. According to the location of its liver, tonight would not go well. A bulge in its stomach, the remnants of a good meal, meant he would get his answers. One sickly lung was blackened and deflated, the other pink and filled with air, Yulric chose not to interpret that. The intestines spilled out first, which indicated a long journey was imminent.

What truly vexed him was the heart. For the greater part of the population, this lump of biologically vital muscle tissue was something about which to sing songs, read poems, and eat little candies with phrases on them. For Yulric, it represented his desire, not just for the coming meeting but for all things to come. In a very limited way, the heart was him. If it had been shriveled or blackened or covered in tumors, he might have been worried. But it was healthy and boisterous and strong: a very good sign.

Except that it was on the wrong side of the body.

"Are you almost ready?" called a voice from upstairs.

"A moment, if you please," he shouted back. He dug a small hole in the already broken concrete floor and threw the cat in. Not the typical disposal method for a sacrificial animal, but he'd been forbidden already from building a fire, and even in ancient times, people got funny about eating cats.

He covered the small hole and then jumped into the large hole that had once been his resting place. Contrary to popular belief, vampires are not very sentimental. When your very existence inevitably results in mobs with torches, it becomes difficult to collect priceless works of art and fine Italian furniture. Even before his original death, Yulric had learned not to get too attached to anything you couldn't fit into a small bag.

That being said, he liked to be prepared. Clawing his way through the dirt, handfuls at a time, he slowly moved deeper and deeper into the ground. Finally, his nails scraped against the wooden lid of a small chest. At one point, it had been finely ornate with delicate carvings and brilliant colors, though that was before it had been buried in dirt for three centuries. If the Austrian carpenter who'd crafted it could see what'd become of his work, he would have killed Yulric. Which was why Yulric had slit his throat before taking possession of the damn pretty box.

Yulric opened it without a second thought. Locks were for mortals and insecure giants; no one stole from a vampire. The contents of the chest found their way into the folds of his robe. Yulric took a moment to consider the state of the box and the likelihood that the boy would be rooting around the cellar after he left. With a smile, he left the box out where it was sure to be found.

Belying the giddiness he felt, he slowly made his way upstairs to face his destiny.

◆   ◆

"Are you ready?" Amanda asked as the vampire strolled into the kitchen. The sight of her seemed to give him pause, and she could feel his eyes sweeping across her body in a disapproving, oddly parental way. He muttered something under his breath that sounded like "never be free of these Puritans."

"What?" she asked, certain she had misheard him.

"Nothing," he replied. "I am ready."

They made their way through the hallway to the front of the house.

"Simon, we're leaving!" Amanda called upstairs.

"Okay," called a voice that sounded busy.

"Stay out of the basement, boy!" shouted the vampire.

There was a long pause before Simon finally answered, "Okay."

Once the two had gone outside, Amanda rounded on the vampire. "What was that about?"

Yulric grinned. "There is a rather tarnished old box that I would like restored."

"Huh," she replied with a smirk. "You're learning."

Amanda made it as far as the car before—

"What are you doing?" cried a voice from behind her. She turned to find the vampire frozen on the stoop, face aghast, as if he wasn't sure whether to run or ravage. Amanda let out the kind of sigh that only saints and people with children make, for only they know the secret of turning oxygen into patience.

"The vampires are not in Shepherd's Crook, present company excepted. Shepherd's Crook is a boring, small town, and no self-respecting vampire would ever set foot here, present company excepted. So we need to go to New York City or New Amsterdam or whatever they called it in your day. And to get there, we need to drive."

"I am not getting into that infernal machine," he proclaimed.

"It can't hit you while you are inside it," she assured him.

"So say you," he replied, having lost all ability for reasonable thought.

"It is a carriage," she explained. "A horseless carriage. A means to transport people from one place to another. It does not have a mind of its own. It is not out to get you. It will not ignite or implode in on itself just because you're inside."

The vampire looked at her as if he didn't believe a word she was saying, and so she continued. "I *am* getting inside. Where the controls are. And you, the person annoying me, will be outside where the controls aren't. And then who knows what might happen."

Angrily, the vampire moved to the passenger side of the car. After she gave him a pointed look, he opened the door and, with a few starts and hisses, got inside, moving toward the middle of the seat, away from the door, which he eyed warily.

Between the corset, the skirt, and the boots, it took Amanda a moment to negotiate her way inside. After she had, she instructed, "Seat belts."

The vampire turned to the strip of fabric hanging off his shoulder. Amanda knew he had learned from the television what they were, so he could not play ignorant this time.

"I have no need for a life saving restraint," he argued.

She was ready for this fight, as well. "If you don't put it on, the police might pull us over and make inquiries."

"Then I will change their minds," he said impatiently.

"Can you also change the mind of the video cameras that will be recording you? Or the people who will be watching those videos?"

It was a bluff. Amanda had talked to her brother on the subject and was pretty sure this vampire wouldn't show up on video. Still, Yulric didn't know that and neither Linske was about to tell him. And so, with some trepidation, he reached out, took the clip attached to the fabric, stretched it across his body, and inserted it into the device meant to receive it.

"Well, here we go," she said. And away they went, the girl and the vampire.

Driving with the vampire turned out to be a lot like driving with a dog. Or a small child. Or a small dog with fingers. As soon as she hit the freeway and they started going faster than Yulric had ever seen anything go, his fear of the car was apparently overcome by awe and curiosity. He watched as they zoomed by the outside world, often choosing to pick objects in the distance and follow them with his head until they had passed. This eventually caused him to lean on the window controls, which Amanda had foolishly forgotten to lock. So, up and down went the window. Then, out of the window went hands, followed by arms, and finally a head. All the while, questions were being asked. "How fast are we going now?" was said with the same annoying frequency as "Have we arrived yet?" or the panicked shouts of "Watch out!" and "No, no, no!" when she weaved the car through traffic.

Amanda had never really understood the theory of relativity. When they had explained it in school, it had gone over her head, and when Simon tried to show her two years ago, it had been during the *Phantom* season finale, so she wasn't really listening. Now, though, she looked on at people passing in their cars, also headed for New York, and finally understood. For those passengers, this trip would only take a few hours. For Amanda, it would be so much longer.

Chapter 12

Yulric had been to cities. To say he'd lived in any would be both literally and metaphorically incorrect. It's hard to live in a place you intend to flee in six months. But he had stayed in dozens, maybe even hundreds of cities, and what he lacked in time spent, he made up for in the quality of the cities themselves. Any college student or ardent world traveler wishes he had the résumé that Yulric could boast.[27]

He had also lived long enough to understand that change and growth were inevitable. In his years, small farming villages filled with serfs had turned to towns filled with merchants and craftsmen, on their way to becoming cities filled with serfs again. Castles and walls had become largely irrelevant

---

27. Not that he did. Boasting was beneath him. At most, he might marvel at an old legend about a dark foreigner who entered Madrid and brought a terrible plague in his wake. When you told him, "No record of the stranger survives to this day," he would merely smile.

fortifications allowing for the outward expansion of dwellings and brothels.[28] What ancient artifices weren't torn down ended up mixing with modern structures, like cathedrals or palaces.

Cities grew. This was the way of things. Unless there was a war or a plague or a mysterious stranger, in which case, a city might crumble, dwindle, or disappear/explode/sink into the sea. But barring any of these occurrences, cities grew, and one need only have looked at Shepherd's Crook to see this fact in motion. Three hundred years ago, it was a small collection of farmhouses around a church, barely worth calling a village. Today, from what Yulric had seen whizzing by, it took up nearly as much land as Paris or London had in his day. However, Yulric's understanding of population growth did not prepare him for the contemporary city.

"Is that a building?" he asked after they'd barely passed beyond what Amanda called the suburbs and into the city proper.

Amanda glanced at where he was looking. "That? That's nothing. An apartment complex probably."

Yulric looked at her aghast. He'd besieged towers in castles smaller than this building. And those had been filled with noble lords and soldiers aplenty. These . . . these were for *regular* people.

Amanda could not help but smile at the vampire's childlike amazement. "Wait until you see the real skyscrapers."

Thirty minutes later, however, Yulric was still waiting.

"Should we not be moving?" he groaned.

"I take it they didn't have traffic back in the 1600s?" said Amanda. She inched the car forward slightly, then stopped.

"What is the point of this hideous monstrosity if it does not go fast?" he protested.

---

28. Sometimes called theaters.

"We'll get there when we get there, all right?" Amanda replied, although he thought she was secretly agreeing with his sentiment.

Yulric looked out the passenger window and pointed. "Why do we not take the empty road?"

"That isn't a road. It's a sidewalk," she told him.

"There are no cars on it," Yulric pointed out.

"That's because it's for people," explained Amanda.

"They would get out of the way," he said absentmindedly. He had just noticed a small boy watching him from the car in the next lane. He smiled, menacingly. The boy started screaming.

"Stop that," scolded Amanda.

"Stop what?" Yulric replied, having adopted the appearance of innocence, both for her and the child's parents, who were now looking at him.

"You know what," Amanda said. She pointed at the windshield. "There, see. There's the city."

"Where?" Yulric asked.

"It was past those condos. You must have missed it," she explained. "Just keep looking."

Yulric craned his neck, trying to peer around the building in question. It was another ten minutes before he realized he'd been tricked, but by that time, it didn't matter because they could finally see the gray tips of distant towers peeking out from around barely moving semis or just above YMCAs. As they inched forward, these monoliths of glass, concrete, and metal resolved themselves and grew. Ten minutes and half as many miles later, they equaled heights rivaling the cyclopean towers of R'lyeh or the ruins of Leng,[29] and still the car had not reached their base. Higher and higher the buildings rose, not

---

29. See *Dig at Your Own Risk: Prehuman Cities and the Archaeologists Who Went Mad* by Professor Tobias Thibnee.

one or two, but dozens, stretching into the sky, some even disappearing into the very clouds overhead, making it impossible to tell if they ever ended.

"I may have underestimated the Dutch." The vampire gaped.

A few minutes later, they were pulling off the road that ran alongside the edge of the island and into an area with an entrance marked by squat, brick buildings, which took up entire blocks. Amanda pointed to one in particular. "That's where we're going."

"A slaughterhouse," Yulric purred.

"Um, maybe. This is the Meatpacking District," Amanda stammered, uncomfortable with his tone of voice. "How did you know?"

The vampire just closed his eyes and breathed in, trying to extract blood from the neighborhood's history. He stopped when Amanda began to drive away from their destination, turning his breathing into a series of inarticulate noises that basically all translated to "Why?"

"We need to park the car," she explained to the still-grunting vampire.

"But . . . there are cars all around," protested Yulric.

"And no space for ours," she replied. Apparently anticipating his next suggestion, she added, "We can't park on the sidewalk." The vampire fell back against his chair in a resentful huff. "Look, we're on our way to a . . . stable for cars." And indeed, a few minutes later they were pulling into a parking garage: a hideous, cement structure built specifically to temporarily house cars for a fee. Which came as a shock. He'd assumed, based on what he'd seen on TV, that such buildings were designed for clandestine meetings and brutal murders. Though when he thought back, there had been cars in those scenes, as well.

Amanda guided the car up, level by level, until they finally found a single, open parking spot. Carefully, she squeezed in the car between a Prius and a brand new Hummer, which had tried to take up two parking spots without getting a ticket. This meant there was an inch and a half of space on the passenger's side to open the door.

"You can mist your way out, right?" Amanda suggested to the vampire. He gave a shrewd grunt of a laugh and then dissolved into smoke, just like she'd had in mind. The mist then crawled over her on its way out the driver-side door, which was very much NOT what she'd had in mind. When the vampire materialized once more, and Amanda was quite certain she wasn't going to vomit, she, too, exited the car. "From here, we walk."

Whatever smugness Yulric's face had gained from his defiant stunt quickly evaporated as he put together what he'd been too distracted to realize before. "But"—his voice became a nervous hush—"what about the—" A distant screeching of tires finished his sentence for him.

"You're not going to be hit by a car," she said exasperatedly.

"They're everywhere," he whispered. The vampire wrung his hands manically, his eyes darting this way and that.

Realizing he would not budge from this spot until certain of his safety, she tried to calm his fears. "In the city, people have the right-of-way. The cars will stop."

The monster folded his arms. "In my day, people on horses stopped for walls and spears and little else. Those who were inattentive or slow were trampled underfoot."

"Well, that doesn't happen now," Amanda said.

"Why?"

"Because people are basically decent and good."

"Ha," laughed Yulric. "Times have not changed that much."

"And we have laws," Amanda added, conceding his point.

"Mmm," mused the vampire. "And how harshly are these laws enforced?"

Amanda had absolutely no idea. "Death," she lied.

"Very well," Yulric nodded approvingly, finally allowing himself to be led away. "Let us go."

Woman and immortal made their way slowly, owing to the former's footwear, to the elevator. The vampire clacked his long nails impatiently on a nearby trashcan with increasing volume while they watched the numbers descend. When the lift finally arrived, the doors opened to reveal a pair of newly minted twenty-one-year-old college boys. They looked to the left at busty blond Goth with a slit skirt and hooker boots, and their eyes spun to "jackpot." Then, they turned to the hottie's dead grandfather, whose eyes—to their horror—were also flashing "jackpot." The boys nervously took a step back and to the right, allowing the newcomers to board.

It was the most uncomfortable elevator ride imaginable. For starters, the college kids were standing behind Amanda, which she knew was a strategic move on their part so they could check out her ass. However, this intention was being nullified by Yulric's inexperience with elevator etiquette. Instead of turning to face the doors like everyone else in the known universe, he was staring directly at the boys, his sharp teeth bared in a malicious, *hungry* grin. Their brains short-circuited as the greatest forces that govern human behavior—libido and self-preservation—fought for control of their actions.

"Hey," one of the boys whispered to Amanda, libido having unsurprisingly won out. "We're headed to a party. If you wanted to, well, you know . . . ?"

Amanda appraised them both, then turned to Yulric. "What do you think, Dad? Can I go with them?"

The boy who'd spoken up immediately went white and shut his mouth. His companion scrunched himself into the corner, trying to distance himself physically and figuratively from his friend. For the rest of the ride, they stood tensely in uncomfortable silence, until the elevator doors opened and the pair of would-be Romeos fled, not even bothering to brush up against Amanda on their way out.

"What?" Amanda said, noticing the vampire watching her.

"How did you do that?" he asked, apparently curious how she had succeeded where the horror of his presence had failed.

She shrugged. "Horny guys fear parents. Everyone knows that. Can we go?"

"Lead the way." Yulric bowed.

◆　◆

Amanda was absolutely right about the behavior of automobiles in the city. Not only did they not jump up onto the far clearer walkways, but they halted even when pedestrians strode out in front of them in defiance of both the metal constructs' potential for death and the signs flashing Don't Walk over and over. They might honk their horns loudly in protest, their drivers might make obscene hand gestures or suggest you remove your head out of various orifices, but that was the worst you could expect to encounter from the cars.

One could not say the same of the pedestrians.

A flood of humanity filled every available walking path in the city. The established convention of staying to the right side, which prevailed on the roads, was here a mere suggestion, flouted as often as it was followed. In some places, crowds obstructed all movement, waiting outside tableless restaurants for pizza with toppings that appeared on no other menu in the world.[30] They jostled, they trampled, they indiscriminately

---

30. For good reason.

plowed ahead, indifferent to the ancient monstrosity in their midst.

A five-foot-four woman texting on her phone walked directly into Yulric. "Excuse me?" she snapped, making it clear that he was the one being unreasonably thick. With an annoyed sigh, she stepped to the left and disappeared into the throng, never even so much as looking up from her cell.

"I thought people knew about vampyrs?" Yulric said, annoyed at the woman's lack of mind-numbing terror.

"Everyone knows about them, but hardly anyone thinks they're real. Especially not the normals." Amanda laughed. "To them, you're just a thing that shows up in movies sometimes." She smiled smugly. "Though not really, because you aren't pretty enough."

"So, when they look at me, what do they see?" he asked.

In response, Amanda drew his attention to a grubby-looking homeless man panhandling at the end of an alley. The vampire hissed in disgust. As he did, a set of stairs caught his eye. "Where do those go?" the vampire inquired.

"To the subway," answered an impatient Amanda.

"Subway," Yulric mused. "I will return."

"Wait!" Amanda called out, but it was too late. Yulric had leapt down the stairs and disappeared. Amanda waited at the top, unwilling to chase after him in heels. A minute later, he reemerged, stowing a subway pamphlet into his robes.

"It always pays to be familiar with underground tunnels." Yulric beamed.

For a fleeting second, she thought of explaining to him what a subway was, but thought better of it. "Are you done now? Can we go?"

He bowed his head and followed her another three blocks to the old, repurposed warehouse. The pair ducked into a dark alleyway that separated it from the building next door. Here, nearly hidden by steam, was a staircase leading down. At the bottom stood a red velvet rope and an intimidatingly large man.

Even seated as he was, the man was nearly as tall as an average-sized person and as wide as two. His neck glittered with gold, as did most of his fingers. Despite the time of night and darkness of the alley, he wore sunglasses, as if light was a meager consideration when compared with style. Not that he wasn't classy; he was, after all, wearing a sports coat over his shirtless torso. Amanda called him a bouncer, but Yulric easily recognized uniform of a guard. And he had ways of dealing with guards.

"Stay close to me," Amanda said. She descended the stairs. With each step, she placed one foot in front of the other. Not forward and to the side, like most people would, but directly in line. This created a sway in her hips that could mesmerize all but the most Yulric of men. In addition, she added a little extra force as each foot fell, so that she bounced and jiggled in all the right places. The bouncer's face remained impassive. Yulric, who recognized the power of Amanda's allure even if he did not feel it himself, made another note in his head. *A eunuch guard, then.*

Yulric thought the man would remain as seated as he was impassive, but when Amanda hit the landing, he was on his feet, moving the rope to one side.

"Welcome, Amanda," he said in a tough, accented voice.

"Thank you, Bruno," she responded. She turned and waited.

Yulric's descent was far less alluring. He glided down the steps, and in his wake, darkness followed. By the time he reached the bottom, his eldritch aura had warped the fabric of reality into a miasmal shadow that reminded the brain of a time when man was once a small, easily eaten primate.

Yulric stopped at the rope and waited. The eunuch remained seated. The vampire glanced over at Amanda, who merely shrugged. Unsure of how to proceed, he reached for the rope.

"Can I help you, sir?" The guard was standing now, right in front of Yulric, so close their chests nearly touched. Then again, the bouncer's chest was such that it could touch you from ten feet away.

Yulric smiled. He'd gotten a reaction. Now he just had to play the right game. The vampire drew up again to his full height, which allowed him to tower over the man, and chose his words carefully. "I require admittance."

The guard stared for a moment. It was impossible to tell what, if anything, was going through his head until he replied, "I'm sorry, sir. This is a private club."

"He's with me," chimed in Amanda, helpfully.

The guard turned and looked at her with as much surprise as you could without actually showing any surprise. "I'm sorry, Amanda. I would lose my job if I let a lich in."

Yulric blinked. "A what?"

"A lich," repeated the guard unhelpfully.

Yulric, who didn't think the man looked nearly German enough to be using that word correctly, turned to Amanda for explanation.

"It's a term for a hideous undead skeleton or desiccated corpse," she explained.

"I thought that was that zom-a-bye thing?" he said.

"Sort of. It's like a zombie, but intelligent," she replied. She thoughtfully left out the bit about it being exclusively used in fantasy role-playing games. Yulric, meanwhile, was thinking of the term people had used in his day to describe a skeleton or desiccated corpse with intelligence: *vampyr.*

A distinct lack of movement brought the vampire's attention back to the bouncer. Yulric weighed his options. Bribery was unlikely to work. Those who accepted bribes were usually not subtle in soliciting them. Attempts at mind control, which had been going on for minutes now, had produced little more than a splitting headache, courtesy of the man's fortuitous taste in eyewear. And given the guard's physique and general attitude, a threat of violence would almost certainly be ineffective.

Which left only *actual* violence. With vicious glee, Yulric reached down and slowly lifted the man by the lapels of his jacket.

"Put me down, sir," he droned, unimpressed.

Yulric smiled. "Very well." His steely muscles flexed with the intent of flinging the man into the nearby concrete. Not through it, the stone looked very strong, but he hoped for, at least, a favorable splat.

A slight swish caught his cloudy eyes, and he turned to see Amanda giving her head a quick shake, indicating that such behavior was not going to be tolerated. Her eyes flicked down. Her left leg had slipped out of the slit in her skirt, and for the first time, Yulric noticed a small black strap. She subtly displayed her inner thigh, and Yulric was met with a flash of pain as the dim light of the alley caught a *familiar* silver cross fastened tightly against her skin. The same silver cross that had helped imprison him for three centuries. He cursed himself for being too distracted to wonder what had become of it, but of course, she had taken it when she'd dug him out.

Amanda caught the vampire's eye. *If you thought I would leave unprepared to deal with you, then you are a fool. Now, put him down.*

Outmaneuvered yet again, Yulric vowed to pay more attention to what was between Amanda's legs in the future.

"Very well. You have made me see the error of my ways," the vampire apologized as he lowered the man to his feet.

"Good," said the bouncer, putting a packet of salt back in his pocket as he sat back on his stool. And that was that. No "Be on your way." No "Hit the road." Nothing. Apparently, Yulric was within his rights to stand there, just so long as he did not try to cross the rope.

Amanda gave him a condescending smile.

"I'll try to bring someone out," she told him before entering the club. Yulric got the impression she had known this would happen.

With very little stimulus coming from either wall, door, or guard, the vampire's attention was drawn to the air. More specifically, he noticed the steam rising from under the ground, the cool breeze that blew it into pleasing patterns, and openings high above, through which both steam and breeze passed into the building beyond.

Chapter 13

"So, where are the vampyrs?"

Amanda spun around to face the hideous ancient vampire.

"You? How?" she sputtered, before moving from shock to suspicion. "What did you do?"

Yulric pointed up. "Windows."

"You can't be here," she hissed quickly, ushering him to a deserted, dark hallway. "You saw the bouncer's reaction," she said. "You'll never pass for a vampire in a vampire club."

He gave a nod to the leg where Amanda was hiding her cross. "Like you, I came prepared." From within the folds of his robes, he produced a golden mask, its features neutral but handsome. He placed it over his face and raised his hood. "Better?"

She wanted to say no. She really did. But the cape-check boy was wearing almost the exact same outfit.[31]

---

31. Vampire clubs, Renaissance fairs, and nineteenth-century opera houses are the only places you are likely to find a cape check.

"Fine," she said angrily, "let's go."

He offered her his cold, bony hand, which she reluctantly took, and like that, they stepped into the club proper.

Yulric Bile had experienced many sounds in his one thousand years of unlife. He had accompanied raging hordes of bellowing Saxon warriors. He had experienced a three-banshee wail. He had been present at the birth of mouthless abominations whose pitiless cries drove men to insanity. None of that even came close to the earsplitting cacophony that assaulted his supernatural hearing within the club.

The racket, which Amanda insisted on calling music, came in two varieties Yulric dubbed *screech-screech* and *thump-thump*. The former consisted solely of loud, shrill scratches. There were no notes or discernible patterns, just a continuous din. After some time, Yulric realized that, contained within the screeching, was a voice, though he could not make out what it was saying because it, too, was screeching. *Thump-thump* was a teeth-rattling rhythm, which caused the body to move against its will. Sometimes this resulted in dancing, other times heart arrhythmia. Yulric was sure some form of mind control was involved.

Amanda led the ancient vampire around the outer edges of the black-clad mass of bumping, grinding, jumping, and writhing humanity. Most of the women were dressed similarly to Amanda, in a style she affectionately called "Transylvanian Ambassador to the Moulin Rouge,"[32] though few could pull it off as well. The men, many with identical hair, jewelry, and makeup to the women's, had no set style and ranged from overdressed to hardly dressed. Shirts were optional. Sometimes, pants were optional. Giant leather boots with hundreds of straps and buckles, it seemed, were not optional.

---

32. Yulric had no idea what this meant.

"Shocked?" Amanda asked when she caught him scanning the crowd.

The vampire turned and looked down at his guide. "Should I be?" They were as far as they could get from where the "music" emanated, and still, he had to yell to make himself heard.

"Just thought you might find this uncomfortable," she prodded. "Indecent, maybe?"

Typical Puritan, thought Yulric. He tapped his mask. "I have been to Venice."

Amanda was visibly disappointed.

"How many of these know the truth?" asked the vampire.

"Some," Amanda answered. "The real members of the vampire community, the staff, the ones who provide blood, a few others. The rest are just Goth posers who like to play dress-up."

"And how can you tell which are the poseurs?" he posed.

"They wear black," she said.

Through his mask, Yulric gave her a look of deepest loathing and then turned back to the crowd, which he found just as repugnant. "Enough of the rabble. Where are the—"

"The coven elders?" she said, finishing the thought that had stalled on his lips. Yulric rolled his eyes. The idea of a group of vampires still seemed unnatural to him, which, considering he was unnatural himself, was saying something.

"Yes, them." He still couldn't bring himself to say the words. "Where are they?"

"For that, you'll need to talk to Tony," she said nodding toward the stairs.

Standing in front of a metal staircase to the right of the dancers stood Tony, the other bouncer. With the exception of his shirt and African descent, he was nearly indistinguishable from Bruno. Same short haircut. Same emotionless face. Same dark sunglasses worn inappropriately in dark places. The same obstacle. And Yulric hadn't really mastered the last one.

"I can't help you this time," Amanda told him. "I've been trying to get him to let me up for months."

Amanda's arms moved to her lower back, which consequently made her chest more prominent. *Another eunuch*, Yulric thought.

"I don't suppose he can be bribed?" the vampire asked, before adding unnecessarily, "With money?"

Amanda held up a wad of paper that passed for currency in the modern world. "Nope." She tucked the bills back between her breasts.

"I will think of something," said the vampire.

"Yeah, good luck with that," replied Amanda. She started to walk away.

"What will you do?" he inquired.

"Why do you care?" she shot back.

"I will need a way back before sunrise," he said.

"I'll meet you outside," she said. "Two hours?"

"Why not four?"

"That'll have us driving home after dawn," she advised.

"I can ride in the luggage space," he said.

Amanda smiled at the thought of stuffing the vampire into the trunk of her car. "Well then, four hours it is. Good luck." And with that Amanda disappeared into the throng.

The vampire's attention turned to Tony the guard. After a moment's thought, he puffed himself up to an impressive posture and stalked his way over to the stairs. When he reached this stoic sentinel, he bowed low and opened his arms in supplication. "I humbly beg an audience with the"—he gritted his teeth—"elders."

There was a long uncomfortable pause. Without rising, Yulric glanced up. The guard was employing that age-old technique of ignoring him.

"May I take that as a no?" he said.

The guard inhaled. Yulric understood that to mean "correct."

The vampire tried to remain humble and polite. "Perhaps you could ask if they would see me?"

Tony the guard exhaled. This meant "perhaps it was time you were moving along."

From within his robe, Yulric pulled out the other thing he'd taken from the box. He untied its drawstring. "I don't suppose I could bribe you into granting me an audience?" He let the handful of rubies and emeralds sift through his fingers back into the small pouch.

The man's breath said nothing. It went in. It went out.

Yulric, frustrated at being thwarted by weak, easily kill-able mortals, bowed slightly to the guard and turned, not to leave, but to gather momentum for slamming the guard's head through the cement floor.

"Wait."

Yulric paused. This was not a translation of breath. This was an actual word spoken by an actual voice. He looked back. Tony had lowered his sunglasses slightly, revealing a sliver of eye.

"You got any diamonds?" asked the guard with a twinkle. It was a twinkle Yulric had seen before from a besotted Austrian duke. Apparently, there was a soon-to-be Mrs. Guard. Yulric removed a diamond the width of a fingernail and dropped it into the palm of the man's hand. Tony held it up to the light, peering into its many facets. Satisfied, he pocketed it. "Follow me."

The second level of the club was far more vampiric. Here, tables and booths were arranged around the floor occupied by fanged clientele. Some of the vampires acted with the same animal lust as the revelers below, mouths and tongues inter-twined, fangs lightly plucking at skin. Others were somewhat more dignified, dressed in their top hats and lacy cuffs, drinking very red wine from ornate goblets. A few raised their glasses in salute as they passed. There were also pairs of vampires rubbing against each other in almost catlike motions. Yulric stopped to observe one such display.

"Psychic vampires," explained Tony.

"Ah," said Yulric, pretending to agree. He may have only recently learned the word *psychic*, but he knew from experience that feeding off life energies should have left quivering, unhinged wretches in its wake.

At the center of the congregation was a circle of high-backed chairs, each intricately carved with arcane symbols and Gothic iconography. Some of it Yulric recognized, some he did not, and the rest he knew only from tattoos he'd seen on the rabble below. There were thirteen chairs total, and while he could make out only a few of their occupants, he spied enough dangling arms on armrests to be sure that all were filled.

Tony approached an elder. After a whispered conversation, he nodded at Yulric.

Everything that had happened since he had woken up all those weeks ago had been leading up to this. All that energy, all that frustration, all that humiliation, all ending with this meeting. If he'd been breathing, he would have breathed heavily. If his heart had been beating, it would have pounded in his chest. As much as a vampire could have butterflies, he did. This was it. Finally, he would have his answers. Finally, he would show the world a true vampire. Yulric stepped into the circle and bowed.

"Arise," said the elder in front of him.

"You wish to speak with us?" said the elder behind him.

"Yes, I . . ." He halted. For the first time, Yulric got a good look at them. There were six men and seven women. Each seemed to represent a type of vampire Yulric had seen coming in, the Goth, the lacy-cuffs, the psychic. A handful were in shape, the majority were very, *very* average, with guts or hips bulging with the fat that comes with middle age. One was so large he could barely fit in his chair. Clothing, jewelry, and skin were littered with ankhs, pentagrams, elder signs, and other symbols of varying occult significance. All in all, they were a most eclectic group. They really had only a single thing in common.

They were all mortal.

Yulric searched the elders for some sign of immortality. You could always tell, in the way someone moved or smelled or, in Yulric's case, looked. But here, there was nothing. No spark, no odor, nothing beyond veneer fangs and dyed hair. The vampire elders were a middle-aged social group.

"Excuse me," he said with a bow and retreated from the circle. He found his way back to Tony.

The bouncer raised a confused eyebrow. "Is there a problem?"

"Could you take me to the *other* vampyr elders?" requested Yulric.

For a second, it seemed like the guard didn't know what he was talking about. A moment later, though, he nodded. "Follow me."

Yulric trailed him, away from the vampire elders, past the other mortals playing pretend, and back down the metal staircase.

"Over there," Tony said.

Yulric found himself staring at the swarm of writhing bodies Amanda had melted into. With a growl of disgust, he slithered his way into the tangled mass, working his way through the cracks between bodies, searching for some sign of undeath. The celebrants didn't seem to notice his passage, with one exception.

Amanda froze as a familiar, cold sensation spread across her back. She turned to find Yulric trying to squeeze by without being dry humped.

"How did it go with the elders?" she shouted. Yulric did not respond. "What? What happened?"

Yulric leaned down, his masked face unnervingly close to her ear. His mouth moved. He was shouting. Still, Amanda could just barely make out the word *mortals*.

"What?" she exclaimed in surprise. "You're kidding me! I've spent months trying to get up to see them. Ugh." She was kicking herself for being so stupid. Or that might have been the leg of the woman behind her.

Meanwhile, Yulric levitated slightly in the air and scanned the monochromatic crowd. A moment later, he was bowling people over, no longer bothering to hide his strength. Amanda followed in his wake.

In a clearing closest to the stage, Amanda and Yulric found them: five vampires—three men and a pair of women—dancing together. All could best be described by Yulric as *svelte* and by Amanda as *anorexic*. Two of the men were well muscled, with lean, strong arms and rippling stomachs. The third's physique was covered by a shirt, but he was likely just as well muscled and rippling as the others. The women were not quite as uniform. One wore a black tank top with black skintight jeans, while the other wore a black strapless blouse with a black skintight skirt. One was a brunette, the other a blonde. One was extremely thin but pleasingly curvaceous around the hips and bust, and the other was extremely thin but pleasingly curvaceous around the bust and hips. Very different, indeed.

All of them sparkled.

He shouted something. She leaned in, failing to hear him over the music. He shouted again and motioned.

"Body glitter," explained Amanda, after a game of charades.

The booming speakers didn't seem to present the same problem for him. Yulric turned his hand palm up. *And that is?*

Amanda paused to figure out how best to simplify *glitter*. Eventually, she decided upon "Makeup." She turned back to the dancing vampires. One of the shirtless ones had noticed her and was giving her a once-over.

"Christ, I thought they were just minor coven members. I didn't realize they were the only vampires here."

With a frown, the shirtless male stopped checking her out and turned away to dance with the man next to him. Yulric tapped the side of his mask.

"What?" Amanda turned toward the sparkling vampire, who now had his back to her. "Did he hear me?"

Yulric nodded.

"Great! Just great!" she growled in frustration. "I need a drink." She punched Yulric in the arm, earning her an annoyed glare. "Don't do anything stupid. Remember"—she gestured to the people all around them—"witnesses."

Yulric pointedly looked away.

"Fine," she said. "I'll meet you outside." And with that, she disappeared again into the crowd.

Yulric stood still. Unnaturally still. Supernaturally, even. The press of the dancers did not move him. The vibration of the music did not sway him. Even the background hum of subatomic exchange that is a normal part of physical matter, for that instant, halted so that he could be unequivocally still.

One by one, the dancing, shiny vampires noticed a chilling lack of movement out of the corners of their eyes and turned to face him.

"Greetings," he said, knowing only they would be able to parse his words from the cacophony of the current *screech-screech* song. "I come to speak with the elders."

"You'll find them upstairs," replied the male wearing a shirt. Yulric assumed that wearing more clothes was some display of rank.

"Mortals, one and all," said Yulric. "I have not come to see pretenders."

The vampires exchanged looks with their shirted leader, who smiled. This was why he had been put in charge of the coven.[33] Deception, intrigue, archaic rules of grammar and hospitality: they were the calling card of role-play, a game the young bloodsucker knew well.

"Wise words, my masked friend," said the shirt. "If it is elder vampires you seek, you will find few older than we in this city."

"Truly?" replied Yulric, trying not to scoff.

The shirted male backed up as much as anybody could in the middle of a rave and gave a little bow. "I am Karos, of the Cavielli line, the last to be sired by the great Cavielli the Black himself, almost a decade ago." As if on cue, the brunette female appeared at the shirted one's shoulder. "Lucretia is also of my line, sired five years ago by Cavielli's eldest, Draka."

"I expect you've heard of him," she boasted. Yulric gave a kind of noncommittal grunt, as if these names meant something.

The blonde approached Karos's other side while the other two men took positions behind the women, looming over them, despite the latter's heels. "Rosetta, Darius, and Henri la Croix are all descended from Count Hedronus, through Gabrielle."

"Of course," Yulric agreed. Again, this siring nonsense. Yulric had poured over all the vampire fiction and was no closer to understanding how it happened than he had ever been. Did you mingle blood? Did you replace the blood entirely?

---

33. Or so he'd been told. The truth was, he was made leader because he was the median height and fit best in the middle when posed.

Sometimes just a bite was enough to do it, but undoubtedly, that would have ended the humanity currently grinding against him, so that couldn't be the case.

Yulric's musings were interrupted by the one called Lucretia. "Why do you come among us masked, unnamed stranger?"

Yulric almost laughed at idea of being challenged. "I was"— he paused for effect—"afraid. Your coven is famous. Your strength, your lineage, and especially your beauty. Though the reports do not do you justice." The vampires beamed at this. Yulric bowed his head in feigned sadness. "I'm sorry to say those of my"—he tried to remember the term they had used— "line are not nearly so handsome."

"Well, your line must be very lenient then." The shirt laughed. "Our sires were all strict when it came to the change, and so are we. We follow the pamphlet's instructions to the letter."

"Pamphlet?" uttered Yulric, hoping to provoke another sharing session. The young vampires traded uncertain glances. Too late, Yulric realized his question was far too suspicious. "Yes, indeed, the pamphlet," he said, trying futilely to cover his mistake. "*The* pamphlet. We lost ours long ago. At least three years."

"You say your line is not nearly as handsome as ours?" Lucretia asked threateningly. She was walking around him now, like the lawyers did on TV.

"Yes," Yulric replied.

Lucretia stopped. "How not handsome?"

"Very," Yulric answered.

"Show us?" she asked with venomous politeness.

"I would rather not," declined Yulric.

"I insist," she said.

"It would dishonor your beauty to sully its sight with my humble plainness."

"Humor me." Lucretia grinned.

Yulric clearly wasn't going to get any more from this conversation and was tired of showing them undeserved deference. And so, with ominous slowness, he pulled down his hood and removed his mask. The vampires gasped. As did the nearest of the human dancers, though a few nodded in approval. Apparently, they thought he would make a great album cover.

"What are you? A mummy?" gasped Darius.

Henri la Croix agreed. "Yeah, definitely a mummy."

"Why don't you go find yourself a nice mummy bar?" Rosetta laughed dismissively.

"Probably 'cause there aren't any mummy bars," said Henri. He regarded Yulric with the disgust usually reserved exclusively for videos of live births. "Really, who would want to be a mummy?"

"Certainly not I," goaded Lucretia.

"I am not a mummy," Yulric barked, letting loose his long-bottled rage. "I am not a werewolf. I am not a ghost. I am not a zom-whatever. I, *dear children*, am Yulric Bile. And I am a *real* vampyr."

And with that dramatic statement, bells sounded from all over the club and the sprinkler system went off.

Screams louder than any Yulric could have hoped to elicit filled the air as cold water fell from the ceiling. The crowd began to run away to avoid the deluge. Where supernatural threats from a thousand-year-old creature of darkness had failed, discomfort and the prospect of ruined clothing succeeded. Not even the vampires were immune to this humiliation.

"These are designer pants," cried Darius.

"My hair!" shrieked Rosetta.

"Bastard. I'll . . . Whoops," said Lucretia as her high heels slipped on the wet floor and she fell. Then, trying to shield themselves from the torrent, they joined the rest of the crowd fleeing in panic. The shirt alone remained behind. With the proper dignity of one chosen for leadership by watching far too many movies, he posed for a good long time before slowly retreating backward. It looked ridiculous, most especially when he had to take two awkward steps to the right to find the doorway.

Yulric was standing there in the pouring indoor rain, cursing the plumbing, when he was approached by a pair of drenched bouncers.

"I think it's time you left, buddy."

"Very well," replied Yulric with a sneer, "I will go."

And he did. After taking his diamond back, of course.

Chapter 14

Outside the club, Amanda milled about with the rest of the soaked clientele. She was wet and cold, and fairly certain she was being ogled just because she was wet and cold. The looks she was receiving, after all, were lustful, not resentful, which is what they would have been if anyone had seen her pull the fire alarm. Sure, it may have saved all of their lives, but it wouldn't fix their makeup.

And so Amanda stood shivering, being objectified, and waiting for Yulric. She didn't really know why. She did not like him. She wanted him gone. This entire outing had been an exercise in exorcizing his presence from her couch. It even had a code name in the Linske household: Operation Get Rid of the Vampire. However, every time she'd made up her mind to abandon him here and try her luck at the vampire clubs up by NYU, what might happen would play out in her head . . .

It was dark in the scenario she imagined. Unnaturally dark for the city. Maybe it was a blackout or something. Who cared?

It was her vision. A minivan sat stopped in the middle of the road, engine smoking slightly. A soccer mom breathed heavily from behind the wheel. Her eyes were wide with fright; her hands shook from adrenaline. She turned to see that her two children—one girl, one boy—were all right. Amanda couldn't help but notice that the boy resembled Simon.

"Stay here," the woman told her children as she unbuckled her seat belt.

"Mommy, what happened?" asked the boy in a voice very like Simon's, if he were normal.

"Just stay here," she replied. "Mommy has to check on something."

She opened the door and stepped out. The rain pelted down on her. (Because this wasn't real, Amanda didn't even wonder when it had started raining.) Slowly, the woman moved toward the front of her car, toward the person she had just hit. Excuses ran through her head. *He just came out of nowhere. I was clearly visible, lights on, but he just walked right in front of me as if he didn't understand the concept of crosswalks or right-of-way. I swear, Officer, that's the truth.*

The soccer mom worried she had killed someone. She worried she would be arrested or charged with something and that her ex-husband would use that as an excuse to take her kids away. Only Amanda knew she should have worried about so much more.

The man was dead, or so the woman thought, up until the moment he started cursing. She breathed a sigh of relief. Not dead meant a charge without the word *homicide* in it. The man—she assumed it was a man based on his baldness—continued to swear in some language she couldn't recognize.[34]

---

34. The words were a gibberish interpretation of how Yulric actually swore. Amanda translated it as comparing the car to the intimate relations of goats.

Foreign, thought the woman. *That's why he didn't stop.* A deeper, darker part of her added, *If he's illegal, it won't even go to trial.* Liberal guilt chiding her, the woman approached the screaming man, who was now attempting to stand.

"Here, let me help you." She grabbed his arm to brace him.

A furious face turned upon contact: a face full of fire and pain and swearing in languages that had died before the last ice age. She screamed as a thousand years of rage literally went for her jugular. The pair fell out of sight, with only dying shrieks, flailing limbs, and the occasional spurt of blood as evidence they had ever been there.

Amanda's focus now fell on the children, sitting in the minivan. Though the hood had shielded them from the grisly scene, they had witnessed the beginning of the attack: a man with scary eyes biting their mommy. Frankly, that was enough. Crying, they called out for her.

Up popped the head of the vampire, his eyes glowing in the headlights, his mouth dripping red. The children bawled louder. If only someone would save them. If only someone would stop him.

If only someone had waited for him outside the club, this could all have been avoided.

And so Amanda stayed. A half hour. An hour. When the only people left were firefighters and cops, many of whom were trying to get her phone number,[35] it was clear Yulric wasn't dumb enough to waltz out the entrance after all, so she decided to wait for him in the car.

Several catcalls and suggestive offers of "rides"[36] later, Amanda finally reached the parking garage. She reluctantly

---

35. "For our inquiries, of course."

36. Which she declined by telling the man in question to go "ride" himself.

fed most of what she had made the week before into a kiosk and took the elevator up five stories, where, after walking the final fifty feet to her car, she did what she had longed to do for hours: take off her boots and put on a dry hoodie.

An hour and a half, she lingered in the parking garage, hoping, sometimes praying, that the vampire would show up. The picture of the imaginary woman and her kids kept playing in her head. She thought about leaving and going to look for him, but what could she do? Drive around a city of eight million people, calling his name as if he were a stray cat?

Finally, she couldn't stay any longer; she had to get home. She drove out of the garage, negotiating the extra two hours with the attendant by taking off her hoodie and leaning out the window. The bright lights of the city were soon left behind and replaced instead by the dull lights of the suburbs. And all the while, Amanda hoped desperately that the vampire would get caught out in the coming dawn.

She really didn't think she was that lucky.

◆　◆

Outside the club, the shirt made a phone call.

◆　◆

Much of Vermillion's face was flayed open when the phone rang. For a moment, its owner considered just letting it go to voice mail. He was, after all, in the middle of very delicate and intricate work, manipulating muscles, tendons, cartilage, and bone into their ideal form. Right now, he was about to give the boy a chin. It was the least he could do, having lipo'd the three others away. But, in the end, he decided to take the call.

It wasn't like Vermillion was going anywhere. His face was pinned to the table.

"Hello, Karos," the man said in his English-accented baritone.

Karos responded with a shocked pause. Even the youngest vampires, who had grown up with caller ID, were willing to attribute anything their leader did to supernatural power. He had long stopped pointing out little things like a name on the call screen. It was faster that way.

"My lord," Karos said. The Englishman rolled his eyes at this reminder of how into vampires Karos was. He usually encouraged such fantasies, but Karos had long ago reached the limit. It was part of why he had neglected to tell the coven leader he was in town.

"My lord," Karos said again, "I hate to disturb you. You are undoubtedly very busy."

"Indeed I am, Karos," replied the Englishman. "If you could get to the point?"

"You told us to call if we ever met a-an old one."

The man on the phone stopped licking blood off his fingers. Things had just taken a *very* serious turn. "What kind of old one?" he asked. He could be referring to a terrible monstrosity beyond time and sanity. Oh, how he hoped the young vampire meant a terrible monstrosity beyond time and sanity.

"It was a—it claimed to be one of us," explained Karos, extinguishing the small glimmer of hope that it was an eldritch, semivegetable horror.

"What did it say? Tell me everything," the man on the phone commanded. Karos obliged. He explained how the supposed vampire had approached, made suspicious inquiries, been unmasked and then driven away by the might of the coven.

"Very good," said the Englishman, not believing that last bit at all. "And did you see where it went?"

"No, my lord," Karos answered sheepishly. "The coward fled too quickly."

"Indeed?" hissed the elder vampire. "Perhaps next time you shouldn't make it flee so fast."

"Er, yes, my lord."

The man rubbed his eyes in frustration. "Is there no way to track it?"

There was a disheartening pause from the young vampire; however, when he spoke again, his voice sounded hopeful. "There might be a blonde, I mean, a *lead*, I can follow."

The Englishman's eyebrow raised. "Well, by all means, Master Karos, follow your 'lead.'" He hung up and immediately scrolled through the contact list on his cell phone until he came across a specific name. It was a name that most would have killed to have in their phones. They would have pressed Send with extreme excitement. There would probably have been ecstatic screaming. The elder vampire, however, did not relish this call. It was dangerous. It was also necessary.

After two rings a voice answered. The voice was strong yet sensitive, soft yet sultry. It was everything that begins with the letter *S*. It was the kind of voice that beckons the brain of every woman with its understanding while simultaneously beckoning to her less brain-related parts, as well, with its mystery. It was, in essence, a siren's call. "Hello?"

"Phantom," said the man. "I have a job for you."

◆ ◆

Outside the club, Yulric Bile brooded atop a garbage dumpster. A part of his brain, the part that had kept him unalive for over a thousand years, screamed at him to move from this exposed and vulnerable location. Another part of his brain, the one with a higher learning curve for this new world, told it to shut up, since there was no way any of the vampires would go anywhere near garbage. Not in those shoes, certainly.

Things had not gone according to plan. Any plan. He had played out a dozen different scenarios in his head, and in none of them did he end up a soaked mess, hiding among refuse. He had no answers: nothing to tell him what exactly vampires had become or how they had become what they were or who he should kill for it. Without that, he was back where he started: sitting on a couch watching TV until something better came along. He did *not* want that, no matter how interested he was in the identity of the father of Caroline's secret love child.

Yulric heard sirens in the distance,[37] announcing the arrival of Authorities. While the hungry, animal parts of his brain longed for the chase that only the discovery of two decimated bodies could bring, rationally, the vampire knew he wasn't ready to face a force with frenzy-sicks: the CSIs, FBIs, and other letter combinations he'd learned from TV. And as they would *definitely* check dumpsters, it was time to move. With the ease of a spider, he scuttled up the wall and onto the roof of the neighboring warehouse. From this vantage point, he could see everything: the big red truck with rubber-clad Authorities, smaller white cars with blue-clad Authorities, the shirted vampire talking into a phone, Amanda, everything.

Amanda. The young girl stood, inappropriately dressed for the cool night air. Surely, she was not waiting for him. Why would she, after all? She loathed him, as well she should, and what he felt for her involved words used only to describe tapeworm infestations. But there she was, naively expecting him to walk out the front door, right in front of Authorities.

---

37. Or rather what were currently known as sirens. He had heard real sirens before, and the two sounds were nothing alike.

Foolish girl, thought Yulric. He walked away from rooftop's edge. After a sound best described as *squelching*, a large bat flew off into the night.

It did not fly far.

The peregrine falcon is the fastest animal on earth. Reaching speeds of two hundred miles an hour, it is known to dive-bomb its quarry from perches high in the air, catching them unaware. This makes them very formidable birds of prey, despite being smaller in size than hawks or eagles. After the use of pesticides resulted in population endangerment, many major American metropolitan areas teamed up with conservation groups to introduce these raptors into their cities as a means of pigeon control. Here, among the towers and spires of the modern city, the falcons have flourished.

None of this was known to Yulric before he transformed himself into a big, juicy, and comparatively slow-moving target.

Several blocks away, something large and Yulric-shaped, going terminal velocity, landed with a crash on a parked Ford Contour. The vampire pulled himself out of the resulting twisted, economical wreckage. Nearby, others among the cost-efficient herd, ones he had not even touched, honked loudly and flashed their lights to raise the alarm against him.

Oh, how he hated cars.

Yulric fled into an alley, away from the heads that were poking out to check on their property. He did not know where he was. He did not know where he was going. All he knew was that there were far too many ways of being caught in a city of ten thousand. This, according to the girl, was a city of eight million, with businesses open all night long and lights that never went out. He was vulnerable, exposed. He needed to find shelter fast.

The vampire headed north, the direction from which he and Amanda had originally come, and when he spotted an underground tunnel, he ducked inside. It quickly became apparent, though, that these were not mere sewers or crypts. They were well-traveled paths, which not only required payment but were also under constant observation. An attempt to enter through the turnstile without paying or understanding what a turnstile was resulted in him being stopped. Trying to bribe the Authority into letting him pass only compounded his troubles, and he was forced to bid a hasty escape. However, where Yulric himself had failed, a large pack of rats skittering suspiciously in unison went completely unnoticed. And so, the vampire found his way into the New York subway system.

Several electrocutions and one bone-shattering impact later, he abandoned the New York subway system.

He emerged out of these deadly underground caverns of gigantic linked cars into brightest day. Failing to dissolve into nothingness, Yulric opened his eyes and gaped at this tremendous display of bottled lightning. Everywhere he looked, TV screens advertised everything from theatrical productions to underwear to banks. So atrociously illuminated was this area of the city that, high above, the night sky became a wash of feeble gray with barely a visible star to be seen.

Even as the vampire marveled at the power of electricity, he became aware of the dangers of his location. The streets were filled with a ubiquitous species of yellow car, one that honked loudly and was less inclined to stop for pedestrians. The sidewalks were filled with humanity. Wealthier, less accepting humanity. The kind of humanity that would notice a hideous man in rags and call over Authorities to deal with such a one. Reluctantly, he turned away from the lights and made his way into the darkness.

It was only a matter of blocks before he found himself in much more comfortable environs. Gone were the massive television screens and crowds, replaced by trash bags, graffiti, and rats. There was still a persistent sense of being watched, but it was a sensation Yulric was more accustomed to, caused not by ever-present video cameras but by eyes behind blinds and figures in doorways. The first time someone tried to mug him, he knew he was safe. And when his would-be assailant told him the name of this neighborhood, he almost laughed out loud. How appropriate that his journey would lead him into the very Kitchen of Hell.

There, stooping beside the blood smear that had been his unsuccessful robber, Yulric licked his fingers and considered his next move. In a few short hours, the sun would rise. He was reasonably sure he could find shelter, but for how long would he need it? Would he remain in the city? The vampires he had encountered were sure to return eventually, and even if they didn't, there must be others. The question was, how much could he really learn from a three-year-old?

Yulric caught a dull glimmer out of the corner of his eye. He turned, expecting to find another ostentatious display of electric light, but instead was surprised to find a simple red glow emanating somewhere northwest of him. There was something familiar about it. And comforting, in a way only an undead mass murderer could appreciate. It called to him. Standing once more, he drifted in its direction. He followed it across several blocks, weaving between tenements and through dark alleys, somehow never losing sight of its glimmering. Finally, after crossing a large abandoned lot, he found himself in front of a shabby bar with two fixtures glowing on either side of its door. One was a neon sign, hanging against trash-bag-covered windows and promoting a popular brand of beer, which, according to Amanda, tasted like watered-down urine.[38] The other was a dull, infernal radiance emanating out of the crude, grinning face carved into a turnip.

The vampire eyed this makeshift lantern suspiciously. He didn't know how hellfire had come to rest within this overlarge root vegetable, or how that had in turn come to rest outside this bar, but he couldn't help but feel it had been left here for him. Was this a trap or an invitation? There was only one way to find out. Yulric stepped inside.

The interior of the bar bore little more charm than the outside did. The tobacco stains on the walls were actually an improvement on the vomit-green wallpaper, which was peeling at the edges. Of the five uselessly circling ceiling-fan fixtures, only three actually had lightbulbs in them, and these looked as if they might go at any second. The molding and pool tables were scarred with innumerable scratches from what looked like vicious attacks, and the stools and tables showed signs of having been mended multiple times. The clientele was rugged, hairy, and had a look about them, as if the bottom of the bottle wasn't nearly far enough down for their liking. Also, to a one, they smelled like wet dog.

Yulric nearly burst out laughing. What were the odds he would wind up at a werewolf bar tonight?

All eyes, and more importantly, all noses turned toward him as his gaze scoured the bar. Yulric paid them no mind. In his experience, werewolves came in two types: self-loathing moralists and French/German psychopaths.[39] He could tell by the quality of the alcohol being served that there were no French or Germans here. Immune to the confused sniffing of the sad-eyed lycanthropic beings, as they tried to

---

38. Not that one. The other one.

39. A new word for monster Yulric had learned from television.

place his odor, a combination of death, decay, and the pine fresheners Simon often slipped into his pocket, Yulric searched the room until finally, in the back of the bar, he spotted eyes that not only gleamed with cunning and mischief but that he vaguely recognized: an unusual occurrence for an immortal and one that was never a coincidence.

Yulric used a small sapphire to buy two of "whatever he is having" from the bartender and made his way to the end of the bar, where his quarry was engaged in a question-answering contest on the television.

"Nice to see the old ways are still remembered," the stranger said, finishing his current glass in a single gulp. Yulric frowned at the sound of the man's accent. Or rather, his brogue.

This was an Irishman.

Yulric did not like the Irish. Like most English, he'd always found it better to kill them rather than deal with them. The two general rules for when you absolutely had no choice were, first, never let them talk, and second, never let them drink.[40] Here he was about to do both.

The man raised his new glass. "Cheers," he said and took a drink, letting some of the beer spill down his long, scraggly beard. Or was it all the beer? Now that Yulric was closer, there was something not quite there about his new acquaintance.

The man's attention turned back to the TV as a new question appeared on the screen:

---

40. The same general rule also applies to Russians, though for different reasons. Instead of finding yourself in some daft misadventure involving a thousand-pound bet and a fiddle-playing goat, someone else finds you in the morning with a note reading *Good-bye, cruel world* pinned to your chest.

The movie *My Fair Lady* was based on the play
Pygmalion, written by what author?
    a) Oscar Wilde
    b) Irving Berlin
    c) George Bernard Shaw
    d) Bertolt Brecht

"George Bernard Shaw, an Irishman," he answered, pressing the letter *C* into a small device on the table. After thirty seconds, the television proclaimed him correct and awarded him one thousand points. "It's been a while," said the Irishman.

"Has it?" replied Yulric, still not exactly sure where he knew the man from.

The Irishman clutched at his heart in mock surprise. "I'm hurt. Though, to be fair, we weren't properly introduced the last time. Jack's the name. Stingy Jack to my friends, if I had any." He gave a little bow. "And you are?"

Yulric paused. Names had power. Even the young vampires knew this, christening themselves with ridiculous pseudonyms as an expression of their new found strength and independence. What this mysterious barfly was doing was testing to see how desperate the vampire was.

With a sense that playing along was his best bet, the vampire admitted his name. "Yulric."

"Yulric? Very uncommon name, Yulric. Almost as if it came from another age." The Irishman looked back at the TV. Little animated words bounced across the screen, announcing the break the game was on. "So, Yulric, what brings you to these parts?"

"I seek a story," Yulric said carefully. He was playing to the Irishman's vanity. The ability to twist language into any shape one desired, to create worlds with words, was an Irish trait, a leftover from the races of fairy folk who had once ruled their island. They called it the "gift of gab" and those possessing it could never resist employing it. The trick was goading them into telling the tale you wanted to hear.

"A story?" The Irishman sipped his beer. "I know many stories. What kind would you like to hear?"

"How about a vampyr tale?" Yulric replied. Metal screeched across wood as several chairs were pushed out, and once again, all eyes turned to the newcomer. While werewolves and vampires had gotten along famously in Yulric's time, these days, the two couldn't stand each other.

"Well, that certainly got everyone's attention." Jack laughed. "What say, everyone? Would you care to hear a vampire tale?"

"Only if it involves those stuck-up little shits getting what's coming to them," barked the bartender.

"So, a story of comeuppance, then. And I . . . What do I want? I want a drink." He drank the last fifth of his beer, which dribbled through him and onto the floor. "Another, if you would? On him."

The bartender looked to Yulric, who nodded.

"So a story about vampires, comeuppance, and drink." Jack turned with a grin to Yulric. "I know just the one."

"Once upon a time in the land of Erin," the Irishman began, "during a month of great portents and storms, a boat came from across the sea carrying with it an Englishman. No one knew how long he'd ridden the waves, but fearing reprisals from the English, he was brought into the nearby village, where the doctor declared him dead. The people of the village gave him what burial they could, though being a Protestant and English, he was not buried in the churchyard, but out by the woods, with a simple wooden cross erected to mark the spot. Without a name, of course." He looked right at Yulric here. "They didn't know his name."

Yulric frowned. He remembered now where he'd seen this man.

"'Twas several days before the first of the livestock died. A week before the infants followed suit. All across the village, people fell ill. The doctor from a nearby town could make neither hide nor hair of it, before he stopped coming at all. The only hope the villagers had left was prayer.

"After a week, the sick began to mend, and the foul weather cleared. The priest declared it a miracle, and everyone took it as such. Everyone except the village drunk."

The Irishman paused his tale to answer a question on the television. "Would anyone happen to know who opposed Richard the Lionheart in the Third Crusade?"

"B," Yulric answered.

"Saladin? Are you sure?" asked Jack suspiciously.

"Quite," responded Yulric, his hand unconsciously moving to the place where his throat had met with the blade of Salah al-Din Yusuf ibn Ayyub.

The Irishman punched the answer into the controller. When it was deemed correct, he continued.

"Several nights before, the drunk had been out a-stumbling, as was his way, when out of the shadows the Englishman appeared. His eyes still dead, his heart still stopped but certainly standing there. 'You look well,' said the drunk, 'for one in the ground.'

"The Englishman just smiled and replied, 'I am seldom in the ground.'

"'Well, the worms have been kind,' said the drunk. He took a bottle from his satchel. 'Care for a drink?'

"'Shortly,' the Englishman said back, letting the man have a final nip.

"What the Englishman did not realize was that this man was a thief as well as a drunk. He'd long since been banned from the pub and was no longer invited into homes, lest people find themselves suddenly bereft. In fact, there was only a single building in all the village that was honor bound never to close its doors to him. Coincidentally, this building was always well stocked in wine. That building was the church, and the wine was the consecrated blood of Christ.

"So as the Englishman fell upon the throat of his drunken prey, and when the first drop of blood touched his lips, it burned them. He screamed and smoked and spasmed and swore. Where the skin did not ignite and turn to ash, it sloughed off like slugs, trying to escape. The muscle boiled, and the organs steamed. The mingled blood of drunk and Savior tore through that unholy beast till naught but the basest bones remained.

"The village drunk took the Englishman's bones and put them back on the boat he'd arrived in. He covered them in a traveling cloak and threw a couple o' dead rats aboard before pushing it back to sea. This done, he clapped his hands together and then got pissed from His Lord and Savior.

"When asked later why he didn't just destroy the stranger, the drunk replied, 'I'd not want to rob the English of his company.'"

The Irishman soaked in the attention of the entire bar. "The moral of the story, ladies and gents—always know what's in your drink."

A number of wolves let out appreciative laughs. A few applauded. One reached over to clap the Irishman on the back, went off-balance when it failed to connect with anything solid, and fell right off his barstool, which incited a much heartier round of laughter. In fact, the only person who wasn't at all amused was Yulric.

"What's the matter?" asked the Irishman. "Didn't you like my story?"

"I've heard it before," Yulric said.

"That's right. I told it to you the last time we met," Jack replied, a playful twinkle in his eye. "You liked it even less then. Hated it, in fact. Right down to your bones."

The Irishman laughed and reached for his drink. His hand came back wet but without his glass. For the first time, he looked distraught. "Damn." He stood up from his seat. "Time we were going, friend."

Yulric did not move. "I'd like to catch up more."

The Irishman raised his hand, which was now clearly see-through. "The sun will rise within the hour. Time for all like-minded shades to be on their way."

They made their way to the door. As they passed, the bartender tossed Yulric back his gem. "For the story."

Jack nodded and made a tiny salute.

Outside, the cold night breeze blew against vampire and phantasm. Neither felt its chill, though it swept up the Irishman's tattered clothes and brambles of hair, as if mercilessly driving him onward.

"Here." The Irishman handed the vampire a small sliver of paper. "I believe this is the tale you were after." It was no wider than a hand, no thicker than a thumb. A pamphlet, in fact.

"If you go several blocks down," Jack said, "you'll find a sewer grate. The tunnel beneath leads straight out of the city, so no worries about subway or sunlight. How are you at crossing water?" Yulric did not answer. "Well, I'm sure you'll think of something."

He turned to the turnip that hung next to the door. Despite his growing translucence, he had no trouble lifting the very solid lantern from the door.

"Your lantern led me here," Yulric stated.

The Irishman nodded. "Aye. An ember of hell resides inside. Tends to attract the wrong kind of crowd: rogues and ne'er-do-wells. It led me to you and then led you to me."

He raised his lantern before him and split the fading night as if it were solid. The wind changed direction, whirling toward the open void.

"Why?" Yulric yelled over the roar of the wind.

The wraith grinned the frightening, malevolent grin of a man mad enough to cross the devil and clever enough to win. A man too sinful for heaven and too slippery for hell. A man of Ireland.

"It's been quiet around here for far too long," he shouted over the roar. "High time things were a bit more interesting."

The Irishman walked toward the tear in the universe. Reality warped around him so that each step was a hundred, and he shrank quickly from sight. However, just before he disappeared, he turned and hollered back, "What's worse than an Englishman?"

Before the vampire could answer, the ghostly man passed through the portal, which promptly closed, allowing the laws of nature to take over once again. And just like that Jack of the Lantern was gone.

Yulric turned the pamphlet over, read the title, and understood why the Irishman had been there, why he had "helped." What is worse than an Englishman? Two Englishmen.

Cursing all Irish, Yulric began to read the pamphlet in his hand: "Proper Vampirism by the Honorable Doctor and Lord Douglas Talby."

Chapter 15

Proper Vampirism™
By the Honorable Doctor and Lord Douglas Talby
Revised Edition 7 Circa 2008

The dictionary defines *vampire* as a preternatural being, commonly believed to be a reanimated corpse that is said to suck the blood of sleeping persons at night. Note that the dictionary has gone out of its way to label the vampire a preternatural being. There is a natural being, as feared and as difficult to kill as the vampire, that is likewise said to suck the blood of sleeping persons at night. This creature is the common bedbug, and according to the dictionary definition, it is our equal. What we have achieved then through our mastery of death is to become a household pest.

You are not to blame.

The dictionary defines *vampirism* as the acts or practices of vampires. Taken together, the two definitions interpret vampirism as simply rising from the grave to suck blood, as well it should. For millennia, our ancestors had no more ambition than to be ticks and leeches. Though capable of so much more, they *chose* to be mere parasites. To use an analogy, they were like a missing link between fish and amphibian, able to journey up onto the land but unwilling to leave the primordial ooze. This tainted legacy weighs us down and makes us monsters.

It needn't be so. We can yet rise above. If vampirism truly is "the acts or practice of vampires," then any action undertaken by two or more of us becomes "an act of vampirism." Charity can be an act of vampirism. Intelligence, sophistication. We need not be limited by the definitions of old. We can make a new definition, one of civilized, worthy beings who have achieved perfection even unto immortality. Something to be idolized. Something to be desired. We can be the princes of the undead.

To this end, I have created a system for a new breed of vampire, a method that emphasizes the traits we find desirable while eliminating those that constrain our kind to the base or the ordinary. It is the way of Proper Vampirism™, and it is the foundation of the modern vampire movement.

The implementation of Proper Vampirism™ depends upon three factors: who becomes a vampire, how they become a vampire, and what kind of vampire they become. Let us explore each of these factors in turn.

Who Becomes a Vampire

Not everyone can be a vampire. It just isn't practical. Biologically speaking, we are apex predators, and as with any ecosystem, our survival depends on there being enough prey species to support us. Seven billion vampires would be impossible to sustain. The planet's animal supply only survives today because many humans live off vegetables, grains, and processed foods.

More importantly, though, not everyone DESERVES to be a vampire. This may be a harder concept to grasp. Many of you have grown up in a democratic society that teaches you everyone is exactly equal. This is patently untrue. Every person is unique, with certain strengths and weaknesses that make him or her more suited to one type of life than another. Certainly, you can seek to improve yourself, achieving through hard work what perhaps you were not naturally attuned for; however, one with no skill, aptitude, or experience cannot expect, for example, to become a doctor. Any society, like any chain, is only as strong, if you'll pardon the cliché, as its weakest link. To include those predisposed to indulge their own desires, to give in to that which we are trying to rise above, undoes us all.

So who are these most worthy, you may ask? Who are these people suited for an immortal life? The rich? The powerful? The beautiful? I think not. Wealth accrues over time. So does power. And as for beauty, what cosmetics cannot fix, cosmetic surgery surely can. High character, however, cannot be bought, intimidated, or seduced into being. It only comes about by overcoming hardship. This resilient and noble kind of person is who we are looking for. These are our vampires.

So when eyeing a prospective vampire, ask yourself these simple questions:

1. Is the person used to getting their way? Do they buy their way through situations with money or looks, or scrape by on the strength of their personality/intellect?
2. What are their appetites? Do they indulge every whim and/or hedonistic desire? Do they delight in mere base, bodily pleasure? Or, perhaps, higher, intellectual

distractions sustain them. Are they willing to sacrifice to achieve their goals?

3. Why do they wish to become a vampire? There are many paths to immortality, and none is perfect. Each has its own drawbacks. Do they merely want to forestall the trials of aging, or are they drawn to us by our culture and society? Do they know anything about us at all, or do they just expect us to be shiny?

4. How old are they? This, unfortunately, must be a consideration. Many of you may be tempted to turn loved ones and family members. Remember, a vampiric life does not magically undo the rigors of a long life. A ninety-year-old with a hip replacement is likely to remain a ninety-year-old with a hip replacement, albeit a stronger one, for all eternity. Moreover, their bad habits would be nearly impossible to break. Young people are able and, more importantly, willing to learn the way of Proper Vampirism™, but those who have aged in normal human society will want to continue living within that society instead of ours. To this end, anyone over the age of thirty-five will not be considered for vampirism. It may be harsh, but a century of experimentation has taught me that it is necessary.

How They Become a Vampire

Once a suitable candidate has been selected, there are steps that must be undertaken by the perspective and actual vampires to improve the outcome.

1. Physique and Appearance: While obviously we eschew the naturally beautiful, aesthetically speaking, beauty is beauty. Oh, standards vary slightly from culture

to culture and era to era, but less than many like to think. Men should always be strong and well-muscled. Women should always have full, firm breasts. You will find those who argue that being fat was once a sign of beauty. This is incorrect. Being fat was once a sign of wealth, which, at the time, was more important than beauty—especially to destitute artists who could not afford bread.

In most cases, a strict workout-and-dietary regimen is all that is necessary to attain the required specifications. However, in the event that more extreme measures must be taken, we offer a number of cosmetic procedures, free of charge. It does not matter if you are in need of simple electrolysis or require facial reconstructive surgery, we will provide them. This is about making you the best possible version of yourself, because how you look reflects upon us all. Just not in a mirror. Haha.

2. Tattoos: This is a new problem that has only arisen in the past few decades. Tattoos have become prevalent, even acceptable, in society, and as our greatest desire is to blend in with the culture around us, you might think that having one would be desirable. You would be wrong. ALL TATTOOS MUST BE REMOVED PRIOR TO BECOMING A VAMPIRE.

There are several reasons for this. You are embarking on an immortal life and, therefore, must be able to adapt to changing times and standards. In a few years, however, the trend will change and tattoos will be dropped in favor of some other method of expressing individuality along with everyone else. Not only that, but depending on the location, style, and subject matter, your tattoo will date you. Remember, you won't just have your tattoo for a few measly decades anymore; you'll have it for an eternity. Laser removal does not yet work on vampires.

Plus, tattoos just look tacky.

3. For the vampire: Each vampire is allowed to sire, at most, three individuals. You may think this is an arbitrary rule but it is very important, and comes as a result of much scientific observation on my part. Since my rebirth as a vampire, I have sought to apply the concepts of genetics and selective breeding to our kind, which does not breed or pass on genes. What I have found is that as vampirism spreads down the line—generation to generation, from sire to sired—its effects become less pronounced. This may not seem like such a good thing, but it is, believe me. I, as one of the eldest-living first-sired vampires, cannot stand the sight of a cross, both figuratively, because I am an atheist, nor physically, because the vampire curse was not yet diluted enough in my time. However, thanks to the three-sire rule, few vampires today need fear garlic, cross, or holy water. Soon, some of you may even be able to step into the light of day. It is my dearest hope and is achievable with strict adherence to the three-sire rule.

4. Approval: Before turning, all prospective vampires must be brought to me for final approval. No exceptions. I have worked tirelessly for over a hundred years to turn us into something civilized and respectable, but we can only continue to evolve down this path with constant vigilance. All it takes is one bad apple, if you'll once more pardon the cliché, to spoil the batch.

What Kind of Vampire They Become

Quite possibly, the most important category, and the reason why we must be scrupulous when choosing candidates, is how a person behaves once they've been turned. Proper Vampirism™ must be reflected not only in the proper aesthetic but also in the proper behaviors. Here is a guide to the minimum that is expected of a vampire.

1. Feeding: First and foremost, blood will be on your mind. It is an insatiable need that has not diminished in the later generations of vampires. It is, however, manageable for those of sufficient self-control. Never has this been more important than now. We can no longer afford to kill anyone we feed on. People are too easily tracked with GPS. Witnesses are too easily believed with video phones. There are more police than at any other time in history, and they are more capable than ever. I don't expect you all to be perfect; accidents will happen, after all. What we cannot have is a killing spree. One of those, and not only will it endanger our existence, it will endanger our reputation.

   Addendum: It is no longer necessary for us to hunt at all. Over the past few decades, a culture has risen up around us, and with it has come individuals willing to let us feed on them. The rules for feeding, therefore, have changed and are the same as the rules for sex, namely that feeding on unwilling humans is NOT acceptable under any circumstances. Those who argue it should be allowed in the event of an emergency would do well to remember they are immortal and can never starve to death.

2. Sex: We are attempting to remake the image of vampirism into something desirable. As such, we cannot just be beautiful; we must back up that promise of beauty in the bedroom. All vampires must be spectacular lovers and will learn to be so. Emphasis on learn. I do not put sexual prowess into the criteria of who becomes a vampire, because I would rather someone with too little experience than too much. A blank canvas, I can work with. Breaking existing bad habits is far more difficult.

    Individual lessons will be given in proper intercourse; however, I will give a general overview. Vampire sex comes in two styles: passionately sensual or animalistic frenzy. There is no in-between. There are no other categories. Talking dirty is beneath us. Role-playing is redundant. Light bondage is acceptable. However, more extreme forms of fetishism are expressly forbidden. Again, you represent all of us, and even here, we must retain a level of respectability.

    And skill. After all, this is not about your own pleasure. Any human can indulge that. It takes an inhuman to give such mind-numbing ecstasy to another. Every act of lovemaking must last an hour and a half minimum and result in the sexual climax of your partner on at least three occasions. No exceptions.

    Addendum: Vampirism does not discriminate based on sexual preference or gender identification. We in the vampire community support our LGBT brothers and sisters and are proud to welcome them into the fold.

3. Language: In maintaining our image, certain words are better than others. A vampire should exude mystery. Your speech cannot be littered with catchphrases or expressions that date you, unless they date you by fifty

years. Likewise, a vampire should never *try* to relate to the modern age through language. The only thing sadder than a vampire who thinks you are "totally radical, dude" is one who thinks you are "totes hott OMG!" A vampire is a timeless being, remember that.

Another faux pas is uncertainty. Vampiric speech cannot be filled with *ers*, *uhs*, or *ums*. Nor should it devolve into incessant chatter. If slow and steady won't win you the race, then quiet always will. There is nothing sexier than the sullen, silent stranger.

Addendum: As previously mentioned in the section on sex, cursing, by and large, should be avoided. While a good *goddamn* and well-placed *hell* are always welcome, other words have no place in the vampire vocabulary. Swear words are meant to be base, low things. Most reference excrement or sex, low concerns closer to those ancient, vile beasts than the modern vampire. Think of your perfect man or woman. Imagine seducing them with your vampire beauty. Now imagine opening your mouth and saying s--- or f--- or a--. You will not have to imagine them walking away.

4. Bettering Yourself/Employment: An eternity is a long time. Believe me when I say you will get bored. You will need distractions. What better way than a job, you say. You can earn money and pass time. But not all professions are worthy of a vampire. A vampire must have a proper job. An artist, maybe, or a musician. A doctor or CEO. You may not be qualified for these professions, but you can be. Take classes. Earn degrees. Better yourself. Now that you are a vampire, you have all the time in the world.

Note: Bettering one's self should occur *after* becoming a vampire. Those who attempt to do so prior to the change are in danger of running into the age limit. Many of the mortal vampire "elders" came to be in just this way.

By adhering to these rules, by screening who can become a vampire, by managing how they become a vampire, and by affecting what kind of vampire they become, we can make the vampire greater than it is today. Imagine a vampire that can walk in the sunlight or one that doesn't drink blood. Imagine if we could create an immortal entity of pure beauty with absolutely no consequence. What a sight that would be. Together, we can make this vision a reality. By adhering to my very basic rules we can make sure that the path to Proper Vampirism™ goes through you!

About the Author

The Doctor Lord Talby was born in England over a hundred and twenty-five years ago. In that time, he has worked to make the vampire into what it has become today and, as such, has earned the title "Father of Modern Vampirism." He maintains residences and medical practices in New York, London, and Beijing, but spends most of his time in LA.

◆   ◆

Yulric crushed the pamphlet when he finished reading it. He continued down the sewer drain, using curse words that pertained to sex and excrement.[41] The Doctor Lord Talby would not have approved.

---

41. Of porcupines.

Chapter 16

Amanda enjoyed three whole days of blissful normalcy. Three days of working, sleeping, and watching TV without a looming shadow falling over her or a furious howl waking her up. Of believing that the rotting old monster was never, ever going to come back. It was wonderful.

Then, just after sunset on the fourth evening, Yulric stormed out of the cellar and made a beeline for the couch.

"So, you're back, then?" she asked. He did not answer, but with an intensity not usually seen in those about to watch TV, threw open a *Phantom Vampire Mysteries* DVD case and inserted it into the player.

"Where'd you go after the club?" she tried, hoping for a little insight. Still, he did not respond. He put on a season-one episode, but skipped over it completely, stopping only to watch the credits go by. At the name of the executive producer, he paused the screen.

"Boy!" he bellowed.

"What?" came an answering call from upstairs.

"Bring me books and maps," the vampire shouted back. The scurry of footsteps could be heard above as Simon ran about his room collecting his favorite things.

"Well, it looks like you two will be busy," she said. "If you'd just keep an eye on my brother while I'm at work." Still, he did not acknowledge her presence. He took out the first DVD and put in another, this one a show from the early '90s about a detective who goes undercover as a vampire, the twist being that he is already, secretly, a vampire. Again, he skipped the entire episode and went right to the credits.

Amanda slung her purse over her shoulder and was on her way out.

"I do not think they will ever let you join them."

Amanda spun around to ask what he had meant by that, but the vampire was turned away, looking for an earlier TV series about a late-night radio psychologist looking for love. Amanda drove away that night convincing herself that he hadn't spoken at all, that it had just been her imagination.

Nearby, a phone call was made.

◆ ◆

It was seven days before anything happened. After all, schedules had to be changed, limos had to be called, jets needed to be chartered, more limos had to be called, suites needed to be booked, room service had to be ordered (for appearances), autographs needed to be signed for waiters' nieces, who were "really big fans," and finally, hotel rooms had to be sneaked out of without the paparazzi noticing, which is a feat only an immortal could possibly achieve.

It was difficult to walk through the Linskes' living room at this time. Books and maps littered every inch of floor space between couch and television, as well as a few other places, the vampire having a habit of tossing books across the room when frustrated. Yulric had not moved in a week, but skittered across his piles of papers cross-referencing the name Talby in book acknowledgments and DVD credits. What Yulric was looking for was not exactly clear; Simon had handed him the man's Los Angeles post-office box, printed from the Phantom Studios home page. The siblings merely supposed the ancient creature refused to believe his quarry would publicly boast of his location.

Amanda knew she should be thanking her lucky stars; this new Yulric was practically a dream. He showed absolutely no sign of killing anyone other than this Talby he was searching for and paid very little attention to the humans at all. His nest of research aside, he had become less trouble than owning a dog or a cat. Yet, Amanda still couldn't shake the feeling that soon the other shoe would drop.

The night it did began with Amanda attempting to push Simon into the bath.

"You are ruining my experiment," he pleaded, trying to keep his sister from stripping him down. "I am testing the benefits of cleanliness versus natural odors and how they pertain to an undetectable approach upon the undead."

"Well, the results are in, and they say that if the living can smell you, you stink too much," she said, managing to wrangle his shirt from him.

"Ah, but the human nose and the immortal nose are attuned differently," he argued. "People smell stink, whereas a monster is more likely to smell soap and perfume."

"I'm pretty sure they smell both," she replied, grabbing one pant leg.

"*Pretty sure* is not certain," challenged Simon. He was now hopping up and down, trying to keep his other leg out of her grasp. "This is why experimentation is needed."

"Look, Simon," she said, finally buckling, "if you take a bath, I will let you take your Houdini kit in with you."

This stopped him hopping.

"Even the straitjacket?" he asked cautiously.

"Even the straitjacket," she agreed.

"And you won't leave it loose, like you normally do? You'll make it nice and tight."

"There will be no way you could possibly escape," she assured him.

"Very well," he replied and finished taking his clothes off. Amanda went and retrieved the straitjacket from his room. She had never really been sure how he'd managed to get his hands on it, but decided to treat its appearance like she did most things having to do with Simon—with silence. After putting the thing on him and chaining his feet and chest below the water, Amanda stood over the bathtub, ready to cover it with a wooden lid.

"Remember to leave the stopwatch on the sink," Simon instructed.

"Wash your hair when you get your hands free," she told him. His head was halfway in the water, which she was sure he would use as an excuse later for having "not heard her." She placed the cover over him and hit the timer as she left the bathroom, her war won.

Unfortunately, the war, like most, had taken longer than the combatants had thought it would, and she was now running late. Going into panic mode, she began undressing in the middle of the hallway. She was doing her best imitation of Simon's earlier hopping when the doorbell rang through the house, after which Amanda's profanity rang through the house. She tore down the stairs, nearly falling, and only just remembered to put on her scrub shirt before opening the door and immediately wishing she hadn't.

Deep brown eyes stared at her from the other side. Sad-but-wholesome deep brown eyes, which bore into Amanda and caressed her soul. Deep brown eyes whose every answer would be "you." A strong nose divided the eyes into perfectly symmetrical halves. Above a strong, stubbled chin, a soft, tender mouth formed a mournful smile that Amanda wanted to comfort with soft, loving kisses. All of this was framed by perfect shoulder-length brown hair.

A cold wind blew across the owner of the deep brown eyes, sweeping his hair across his face and his long black coat across his body. His body! Amanda hadn't even made it past his head. A black button-down shirt hugged his ample muscular chest. The pants were black and long and not particularly tight, but Amanda had seen enough on TV to give her a fairly decent idea of what lay beneath, and what she hadn't already seen, she could imagine. Oh, how she could imagine.

Amanda couldn't catch her breath. She couldn't speak. She couldn't even respond to the urge to tear her clothes off. She was frozen in place with both the door and her mouth gaping open stupidly.

"Hi." Words, blessed words emerged from the lovely, sad mouth. "Amanda, right?"

Amanda nodded. In a deep part of her brain, she realized she should say something and so muttered, "Ph-Phantom." Before she could stop herself, she reached out and poked him to make sure he was real.

"I'm not really a ghost; I just play one on TV," he quipped, taking the extremely awkward moment in stride. "Hey, you post on the fan site, right?"

Amanda's eyes went wide. If he'd actually read what she'd posted . . . *everything* she'd posted, the fan fic and everything . . . Suddenly, Amanda wished her arms had the strength to close the door.

Phantom, unsure of what this silence meant, continued. "You are PhaNora4EVR640, aren't you?"

"Y-yes," answered Amanda, realizing he actually expected her to respond.

"Wow," he said. "It is really great to meet you. The writers have said your posts are some of the most trusted and constructive they've ever read. Didn't you, guys?"

Phantom said this last over his shoulder. He moved to the side, and for the first time, Amanda saw that Phantom was not alone. Reclining against a limo were others. A man and woman waved in response to what Phantom had said. Amanda would have assumed these unfamiliar faces were the writers—would have, except her eyes had already found the others: Berwyn, Phantom's main rival for the affection of Sasha and a rebel-without-a-cause stud muffin of the first order; Cassan, the strong, silent leader of the coven, with a tragic history as an African slave; Victoria, Cassan's wife, whose full, supple body was much touted as a return of curves to the airwaves; Lord Dunstan, the villain from the third season, who had been summarily defeated so that he could turn good in the fourth; The Gorgon, this season's Big Bad, who had kidnapped Sasha, convinced Phantom she had left him forever, and was sleeping with the person to his right, the person who, other than Phantom, Amanda was most excited to see—Nora, the strong, smart blond vampiress who served as the group's enforcer. The one Phantom truly belonged with, because she was a real woman—she owned her sexuality and refused to be beat out by a man.

Nora was right there. The main cast was right *there*. All except Sasha, and really, who needed her? The tramp.

"Anyway," began Phantom, likely judging that he had given her long enough to let their presence sink in, "we were just in the neighborhood, tossing around story ideas, and I said, 'Hey, you know who we should talk to as long as we're here? Amanda Linske.'"

Amanda's brain should have been screaming warnings. It should have been asking itself what the hell a bunch of TV stars were doing riding a limo through Shepherd's Crook. It should have been asking how he was able to get her full name and address from a secure forum account. But her brain was currently mush, and so she just stared dreamily at him.

Phantom started to look a little impatient. "So, we stopped to talk to you, Amanda. Do you think we could maybe come in?"

Amanda's eyes went even wider, now with terror. How could she be so stupid? She hadn't invited them in. And they needed an invitation, didn't they? Oh, Phantom probably thought she was rude now. She really hoped Phantom didn't think she was rude. But he probably did. She wished she could have asked him, but she knew he would lie like the gentleman he was. And he was.

Phantom waited on the doorstep until the whirlwind of thoughts in Amanda's head came back around to what he had asked. Finally she said, "Yes, of course. Come right in."

Behind her, there was an explosion of glass. She tried to scream, but Phantom was crushing her throat.

◆　◆

Yulric was slightly aware that Amanda had been standing at the door for an inappropriate length of time. He was also aware of the smell of hair spray, cologne, and large amounts of makeup wafting in from outside. Yulric's brain should have been able to put together that only those club vampires operated at that level of grooming, but currently, the vampire was too busy searching for hidden messages within every fifth episode of *Dark Shadows* using the so-called vampire language from a role-playing game as a cipher key. And so Yulric paid these facts no mind.

That is, until the room exploded.

Glass flew through the air as four massive objects crashed through the windows around him. Yulric tried to dismiss this as more mortal nonsense meant to distract him, but his self-preservation sense was telling him that massive objects thrown through windows don't usually land lightly when they hit the ground. Extremely powerful and athletic people do. He turned and managed a feeble "Berwyn?" before a fist backed by big, heavy muscles met his face and sent him over the end of the couch.

Yulric hit the wall and bounced off, landing on his hands and feet in a spiderlike crouch. His brain tried to analyze the sight it had briefly glimpsed, but a kick to the ribs sent him back into the wall, and a fist to the back of the head tried to put him down.

If I may? proposed Yulric's instincts.

Very well, relented his conscious mind.

And with that, Yulric's arm shot out and broke an ankle.

The owner of the ankle fell to the floor, howling in pain. A moment later, he was howling in terror as a still-grounded Yulric made to eat his face. Someone grabbed Yulric's robes and pulled back to stop the sprawling attack. The vampire let his assailant place him back on his feet before spinning around and smashing her head into a wall, then another wall, then a chair. He was about to make his way to the kitchen to see if her head could be smashed through the refrigerator when he was attacked from behind by a spray of holy water.

The holy water struck him in the back, soaking through his robes and burning his skin. Yulric released the head he was holding and turned, just in time to get another spray full in the face. Yulric clawed at his skin, tearing away chunks where the water had touched. One of his eyes bubbled and boiled. He was in the middle of plucking it out when he was forced back against the wall again. His arms were stretched out and pinned. Yulric tried to struggle, but the two men holding him were pressing crosses into his skin.

These weren't just any men, though. Deep in the recesses of Yulric's brain, behind the pain and snarling instincts, there was a moment of recognition.

That's Berwyn, thought his conscious mind.

Can't be, replied his animal instincts.

It is, assured the conscious mind. *And the one on our right arm is Cassan. Look.*

It . . . It is! said animal instincts. *Would you—*

Only if you don't mind, replied conscious mind.

By all means, said instincts.

Reason returned to Yulric. The situation was easy enough to assess. He was pinned by crosses, being sprayed with holy water, and facing down at least seven assailants, nine if the footsteps upstairs were to be believed. But who his assailants were, that was the surprise. Cassan and Berwyn held his arms. The Gorgon held a bottle of holy water. The two trying to stand up were show writers Damien Black and Sanguina Marlowe. Back by the archway, Nora leaned against a wall, and standing next to her, holding Amanda by the throat, was Phantom in the far-less-than-spectral flesh.

"We've got him," Phantom yelled, presumably to those upstairs. "Find anything up there?"

"The bastard had a kid chained underwater," called down a voice from one Yulric loathed—Lord Dunstan, the redeemed vampire. Oh, how he wished to get his hands on that "man's" throat and show him the error of his now-virtuous ways. "Just give us a minute."

"Good. We'll take care of things down here," replied Phantom. He turned to the struggling Amanda. "Don't worry. I'll let you go once we've broken his power over you." He turned away too quickly to see her roll her eyes at that.

So, thought Yulric, *they think I am controlling the girl and her brother. And they mean to break that control. Which means . . .*

"Nora," said Phantom, "would you like to dust him?"

"Always," replied Nora.

Surely not, thought Yulric. A plan formed. Not a great plan, but it would have to do.

Nora sprang away from the wall and grabbed the wooden stake from Phantom's outstretched hand. The two seemed to share a moment, ending in a wink from Phantom. Amanda's eyes went wide, taking in every detail, and she hopped excitedly from one foot to another. It was the best shipper end-zone dance she could manage while being held by the throat.

"Ready to die, beast?" Nora asked.

"Dhyhol a ver ph'logga shee—" began the ancient vampire.

"Stop him!" shouted Phantom. Cassan punched Yulric square in the jaw, dislocating it and preventing him from finishing the spell. *No matter,* thought Yulric. It had been only a distraction anyway.

Sprinting forward, Nora thrust her wooden stake through his chest with all her vampiric strength. Yulric let out a single cry of pain as the spike pierced his heart and lodged itself in the wood and plaster behind him. A moment later, all his skin turned to dust and fell to the ground, leaving a twisted, robe-clad skeleton hanging on the wall.

The two vampires let go of the skeleton's arms hesitantly.

"What the hell was that?" Nora gaped.

Cassan shook his head. "The Doctor said he might have powers, spells and transformations and stuff?"

"Is he supposed to dust like this?" asked Berwyn.

"Maybe all ancient vampires leave skeletons behind," replied Phantom. "Oh. Oops." He had just remembered he was holding Amanda by the throat. He let her go. "Sorry about that, Amanda. We had to be sure. You're free now."

He touched her face when he said that, which would have been a kind and loving gesture if (a) he hadn't just been choking her or (b) she had actually been under any sort of spell. There was an awkward pause. Amanda looked at Phantom. Phantom looked at Amanda, expectantly. If this were the show, this would be the moment they'd kiss. And Amanda realized that was exactly what he was expecting, for her to throw herself at him. Her heart sank along with her ship. He and Nora weren't together, Phantom was just a huge flirt.

Amanda took a step back and crossed her arms sullenly. "Thanks."

"Uh, you're welcome," he said, obviously trying not to sound surprised.

The male vampires all snickered. Nearby, Nora caught Amanda's eye and mouthed, "Thank you."

"Ah. Here's Victoria," said Phantom as Victoria came around the corner. "Where's the boy?" He gave Amanda a worried look. "He's not—"

"I am here," replied Simon, coming out from behind the new arrival. All the vampires smiled and relaxed. All except Victoria. Only Amanda noticed how stiff and nervous the vampiress seemed, her arms stuck to her sides, her eyes staring straight ahead. Amanda's eyes narrowed on her brother; none of them had seen Simon hide something up his left sleeve or realized that a normal child would have said "Here I am."

"See? All safe and sound," Phantom said, smiling at Amanda.

"The monster's power is broken. His hold over you is gone," added the Gorgon in his raspy, lizard-like voice.

"Gorgon, can you not, please?" sniped Damien Black.

The raspy voice gave way. "I have to stay in character, Damien. I'm method."

"One acting class does not make you method," retorted the limping writer.

"So you staked the vampire?" Simon asked.

Phantom approached Simon and crouched down to talk with him. "Yeah, we staked him, little man." He turned, apparently to make sure Amanda was seeing how good he was with children.

Nora sidled up beside Amanda. "He's always like this," Amanda explained tersely.

Under the pretext of being in awe of the vampire, Simon continued to examine Yulric's corpse.

Meanwhile, a nagging doubt finally found a voice. "Where's Lord Dunstan?" asked Berwyn.

The question was casual, but it seemed to shake Victoria awake. Whatever trance she'd been in cracked, and her eyes went back and forth as the inquiry reverberated around the room.

"Yeah, where is Lord Dunstan?" repeated Cassan.

"He was upstairs with you, Victoria," said Berwyn. "Where'd he go?"

Audibly swallowing, Victoria's eyes went straight to Simon. She looked as if she wanted to say something but was too afraid.

Simon paused in his examination long enough to answer. "Oh, the other guy? I told him about the vampire's attic workshop, where it kept all of its secret artifacts. He went up to investigate."

"Secret artifacts, you say?" asked the Gorgon, back in character.

"No!" said several people together.

"I'll go look for him," volunteered Berwyn.

Simon pointed up at the stake holding Yulric's skeleton to the wall. "So, is that like magic or something?" he asked, doing his very best impression of a normal child. He inappropriately used the word *like* and everything.

Phantom seemed all too eager to play to a kid. "Yeah, buddy," he said. "It's a shard from the staff of St. Hadrian of Toulouse, who wards away evil."

Simon's face twitched. Amanda could tell that he knew about St. Hadrian[42] and was fighting down his natural urge to correct the vampire. "Cool," he said through a tight smile.

---

42. St. Hadrian of Toulouse (1178–1212?) was a hermitic monk who lived outside Toulouse. When a great army from the Almohad dynasty began invading the Christian kingdoms of Spain, Hadrian was sent by God to delay their forces long enough for the Christian armies to stop arguing with one another and defend themselves. And so Hadrian walked from Toulouse, France, to the snow-covered peaks of the Sierra Morena mountain range where, through a series of miracles, one of which involved a rabid donkey, he managed to delay the attacking forces. There are no records on how he eventually met his end; however, when the Christian army eventually got around to fighting their enemy, they found in the Caliph's abandoned tent the still-frozen, now-severed feet of Hadrian of Toulouse. An important part of St. Hadrian's legend was that he ventured into the mountains specifically without shoes or *staff*. That is why he is the patron saint of hikers, podiatrists, and frostbitten toes.

Then, he lowered his eyes, toed the ground, and made a big show of embarrassment. "Can I see it?"

Phantom turned to the others. "I don't see why not. Cassan?"

Cassan, who on the show would have known all the answers, shrugged his shoulders. "I don't know." He turned to the writers. "What do you think?"

The two writers conferred on the subject, if *confer* was the right word. *Nerd bait* might be a more accurate term. Damien seemed convinced that all was perfectly safe and that the immediate disintegration of the vampire's blood-filled tissues served as evidence of this. Sanguina was more hesitant, maintaining that there was an inherent danger in removing the stake, and that if anyone needed her, she'd be investigating a murder on the Orient Express. Vampires, as it turned out, could suffer concussions. In the end, the more coherent writer won out.

"Come on, little buddy. You can do the honors," said Phantom, taking Simon by the hand. They approached the skeleton. Simon hung back, pretending to be scared.

"Don't worry," said the vampire. "I'm right here."

He bent down and put his hands around the boy's waist.

"Ready?" he asked. "One. Two. Three."

The vampire bounced Simon two times and then picked him up so that he was level with the skeleton.

"Go ahead. Take it," Phantom encouraged. Simon grasped the end of the stake and pulled.

In that moment, several things happened at once.

Phantom looked down at the ground and asked, "Hey, Cassan, is that one of those sigil things?"

Berwyn came running from upstairs and screamed, "Lord Dunstan's dead!"

Victoria finally found her voice and shrieked, "It was him! It was the kid!"

Simon, using both hands, extracted the stake from Yulric Bile.

It took everyone several moments to register all that had been said and done. By the time they had, they were no longer turning to look at a small boy who had murdered their friend; they were instead facing the skeleton that was dusting itself off. Phantom, who was still holding the boy, stared into the gaping eye sockets of Yulric Bile's skull. The skull grinned back viciously. It couldn't actually not grin, being a skull, so it grinned extra hard to make the viciousness clear.

"Phantom," chittered the skull. An impressive accomplishment without lips or vocal cords. "Big fan."

There was a flash, and Phantom was gone, having been knocked into Sanguina and then into the wall of the next room. Simon had barely begun to fall when Yulric plucked him out of the air.

"Get him," screamed Berwyn. The vampires readied themselves to fight again. This proved to be a mistake, for once Yulric had set Simon on the ground, he did not ready himself to fight; he simply fought.

The Gorgon went for the holy water. Unfortunately, he'd put the bottle back in one of his trench-coat pockets. By the time he had hold of it, it was too late. A light smack of skeletal fingers sent the glass container flying to the floor, where it shattered. The Gorgon then found himself next to Phantom and the twice-concussed Sanguina.

Berwyn and Cassan took out their crosses and bore down on the ancient vampire from opposite sides. Yulric yowled in pain and frustration. He picked up a glass paperweight from the table, and with as much supernatural force as he could muster under the influence of two crosses, threw it into Berwyn's groin. Bent over in pain, the young vampire was in no condition to maintain his grip on the cross.

"Hey!" Amanda shouted at the skeleton. It turned as she bore down on it. "That was my mother's."

The skeleton Yulric kicked Berwyn a bit to the left, revealing that the useless little knick-knack was intact.

"Okay then. Just . . . try not to break stuff," replied Amanda. She took the cross from the ground, snapped it in two, and walked to a safe corner.

Cassan approached, one hand grasping his intact cross, the other protecting his intact junk—not the best fighting position. Yulric picked up a couch cushion and tossed it at him. In the split-second impact it blotted out the holy symbol, Yulric ran up and struck the near helpless Cassan in the head. Cassan, too, dropped his cross, but just as the skeleton was about to capitalize on his sucker punch, Nora snatched it from the ground and held the monster at bay.

"AAAAH!"

A bloodcurdling scream rang out, distracting everyone. They all turned just in time to see Victoria—beautiful, busty, full-figured Victoria—fall to pieces before them. Where once she'd stood, there was only dust and ash and Simon.

"No!" Two voices cried out in unison. Neither was a young vampire.

"What did you do?" shouted Amanda.

"What have you done?" shrieked skeleton Yulric. He reached down and sifted through the powder on the floor. It spilled through his fingers with no signs of life.

"I—I killed a vampire," Simon said in a tone of complete innocence.

"And who asked you to do that?" replied Amanda.

Simon looked at his sister. He hadn't expected this kind of reaction. In his mind, she should have been proud that her eight-year-old brother could kill a vampire. In a pleading voice, he said, "They were fighting." He pointed to the red hand mark on her neck. "And they attacked you."

"That's no reason to kill her," scolded Amanda. "I mean, that was Victoria. Victoria! How will we ever know if she was really the woman who bought Cassan as a slave?"

"Or what she did to save him from the Helsings?" added Yulric.

"Or if they'll stay together when she learns that he turned her last living relative?" concluded Amanda.

Simon peered confused from one to the other. He had defended himself. He had saved them both and all they cared about was a stupid television show.

"Is she really dead?" Amanda asked Yulric, hoping against hope.

"I . . . think so," he told her, once more turning his attention to the remains. "This doesn't appear to be a trick or illusion."

"Well, how did you do it?" she asked him.

"Sigil on the floor, carved with my toe. The curse of dust. One touch and—" He turned to Simon. "What did you do? *Exactly.*"

"I staked her through the heart with this," he explained, showing them the stake.

"And?" waited Yulric.

"That's it," replied Simon.

"You cannot kill a vampyr just by stabbing it through the heart," Yulric exclaimed.

There was an uncomfortable squirm from the young vampires.

Yulric gaped incredulously. "Really? A stake through the heart? That is all it takes? No removal of the head? No purification by fire? You do not even have to be staked to anything? Just"—he made a stabbing motion—"and you are dead?"

The vampires looked at each other awkwardly. You weren't really supposed to discuss your weaknesses with the enemy.

"How is this possible?" Yulric roared in frustration. He turned on Simon. "Very well. No more killing, understand?"

Simon made a face. It was not a good face. It was a face that said, "Oh, if only you'd told me earlier."

"What?" Yulric barked, unaware. He turned to Amanda. "What?"

"I think he killed Lord Dunstan, too," she explained.

Yulric let out what could only be called an unholy racket. "The traitor! You killed Lord Dunstan before he could return to his evil ways?"

"Lord Dunstan wasn't going to return to his evil ways," chimed in a voice from behind him. It was Damien Black. Yulric turned to face the brave little writer.

"Well, why was he collecting the keys of Sekhmet, if he wasn't going to unleash the blood goddess and sit atop the end as Lord of Destruction?" he asked testily.

"He only said that to gain the Gorgon's trust. In the end, he would have opened the prison and thrown the Gorgon inside, finally redeeming himself completely," explained the writer.

"That makes no sense. Why would he do that?" disagreed Yulric.

Amanda knew why.

"*No!*" she shouted. "No. No. No. No. No!"

"What?" asked a confused Yulric.

"He does it to save Nora, doesn't he?" she challenged.

"She is the intended blood sacrifice," said the writer smugly.

"You're trying to set Nora up with Dunstan," she accused. The writer gave a noncommittal shrug, which further set her off. "Nora belongs with Phantom!"

"Well, we've set up from the beginning that Phantom and Sasha will end up together," Damien explained.

"He belongs with Nora." She began counting on her fingers. "They have known each other longer. They have more in common. They have better chemistry. And Nora is a much stronger character than Sasha is."

"Not going to happen," retorted the exasperated writer.

"Weren't we in the middle of a fight?" interrupted Berwyn.

"*In a minute!*" barked Yulric, Amanda, and the writer.

"So, your great plan is to just pawn off Nora on Lord Dunstan? *Dunstan?*" cried Amanda.

"Would you prefer she end up alone?" replied the writer.

"Rather than watch her throw herself at Lord Dunstan? Yeah, I would. I don't care what he did. He could save the world a thousand times over and you'd still have to give her a lobotomy before she'd choose him." Amanda turned to Yulric. "You agree with me, right?"

Yulric nodded. "Lord Dunstan is far too powerful to simply fall in love and 'turn good.'" This last was said with air-quote fingers. He'd figured out how they worked.

"See," she said.

"He didn't actually agree with you," the writer pointed out.

"Well, neither of us thinks Nora and Lord Dunstan should be together," she spat back.

"Indeed," agreed Yulric.

"Look, you can complain until you're blue in the face"—the writer turned to Yulric—"or until you have a face, but this is not a democracy. It's a monarchy. A dictatorship." He lifted the concussed Sanguina to her feet. "And we're in charge. We control it. We are God."

"We are?" Sanguina eyed her omnipotent hands.

"We decide how the story goes," Damien continued. "We decide how the characters act. If we say they fall in love, they fall in love. If we say they turn good, they turn good. I once invented a hopping curse because Phantom pissed me off and

I wanted to watch him hop on one leg for an entire episode. Which got me nominated for a Hugo Award by the way. So, let me be clear, Phantom and Nora are never going to be together. Lord Dunstan is never . . . was never going to be evil again. And by the end of this season, Dunstan and Nora were going to get it on and make little vampire babies."

Silence fell. A silence that can be broken only by someone without a clue.

"Vampyrs cannot have babies," Yulric corrected him.

"They can if I say they can!" yelled the writer in frustration.

"Really? You were going to have vampire babies?" said Amanda, disgusted.

"No, I—"

"You were going to put a pregnancy belly on me? On this?" Nora questioned, outlining her figure as she spoke.

"You weren't going to be pregnant, okay?" assured the writer. "I was just making a point."

"Okay, because I don't want to have to wear a one-piece for *The Phantom Vampire Mysteries Magazine* swimsuit special."

"You won't," said the writer. "You won't."

Silence fell again.

"So, are we done?" asked Phantom. "Can we fight now?"

"Certainly," replied Yulric.

"Yeah," said Damien.

"You're mine, writer boy," growled Amanda.

"Well then . . . ," said Phantom dramatically. "Here we go."

"No killing!" Yulric and Amanda shouted at Simon. He nodded with a bit of a pout.

And with that, the fight began again in earnest.

Berwyn, Phantom, and Nora went for skeleton Yulric—encircling, pecking, and generally trying to stay out of arm's reach of the great old vampire. Cassan and the Gorgon charged Simon—the former grief-stricken at the loss of his on-screen wife and offscreen girlfriend, the latter just now remembering he was missing his favorite celebrity dance competition show.

This left the two writers for Amanda. While one of them attacked what turned out to be a coatrack, the second lunged forward to grab her, unsuccessfully. He might have been supernaturally fast and strong, but Amanda was a woman with a nighttime job, who had watched *The Karate Kid* at least a hundred times growing up. Damien Black reached his intended quarry just in time to have his already injured leg swept out from under him. He fell hard.

With her opponent on the floor clutching his ankle, Amanda spared a glance to make sure her brother was okay. Miraculously, not only was he fine but his vampires were shrinking back from him, holding their groins. Clearly they had forgotten a basic rule—that an eight-year-old will always find a way to hit you in the nuts. A flash of green light and glimpse of something tentacled told her Yulric was still alive, too.

Quickly, Amanda ran over to where Sanguina Marlowe was losing her fight with the coatrack, snatched up her purse, and began rummaging. She passed over a compact, lipstick, wallet, keys, individual cough drops, gum, gum wrappers, gum wrappers with used pieces of gum in them, pens, crayons, Kleenex, used Kleenex, napkins, wet wipes, feminine-hygiene products, hair ties, hair clips, a pink wig in a baggy, fishnet stockings, regular stockings, an extra lace bra, an extra plain bra, a white tank top, her cell phone, the latest *Phantom Vampire* novelization (coincidentally written by Damien Black), a half-eaten donut, a banana, a spoon, and a bag of M&M'S she'd forgotten she had. Finally, at the bottom of the bag, among the loose change and crumbs, she found what she was looking for.

Wham! She flew back into the wall. The fact that she barely missed hitting Sanguina was a lucky break for the vampire, though not for Amanda, whose head bounced off a stud instead. Her vision filled with light, then darkness. It was a few seconds before she realized her eyelids were shut. She opened them to discover she could still see, though it was kind of fuzzy. And spinny. And starry. Having lost her contacts would account for only one of these.

Something reached down and, with a bulge of muscles, lifted her up with unnatural strength. Its bared teeth shone bright; its eyes burned with malice. Whatever this blurry, ominous figure was, it was truly terrifying.

Then, Amanda blinked, and the apparition resolved itself back into the attractive-but-twerpy little writer again.

He held her by the throat and quipped, "What about Nora and Dunstan now? Any thoughts?"

Amanda did have one thought. *I'm getting really sick of being picked up by the neck.* She raised her hand to his ear and pressed the button of her mini foghorn.

The foghorn was part of the rape-prevention defense package her brother had given her when he was four.[43] It was meant to audibly incapacitate an attacker with sound loud enough to cause physical pain. An attacker with normal hearing, that is. As for attackers with supernatural hearing . . .

The writer fell to the ground clawing at his ears and screaming till his voice was raw. Or he may have been screaming that loud only because he couldn't hear himself. Amanda didn't know nor did she care. She just pressed the button again. And again. And again. Her opponent went from kneeling, to crawling, to thrashing on the floor.

---

43. He had been reading about the Vikings at the time. Incidentally, he had also created a pillage-prevention defense kit for the house. Their parents had thought it was cute, cardboard-pole arms and all.

"I think Nora and Dunstan is a stupid idea!" shouted Amanda, her voice a bit raspy from being choked, twice. She punctuated her words by hitting the bullhorn. "Did you hear that? I said it's stupid. *Stupid!* Nora belongs with Phantom. With Phantom!"

She went to hit the button again, but it was snatched away from her. Amanda looked up. Yulric's empty eye sockets stared back at her. One skeletal hand held the bullhorn, the other protected the hole where an ear would be on a flesh-covered face.

"No more!" Yulric said, quite a bit louder than was normally necessary.

"Sorry," she apologized. She'd forgotten that the one with the most supernaturally acute hearing was on her side. Phantom, Berwyn, and Nora also looked relieved. Phantom gave a nod of thanks to Yulric that turned into something else. It was an anticipatory stare, directed, not at him, but at her.

A hiss from behind alerted Amanda to danger. She glanced over her shoulder just in time to see the writer's open mouth ready to sink its fangs into her neck. Yulric was facing the other way. There wouldn't be time for him to do anything. This was it. The end. She was going to die at the hands of a pathetic little writer with no understanding for the intricacies of relationship chemistry. *I'm sorry, Simon,* she thought as she braced for the bite.

It never came.

A scream made Amanda open her eyes, just in time to get a face full of dust. Through her stinging corneas, she could just make out her brother, stake in hand, standing at the epicenter of the vampiric explosion.

"Simon . . . ," she began, before coughing up some writer that had gotten into her mouth. Finally, she was able to compose herself to scold, "Simon, what did we . . . *No!*"

The Gorgon's attempt to sneak up behind her brother failed miserably as the eight-year-old flung it into his would-be attacker's chest, piercing his heart. Amanda watched as he, too, went gray and fell to pieces.

"Stop killing vampires!" yelled Amanda. Simon gave her a look most younger brothers reserve for finding their sisters making out with boys.

Another scream sounded, and they forgot their tiff as they turned as one to stare at the vampires.

Yulric Bile had transformed into thousands of tiny white spiders. Nora and Cassan were shrieking and swatting as the bony arachnids crawled all over them. Phantom picked up a piece of broken wood and threw it. It hit Simon in the forehead, knocking him to the ground.

"Simon!" Amanda cried out. She wanted to see if he was all right but was hit again from the side, more gently this time but still hard enough to send her flying. She expected to hit the ground or the wall or something hard and unforgiving but didn't. She looked up to find Berwyn's face hovering above her. He had literally swept her off her feet and was carrying her out of the house. Phantom followed quickly behind while Cassan and Nora pulled up the rear, still shaking off the spiders.

Amanda was stuffed unceremoniously into the limo outside. The other vampires got in quickly, and following a double tap on the dividing window, they took off. Amanda was now alone and in the clutches of vampires. Finally.

◆ ◆

Yulric reconstituted himself just in time to watch the long car of the young vampires fade into the distance. Moments later, Simon joined him. The small boy and the old vampire stood side by side, unable to chase after them as neither knew how to drive.

"Where did you get a hatchet?" asked the vampire, referring to the weapon the boy was now holding.

"I always have a hatchet," responded the boy. "Ransom?"

"Ransom," Yulric concurred.

The taillights of the limo disappeared over a hill.

"What about us?" asked Simon.

"We wait," replied the vampire. A crash made them turn. Stuck in the doorway was the very concussed Sanguina Marlowe.

"Wait for me, guys. I'll drive," she cried, making vroom noises with her lips and scooting a chair on its side into the doorframe.

The odd pair looked from loopy vampire to each other. Simon raised an eyebrow.

"Very well," said Yulric. The boy skipped across the lawn, surreptitiously stowing the small hatchet up his sleeve. The skinless one was now alone, his thoughts on the horizon and what would come next. Behind him, a scream rang out followed by the sound of small particles hitting wood. Yulric made his way back into the house, being sure to tread in the ashes on his way.

Chapter 17

The phone rang.

Yulric had learned enough from television to figure out how phones worked, in theory if not specifically.[44] Through them, you were able to talk to others over great distances. They used to be attached to walls or in booths, but more and more these days, people were using little metal blocks like this one. All things being equal, Yulric had discovered how to communicate from afar long ago. The difference was, now you had to pay for data plans and overage fees, whereas in his day, it cost only the blood of three pregnant goats and a virgin's left eye. The jury was still out on which system was better.

Cautiously, he picked up the device. His long, spindly fingers reached over to the Send button and pressed down. This was how to start a call, or so he'd been told. Then the "cell" was placed to his ear.

---

44. He was still trying to catch lightning in jars.

"Yes?" answered the vampire. He was not a *hello* type of person. He was not, in fact, a person at all.

"Is this Mr. Yulric Bile?" asked a woman's voice. It was not the one he had expected. This voice was pleasant but formal.

"Yes," responded Yulric.

"Please hold for The Doctor Lord Talby," instructed the woman, and with a click she was gone.

Yulric hung up. A few minutes later the phone rang again.[45] Yulric answered it.

"Yes?" he said again.

"Mr. Bile?" asked the woman's voice. "I'm sorry. We must have been disconnected. I apologize for the inconvenience. The Doctor Lord Talby will be with you in just a—"

This time he hung up while she was still talking. Yulric Bile might have been three hundred years out of time, but he still recognized a lackey when he heard one.

After a much longer pause than before, the phone rang again. Yulric picked up. "Yes?"

"Yulric Bile."

This time it was not a question. It also wasn't a woman.

"Speaking," replied Yulric.

"You've been quite rude to my assistant," said this new voice. It was strong, confident, and properly English, which usually lent it an air of authority. Not here, though. Back when Yulric had lived, Anglo-Saxon wasn't just a term of ancestry, it was the current political state.

"You shouldn't have used her to be rude to me, Talby," retorted Yulric. He could almost hear the other man smile.

"Touché," said the Doctor.

---

45. But not really. Phones did not actually ring so much as play music: in this case a *screech-screech* song whose lyrics were unsurprisingly unintelligible.

Yulric smiled, too. Thus far, he had faced children and mortals, and the only real challenge he'd found among them was a mortal child. This one was different. He knew how to play the game.

"I assume you know why I'm calling?" asked Talby.

"The girl," said Yulric.

"She's quite safe," Talby replied, mistaking Yulric's statement as a sign of concern. "Both from injury and you finding her."

"I doubt that," said Yulric.

"Ah. You are referring to your 'powers,'" said Talby. Yulric noted how far out of his way the Doctor went to avoid saying *magic*. "As with vampires, witches are open and abundant these days. A few are even real. I think you'll find any attempt to track Ms. Linske will lead you to the nearest church."

Yulric knew this. He'd already tried. "Well then, I assume you require some sort of ransom."

The Doctor laughed. "So open. I thought for sure you'd refuse to negotiate."

"In my day, ransom was common. Princes and kings held by other princes and kings," explained Yulric. "A noble business."

"Indeed. I must brush up on my history," replied the Doctor.

"Name your terms," Yulric demanded.

"The price for her release is you," said The Doctor Lord Talby, who then had to deal with an earful of barking, shrill laughter.

Eventually, Yulric composed himself enough to respond. "I don't think you realize what you're dealing with."

"Oh, I think I do," said the Doctor. "Yulric Bile. Born sometime between the eighth and tenth centuries, last sighted in Shepherd's Crook, Massachusetts, in the seventeenth. Supposedly killed a dozen times before that. Vampire, sorcerer, madman, and monster. Alignment—chaotic evil, whatever that means. Modus operandi usually involves creating a cult of thralls, with no other goal than the sowing of violence, madness, and death. How am I doing?"

Yulric was a bit uneasy. He had always been very careful to destroy any record of himself.[46] More than that, he had thought himself unpredictable. That he could even be categorized made his newly re-formed skin squirm. He slapped at it, to be sure it didn't crawl away. Skin dormant again, he made sure his voice was calm before responding, "You've done your research."

"Actually, I couldn't find anything about you at all," admitted Talby. "Couldn't even get the bank to divulge its information. I also use La Première Banque du Suisse, incidentally. No, all of this I got from Ms. Linske. Apparently, she did quite a bit of homework on you."

Yulric frowned. The only thing worse than his enemy knowing so much about him was the girl and her brother knowing so much about him.

"Well, since you know everything," growled Yulric, "you know how likely it is that I will just hand myself over to you."

"You misunderstand me," replied Talby. "I don't mean an exchange. I simply want to meet you. To talk. Maybe come to an arrangement of sorts."

"Is that why you sent the Phantom to kill me?" retorted Yulric.

"That was a mistake," sighed the Doctor, "on so many levels. We've had to completely reconfigure this season to make up for our . . . losses." The Doctor seemed on the verge of anger for the merest moment. He regained himself quickly. "You are too dangerous and powerful to fight, and so, I've chosen to deal."

Yulric wanted to say "to beg." He wanted to laugh and gloat and challenge this man. But he was careful, very careful. He

---

46. Except in banks. Those, like him, were necessary evils.

nearly hadn't walked away from the last encounter, and there had been just the slightest emphasis on *powerful*. The Doctor Lord Talby was trying to push Yulric's buttons. He shouldn't even know there were buttons to push.

"You mean to trap me," Yulric said. It was not a question.

"Well, certainly," replied Talby jovially. "If not one way, then another. There is an old saying, or maybe for you, a new saying. 'If you can't beat them, join them.' We cannot beat you. I am equally certain you cannot beat us. Therefore, coming together is the only rational, civilized thing to do."

Yulric said nothing. The same thoughts had crossed his mind, though he wasn't about to say so. Talby likely recognized this and so continued, "Just come to the studios in Los Angeles, and we'll have a little chat about the future. Our future. Anyway, must go. The bandages are coming off today, and, well, that's another story. See you soon."

He hung up.

"Well?" Yulric asked.

"Duplicitous, at best," Simon assessed. He was sitting on the floor, legs crossed, listening on something called a "cloned phone." Yulric understood only that it had enabled the boy to hear the whole conversation.

"He means to lure me to his place of strength and kill me there," said Yulric.

"Possibly, as a last resort. If you don't agree to his arrangement," replied Simon. Yulric appreciated how the boy's mind worked when it was not trying to kill him. "What about my sister?"

"She is fine," answered the vampire.

"How can you be sure?" asked Simon with a little boy's concern in his voice. Most little boys, however, wouldn't have added, "He didn't offer proof of life."

"Only because he did not think he needed to," explained Yulric. "He fancies himself a great man, civilized, honorable. She will be fine."

"We'll need to know everything we can about Phantom Studios," said Simon. He tapped a few times on his magic Pad of Eye and brought up a view of the entire structure.

"If you were holding my sister, where would you keep her?" he asked the vampire.

Yulric scanned the layout. "There."

"The front gate?" Simon asked suspiciously.

"Yes," replied Yulric. "She would be tied to it. Her corpse would anyway."

"So, that really doesn't help us, does it?" said Simon, leaving out "foul creature." The term was implied, though.

"I suppose not," said the vampire, very bored and not really caring. The small boy continued to plot and strategize how to rescue his sister while Yulric considered *The Phantom Vampire Mysteries* third-season episode "As You Wish" and the plot holes concerning who turned Phantom. After all, if it was Nora, like so many on the online forums insisted, then how could one account for the fact that in that episode she was controlled by the sire call of the Dead Pirate Rowan[47] and he was not? He vowed to have Amanda post a "flame" on the message boards upon her return.

After an hour of careful study, Simon leaned back in his chair and rubbed his eyes. "I'm afraid the other vampires have the advantage. Even if we were to cause a distraction and try to sneak past, I'm not sure . . . What? What are you smiling about?"

Yulric sat up and spoke only two words:

"Other vampyrs . . ."

---

47. Yulric did not get the reference.

Chapter 18

Leaving a country used to be such an easy process; you would simply get on a horse or a boat or, if you were poor, walk and physically travel from where you were to a place where people spoke a different language. Occasionally, you might find yourself in a country where the border was fortified with various checkpoints and magistrates were charged with keeping out certain undesirables: gypsies, tramps, the English. This made a crossing slightly more difficult but was easily overcome by a judicious application of currency.

In the modern world, though, leaving required detailing personal information, which was checked, double-checked, and then double-checked again until they found some reason to stop you. It was no use explaining to them that you were a five-year-old girl in a wheelchair; if your name was on their list, they assumed you were really a six-foot, thirty-five-year-old murderer in disguise and refused to let you travel. And that was supposing you got that far. Identification was required just to fill out a form to receive identification. If you were an eight-year-old who didn't understand why a library card didn't count as ID, no matter how many books you'd read, this was a problem. If you were a one-thousand-year-old vampire with only a handful of cautionary mentions in the biographies of certain saints, it was impossible. Worse yet, those in charge of customs no longer accepted bribes. In fact, they became very cross when you tried. Alarms were pressed. Authorities were called. Guns were drawn.

When did everyone become so honest? thought Yulric as he speedily fled an airport.

"I told you so," said Simon later, back at the designated flee-to place.

"You didn't fare much better, I see," retorted Yulric.

The boy mumbled something about travel-sized holy water containers. "What we need is proper documentation," he said.

The vampire gave it some thought. "In the TV, people forge their documents. Could such a thing work?"

"It couldn't hurt to try," replied Simon.

He was wrong. It did hurt. At least, it hurt Yulric, who took the full brunt of the 240-pound dock official's tackle. The look of terror on the man's face when the vampire exploded into a thousand spiders and crawled all over him was barely consolation.

"I think we need better documents," said the boy as the vampire reconstituted himself back at the house.

Yulric examined the parchment documents with their impressive calligraphy and hand-drawn borders. To him, they looked more official than anything machine-made. "What do you suggest?" he asked, ripping apart two days of painstaking artistry.

"Well, once I have an adult with me, I can get a proper, legal passport," Simon reasoned. "The problem is you. You don't have a social security number or birth certificate."

"Bah," the vampire scoffed. "I can find my way on board easily enough."

"And what happens when someone opens the cargo hold in the middle of the day?" asked the boy.

"What of the Dracula plan?" Yulric suggested.

"Shipping you in a coffin? We'd still need a grown-up to be my"—Simon rolled his eyes—"chaperone."

"That should not be difficult to provide," Yulric offered.

Simon glared at his counterpart. "A *willing* chaperone."

The vampire glowered. "I thought you wanted to save your sister."

"If we rescue her and it isn't to her liking, she'll take away my library card and won't pay the cable bill."

Yulric hissed.

"Exactly," Simon went on, "so unless you know someone with a lot of spare time on their hands, who owes you a favor, we move on." Simon flipped a few more pages in his notebook. However, there was a decided lack of clacking from the vampire. He looked up. The vampire was smiling again. "I'm not going to like this, am I?"

"No," replied Yulric, "I very much doubt you will."

◆　◆

Catherine Dorset was baking a cake in her mind when the ghost came back.

"I have an offer for you," it said without preamble, causing her to jump and smash the cake into the stove before dropping it on the ground.

She wheeled on the ugly old man. "Look what you made me do!"

The ghost looked confused. "It is not real."

"That's not the point," she sputtered. "It isn't polite to just pop into someone's mind unannounced. I could have been naked."

The ghost raised an eyebrow. Catherine sighed. Living the life of the mind could be hard sometimes. Trying not to think of an elephant often resulted in an elephant barging through your room and treading on anything you told it not to. Saying "I could have been naked" posed similar problems.

"Turn around, please," she told him, covering herself with her arms.

"I assure you I—" began the ghost.

"Now!" she demanded. The ghost rolled its eyes and turned around. She quickly ran upstairs where she found the clothes she had been wearing not moments ago, folded in a dresser drawer, and put them on. She would have gone back downstairs but found the ghost behind her, the same distance away, still with its back to her.

"All right then," she said, signaling that it was okay to look. "First of all, hello again."

"Greetings," it said reluctantly. "I have an—"

Catherine held up a finger. "I didn't get your name. Before you make any offer, I feel it only right that I know who keeps invading my mind."

A look of deepest disgust crawled across the ghost's face. Literally crawled. It slapped its own face, hard, to make it stop.

"New skin," explained the ghost to answer the look of disgust that had much more metaphorically crawled across her face. Then, with a low and patronizingly theatrical bow, he introduced himself. "I am the vampyr Yulric Bile."

Catherine tried to catch a snicker before it came out. She failed. Yulric Bile rose back up, angrier than before.

"So you said something about an offer. Is this about me dying again?" Catherine asked hopefully. She had made up her mind on this, or rather network TV had made up her mind for her by canceling her favorite sexy-lawyer show.

"Actually, I need you to accompany me on a trip," said Yulric.

"Excuse me?" Catherine uttered. She was sure he must have misspoke. Or been kidding. Or . . .

"I will be traveling overseas and require someone to watch over a small boy," he clarified without kidding or misspeaking.

"You're talking about . . . in the real world, right?" she asked, feeling this point needed further clarification. She had, after all, done quite a bit of traveling in her head: Paris, London, Sheboygan.[48] But that was very different and somewhat unsatisfying, as she had never been anywhere outside Massachusetts before and could draw from only old black-and-white movies she'd seen. In other words, everywhere she went looked like a gray California.

"The real world, yes," he responded.

Catherine sighed. "I thought we went over this last time. I'm in a coma. I can't wake up."

"What if you could?" he asked.

Catherine's metaphorical heart skipped a beat. Or was that her real heart? Whichever it was, it lodged itself in her throat. "What—what do you mean?"

"If I could give you a measure of control over your body, would you serve my needs?" he proposed.

Catherine raised the suspicious eyebrow of someone who watched too many sexy-lawyer shows. "Serve your needs how?"

---

48. Don't ask.

"Mostly what I already said," he explained. "Watch and care for the boy while we travel. Also, you will be required to pick up my coffin at our destinations."

"And the, uh, sleeping arrangements?" she said, trying to put it delicately.

"You can work that out with the boy," he replied. "I will be spending my nights out."

She felt this point needed clarifying. "What I'm trying to get at is . . . Well, I'm gay, so even if you were thinking about—"

"You may prostitute yourself on your own time, so long as you fulfill the duties you are given," replied Yulric with his seventeenth-century definition of the word *gay*.

"Whoa!" Catherine cried. "I am not a prostitute, okay? I—I'm trying to say that I like girls. Women. Not men."

Yulric glared at her. "I do not see how this is relevant."

"So . . . no kissing, right?" she said.

"No. No kissing," he answered, as if kissing *her* was the most disgusting thought a person could have.

"Just so we're clear," she muttered. "So, what's the catch?" She remembered his problem with words. "The drawback? The downside? The—"

"I will show you." He cut her off. Yulric raised his hand and passed it through the space in her mind. A hospital room appeared around them. It was very white and very sterile, without any personal touches that might distinguish it from any other room in any other hospital. A TV hung on one wall, sadly turned off. The curtains were drawn on both the windows and the door. The room was dark, brightened only by the reds and greens of various computer displays and a book light being used by a little boy in the corner.

"Where is this?" asked Catherine, who had never seen a room like this before, except on TV. She checked the patient to see if she was a famous celebrity. She wasn't, not by a long shot.

The woman in the bed looked awful. She was bone thin, and wired up to so many machines, it looked like a plastic squid was erupting from her face. Her hair was matted and scraggly and hadn't seen product in years. Four years, to be exact.

"Is that . . . me?" she asked.

"Yes," Yulric answered.

Catherine flickered for a moment, her mental image switching between her full-bodied normal self to the wraith she saw lying in the bed, and back again. She'd known that she didn't look good, but it had never been an issue because she'd never been able to look at herself. It was such a disturbing sight, she didn't even care that a second version of the vampire was crouched on top of her, looking into her pried-open eyes.

She turned away, unable to take any more, and found herself facing the small boy. She'd have thought he would stir at the sudden and miraculous appearance of a hideous man and flickering-mind woman in the middle of the room. There he was, though, paging through a biography of Oliver Cromwell like they weren't even there. She went up and waved her hand in front of his face. He licked his finger and turned the page.

"This isn't real," she said, very disappointed.

"On the contrary," corrected the vampire. "This is very real. This is your room, as I see it."

"Okay," said Catherine, "I'll give you that, but—"

She was cut off. Catherine's hand, her *real hand*, was waving at her. Catherine gaped at herself. "How is that possible?"

"A vampyr can control the actions of the weak willed," he boasted. "A person who lies forever in sleep is particularly weak willed."

"Uh-huh," she replied, trying not to take offense. "Great. You can make my weak-willed arm move. Good for you. What do you need me for?"

"Due to your condition, such control requires concentration and . . . proximity," he explained.

"I assume that's why you're on top of me?" she added. She made a quick glance to make sure his hands weren't anywhere they shouldn't be.

"Indeed," he said, choosing to ignore her lack of trust in him, "it would be more beneficial if you could move yourself."

"Believe me, I'd love to," she said.

"I can show you," he told her.

Four words. Four lovely words. Yulric held out his hand. Catherine, shaking with nervous excitement, took it. His other hand reached out and touched the projection of her comatose body. It shuddered, sending the machines into apoplexy. The boy ran over and silenced them.

"Please, lie down into your body," Yulric instructed.

"Um, can you move?" she asked him, referring to his real form, still crouched on the bed. He glowered, obviously having no intention of changing his position. Swallowing the discomfort of his hovering body near her spectral head, Catherine sat on the bed, letting her feet line up with her feet and her legs line up with her legs, or at least where they appeared to be under the blanket. It was weird, as her mental legs took up far more room than her real legs. It felt like trying to squeeze into jeans that were now too small for her, a sensation she was all too familiar with. Once her bottom half was in position, she lay down, slowly at first, then more quickly as her mind abdominals grew tired. She passed through the real Yulric's body—a cold and endless void filled with screaming maggots and burning flesh—and finally settled her head down into place.

"Close your eyes," instructed the Yulric standing beside the Yulric crouched on top of her. Catherine wasn't sure which she preferred. She did close her eyes, though.

"Now open them."

She did.

"Now scratch your nose."

"Not funny," she said. At least, she tried to, but she couldn't. Something was in her throat, gagging her. With a panicked thought to the monsters surrounding her, she scrabbled at whatever it was with her hands . . . and stopped. These were not the hands she was used to. They were paler, more veiny. They had longer nails and rougher skin. An IV stuck out of one of them. They were skeletal and weak and utterly goddamned beautiful.

These were Catherine's *real* hands.

She laughed, or tried to. The sound was once more strangled by the tubes in her mouth. With her two real hands, she pulled them out, gagging as she did so and probably scraping her trachea or esophagus or both, but she didn't care. She was finally going to get out of this bed, just as soon as the vampire got off her.

"Excuse me," she said to the Yulric in her mind. Her voice was dry and scratchy, but it was real and she could hear it with her ears.

Mind Yulric just stood there, staring at her, as unmoving as his real body.

"Fine," she said, and with a swat of her arm, she knocked the vampire's body onto the floor.

Everything went black.

Catherine looked around in a panic. The room was gone. The boy was gone. Both Yulrics were gone. She looked down at her hands. They were back to normal. Normal for her mind. Tears welled up in her eyes. Not really, though, since the tears were just imaginary. And with that thought, she started to cry.

"That would be the problem."

Catherine looked up. Mind Yulric was standing over her once more, mocking her with a little wink.

"Bastard!" she screamed, running and flinging herself at him. *"Goddamned bastard!"*

She hit him, but without the will to do much else, she just sort of melted down his front in a pile of sobs. He knelt down beside her.

"You can only control your body by inhabiting its image in your mind, but you can only maintain that image through my sight," he explained. Catherine looked through tear-filled eyes up into Yulric's face. It was cold and hard but free of malice. What she had taken as a wink was clearly something more. The vampire's left eye remained closed.

"So"—Catherine cried—"what does that m-mean?"

"Sacrifice," said the vampire, his voice echoing through the blackness of her mind. "On both our parts."

"What kind of sacrifice?" she asked.

"The very oldest," he told her, lowering his gaze. Hers followed suit and fell upon his balled-up left hand, which unfurled to reveal its contents—a clouded eyeball with a pinprick black pupil.

"An eye for an eye," he said.

Catherine understood. This was the price of feeling, of moving, of being alive, truly alive. One measly eye.

"Yes," she agreed.

The vampire picked her back up off the floor of her mind.

"It shall be quick. You will not feel it," he said as he faded back into the real world.

"Be seeing you," she called after him. That single eye rolled in its socket. Catherine smiled and closed her own. Then, she opened them and got up.

◆ ◆

Back at the Pink House, Yulric and Simon sat at the dining room table and pretended they could not hear the ecstatic singing of their new compatriot as she took her first hot shower in four years. The boy tapped on a laptop keyboard. The vampire rubbed his eye and looked irritable.

"It is misty," Yulric complained.

Simon, completely ignoring the vampire's moaning, finished his typing. "I've arranged a coffin for you."

"Comfortable?" Yulric asked.

Simon raised his eyebrow. "We're on a budget."

"I have three hundred years of back rent and compound interest in a bank in Switzerland," Yulric pointed out.

Simon paused in his typing. "Fine. Satin lining, it is."

"Can you arrange for it to be picked up and taken to this airport of yours?" the vampire asked.

"Certainly," Simon answered. "I just need to know where we're going first."

Chapter 19

Vermillion (née Rusty) had never actually been to a vampire club before, never inside anyway. That was the unspoken secret he and his coven—correction, his former coven—kept. Every weekend they would go to a vampire club, wait in line, be turned away, and then head for the nearest Applebee's before retiring to Grimvice's (née Derek's) uncle's comic shop for some role-play. The closest any of them had been to the inside was when Sara (née Sarah) forgot her feminine-hygiene products and had to buy a sanitary pad from the ladies' room. The bouncer had actually let Sara give her quarter to a much more attractive girl to buy one for her. The girl hadn't come back, and Sara's skirt had been ruined, but the quarter had been there; it had seen, and they all had imagined what the sanitary napkin would have looked like. It would have been black.

Now here he was—new beautiful face, new buff body, ill-fitting robes traded in for form-fitting slacks and a shirt best described as *flowy*, hair cut short and well gelled, eyeliner caked on—waiting to be let in. He couldn't believe it. Literally, he couldn't. Despite all the cosmetic surgery and The Doctor Lord Talby's instructions on proper dress and behavior, despite all the lusty stares he was enjoying by hot girls and hot guys alike, despite it all, he still expected to be turned away.

The line moved . . . slowly, which was odd. Normally, it was all over in a few seconds. The bouncer would either nod and pull the rope aside or make no motion at all, which was your cue to start toward Applebee's. The hopeful turned away, those who were too beautiful to need hope admitted, easy. Today, though, it was taking forever, and there was talking up ahead—loud, high-pitched, frantic talking. If Vermillion didn't know better, he'd swear people were being allowed to plead their case.

"I nearly had him convinced that I had to run this inhaler to my sister inside," one rejected passerby told his friend. "He actually checked the name of the prescription before telling me to get lost."

"I tried the ol' lean over and flirt," said his female friend. "His hand moved for the rope. I think if I'd worn my pushup bra, I'd have had him."

Vermillion stopped one of the ecstatic rejects walking away. "What's going on?"

"New bouncer," said the reject, flipping his dyed black hair out of his eyes, which were also black.

"What happened to Bruno?"

"Oh, you know . . . nothing," muttered the reject with a wink-wink at the end. He snickered, obviously assuming that Vermillion would not understand.

"What kind of nothing?" he pressed, adding a rather pointed wink-wink of his own. The other man's eyes went wide at the sight of the countersign marking those who "knew."[49]

"You didn't hear?" the reject leaned forward conspiratorially. "A lich came by a few weeks ago."

"A lich?" whispered Vermillion. He'd always thought liches were role-playing-game inventions.

The reject, who'd thought the same, continued, "It sneaked in, tore the place apart, and killed Bruno and Tony before the real vampires scared it away."

"They're dead?"

"Yeah," sighed the reject. "They're taking up a collection for Tony's girlfriend up at the front. Give if you can."

"I will. Thanks."

"Anytime," replied the reject. The two awkwardly stood there for a minute before the reject gave a small wave and walked away. Vermillion kicked himself. He hadn't been authoritative enough with his dismissal. He'd work on that in the mirror later.

The line moved forward again, this time dramatically enough for him to reach the stairs.

A large group must have been turned away. He was right. Coming up the other side of the staircase was his old coven. Vermillion's heart beat faster. It seemed like a million years since he had last seen them: Grimvice and Ulster, Phoenix and Gorellis. There were his friends, all chatting excitedly about how Phoenix, pretending to faint, had almost gotten them inside. He wanted to call out to them. He wanted to show them what he'd become. He wasn't really sure why he didn't, why he

---

49. Ironically, people who could not get into vampire clubs were far more likely to believe in real vampires than those who could.

watched them walk by. Maybe it had something to do with the fact that not one of them recognized him.

"Rusty?"

Well, almost.

Vermillion turned back around to find Sara standing up from tying the strap on one of her knee-high boots. Her face was all astonishment—wide eyes, comically open mouth. Even her nostrils were somehow astonished.

"Rusty?" she repeated, moving slowly toward him.

Sara was not what anyone would call a conventional beauty. She was a big woman, structurally speaking, very tall, very broad, and pleasantly soft, despite being so literally big boned. She may not have had the symmetrical facial features that inspire misspellings like *hott* or *phat*,[50] but she was, in fact, quite pretty, if you could get past the lathered-on Goth makeup, which reeked of desperation. She might not have turned your head immediately, but she tended to grow on you over time, until one day, her smile made you wonder why you'd never asked her out. For Rusty, the answer to that question had always been found looking back at him in a mirror.

"Rusty, is that you?" she asked, adjusting the top of her dress. Vermillion raised an eyebrow, just like he'd practiced, and she realized her mistake. "Sorry. I mean, Vermillion."

"Hello, Sara," he greeted her.

"Oh. My. God," she said with a hug. It was one of her patented big, tight hugs, which went on a fraction longer than you thought it would. Rusty had always liked that.

"Look at you," she continued. "Wow. I mean, wow."

She was pressing his pecs with her finger. Vermillion tried not to flex. Too much.

---

50. or *pulchritudinUS*.

"What happened to you?" she asked him. "You fell off the face of the earth. We thought you'd gone Darkmyst on us."

"You what?" he replied, anger rising in his voice. "How could you even think I was like that traitor?"

Sara's face turned apologetic. "Sorry. It's just no one could get a hold of you for the longest time. So I thought, er, we thought . . ." She trailed off and looked away, ashamed apparently of what she had thought. "But, obviously, now we know where you were—the gym."

"Yeah. The gym," Vermillion said in an all-too-Rusty tone.

"You look great," Sara complimented.

"Thanks," he said. "You, too."

"Oh please." Sara laughed. "I look the same. You, though. Did you get a nose job?"

"It's good to see you," Vermillion said, quickly changing the subject.

"Yeah. Hey, listen . . . ," she began.

"Um, the line," interrupted a cadre of Goth schoolgirls in high heels behind him. Vermillion looked to see that the line had moved. In fact, ahead of him, there was no line. The new bouncer motioned him forward, the rope in hand, ready to let him in.

"Go ahead," he told the girls. They filed past, being sure to let their chests brush up against him as they did. The last one gave him a little wink.

"Anyway," continued Sara, looking after the girls with utter loathing, "we were all heading over to Applebee's, if you want to join us after you get rejected."

"Um, I don't think I'm going to be rejected," he said, trying to put it as delicately as possible.

"No," she said with a frown, "I don't suppose you will. Oh well. It was . . . just . . . It was good to see you, Rusty. I mean, Vermillion."

She started to go.

"Wait," Vermillion called after her. He grabbed her wrist, and electricity shot through his body. He was normally very careful not to touch anyone, least of all Sara. This physical contact, it was . . . nice. By the doe-eyed look on Sara's face, she thought so, too.

"I guess I could go with you guys," he continued, trying to sound casual. "I mean, I haven't seen you in a couple of months."

"Great. That's"—she couldn't seem to find the right word—"great. Grimvice just picked up the new expansion, and we—"

She was interrupted by the ring of Vermillion's phone. He checked the ID.

The Doctor Lord Talby.

"I've got to . . . ," he said apologetically.

"Yeah, of course," she replied with a bit too much gusto. All the nervous energy was apparently going to her head.

Vermillion answered the phone.

"Hello, Vermillion." The Doctor's smooth, accented voice put a chill in his heart.

"Doctor, hey," Vermillion replied cautiously.

"Excuse me?" said Talby in a sterner voice.

"I mean, hello," he corrected himself. "How can I help you?"

"As ever, it is I who can help you," said the Doctor. "May I ask why you have not yet entered the club?"

Vermillion looked around suspiciously.

"There was a line," he explained.

"My dear Vermillion, do we wait in lines?"

"No, Doctor. Sorry."

"Try to remember that for next time," said Talby.

"I will."

"The line appears to have gone down, though. May I ask why you remain at the top of the stairs?"

Vermillion's suspicions were confirmed. The Doctor Lord Talby was watching him. A more thorough glance revealed a camera on the top of the adjoining building.

"I was, uh, talking. To an old friend."

"Indeed? And what does she think of you?"

Vermillion turned to look at Sara. She was standing a bit off to the side, obviously trying to find ways not to eavesdrop. Currently, she was adjusting her stockings. His mind filled with white noise for a moment. When he came back, he remembered the Doctor had asked him a question.

"She, uh, she's impressed," he answered, barely remembering what had been asked.

"I should think so," said the Doctor. "I worked very hard on you. You worked very hard on you. And now you are a masterpiece."

"Um, yeah. Yes, I mean."

There was a pause on the line.

"Did she say anything else?" asked The Doctor Lord Talby.

He knows! Vermillion thought. *This is a test and he knows.*

"Well," he said hesitantly, "she invited me to go . . . hang out."

Sara smiled at this, then covered it up and went back to not listening.

There was a sigh on the other end of the phone. A long, disappointed sigh. Followed by tuts. "And I assume you were going to accept said invitation?"

"Yes," Vermillion answered. "I mean, I've been away, and it's been so long since my coven's seen me so . . ."

"Your old coven, you mean," Talby corrected.

"Yes, of course, my old coven," he said quickly. The Doctor sighed again, prompting Vermillion to ask, "Is there something wrong?"

"Well, it has been even longer since your new coven saw you. Ever, in fact."

"Oh!" he exclaimed. He'd been told only to come to the club. He'd had no idea that *this* might be happening tonight.

"Yes, *oh*, indeed," said the Doctor. "It was meant to be a surprise, but as you were about to run away with your 'big-boned' friend, I thought it best to intervene."

"Oh," said Vermillion again. He looked back at Sara. She smiled a worried little smile.

"I—I don't think I'm ready, sir," he said.

"You are more ready than I was."

"I don't suppose we could do this tomorrow?" asked the soon-to-be vampire.

"Karos is waiting for you inside," said Talby.

"It's just . . . ," began Vermillion.

"The girl?" the Doctor completed his thought.

"Yeah."

"Do not worry. This happens to everyone. It's the confidence your newfound beauty gives you. The first thing you want to do is find someone you've pined over for so long and play out your every romantic fantasy." The Doctor paused. "It is, of course, an urge you must resist."

Vermillion's heart fell.

"My dear Vermillion, you could run off and indulge these feelings you've harbored, but what then? You have a grander destiny, one that she is not a part of. Would you really want to use her like that?"

He wasn't thinking about using her. Well, he was, but he was also thinking about other things: eating together, walking together, the two of them reading on a couch with her legs draped over his. He didn't think that was using her. He tried to plead with the Doctor. "I don't suppose—"

"No," the Doctor said sternly.

"You didn't let me finish," he said, his voice rising.

"You were going to ask me if I could turn her, as well, were you not?"

"Well, yes," answered a mollified Vermillion.

"No," said Talby again.

"But—"

The Doctor cut across him. "Vermillion, I watched for a long time before choosing you for our ranks. I watched your friends, as well. At that point, I was not sure which, if any, of you might be worthy. Of all of them, only you had the will and strength of the vampire."

Vermillion wasn't convinced. He didn't really think he was better than any of his friends. Well, looks-wise, he was *now*, but that was only because of all he'd done these past few months.

"You are thinking that you are not better than any of your friends," said the Doctor with a disconcerting amount of insight. "You are thinking that any of them would be worthy if they had gone through what you have gone through, if they had endured what you have endured."

He did not answer. He didn't have to. The Doctor continued. "But that is the point, Vermillion, the very point. They would not have endured, would not have done all that you have. *She* would not have, because deep down, she believes that there is nothing wrong with her. She has bought the lie people today tell themselves to feel good. Think of what you were. Think of Rusty. Do you really believe that he was equal to what you have become? To Vermillion?"

He shook his head.

"She would," said the Doctor with increasing fervor. "She would have you believe that you were fine the way you were, that you did not need to change. She, who was so surprised by your appearance. Why so surprised? Because she could not imagine you as something better. She could not see you for who, for what you truly were all along."

Vermillion glared at Sara. She shifted, looking uncomfortable.

The Doctor's voice became soft and resigned. "She would hold you down, my dear. Make you common and ordinary and, yes, probably fat again. But it is up to you. If you are content with being merely Rusty, go with her. If not, Vermillion is expected inside the club."

Vermillion, not Rusty, hung up the phone.

◆　◆

The Doctor Lord Talby put down his cell phone.

"Crisis averted," he said, watching the security monitors. There was no sound, but a picture was worth a thousand words and the pain of the fat girl's tears were worth their weight in gold to him.

There was a knock at his door. "Enter," the Doctor called.

The blond vampiress entered the room the same way she entered the dreams of so many teenage boys—perfectly. Not a hair out of place, not a smudge of makeup astray. Her clothes clung to her body as if they were her skin. Jeans accentuated her legs and hips when she walked, her shirt doing the same for her breasts and abs. The leather jacket was purely for attitude. Talby sat back, admiring the fine job he had done with her.

"Nora, how wonderful it is to see you," he greeted. "What can I do for you?"

"She wants to see you," Nora interrupted.

The Doctor frowned. "She has a problem with the accommodations? I was very clear that, as our guest, she be provided with anything she might require."

"She says what she most requires are answers," explained Nora.

He stood and stepped up to his mirror and gave himself a once-over. It wasn't actually a mirror. They didn't show his reflection. It was a plasma-screen TV with a sensor in it that played a computer-generated rendition of his image whenever it was triggered. He couldn't check his hair in it, but it did allow him a sense of normalcy. And vanity. It was, after all, a very good likeness.

"As her host, if she wishes to see me, I am at her beck and call," he said, adjusting his tie unnecessarily. "Please, show her in."

Nora nodded and, with a perfect sway to her hips, left the room. Talby smiled. They had worked on that sway for nearly a month, trying to get it right. Now it was second nature to her. He was very proud.

The Doctor Lord Talby spent the next few minutes making small adjustments to the room. A file placed here, a portrait adjusted there. He made sure both tea and coffee were available and that the cookies were soft and moist. Small things, really, but it had always been his philosophy that it was the small things that count most.

Talby was straightening his suit when Nora knocked again.

"Hello," he said, opening the door. "You must be Amanda Linske. Please come in." Amanda stepped inside. Nora tried to follow, but Talby blocked her entrance. "If you would wait outside, please, Nora."

"Actually, I'd rather she stayed," said Amanda.

"Oh, it's fine. With our hearing, it's like she's here with us," he said, shutting out the blond vampiress. "Besides, you two see so much of each other."

"Because she's my jailor," interrupted Amanda, crossing her arms.

The Doctor ignored her remark. "I'd like to get to know you a bit better myself," he rolled on. "Please have a seat. Cookie?"

"No, thanks," replied Amanda, sitting down in the chair offered her. "Shouldn't you call them biscuits?"

The Doctor laughed. "Yes, of course. Sadly, not everyone has such a grasp on English slang. Most just look at me and wonder why I would offer them a dinner roll with their tea. Speaking of—"

"No, thanks," she repeated.

"You don't mind if I—" he asked.

"That's fine," she said.

"Much thanks," he said, fixing himself a cup of tea. "I have tried to assimilate to this country and this time, but sadly I still can't stand coffee. Every decade, I try to make the switch, but . . . old habits and all that."

Amanda leaned back, taking the time to study him while he busied himself. He smiled as he stirred. She thought it was a pleasant, handsome smile. There was not a trace of vampire underneath—no fangs, no bloodlust, no look of nefarious intent—just a man making pleasant small talk with her. He moved his chair around the desk and sat across from her.

"Ah, that's better," he said, continuing to stir his tea. "First, let me thank you for the information you gave me about Yulric Bile. It was most useful."

"Well, it pays to give one's kidnappers what they want," she retorted. It was much easier to put on a brave face in this vampire's lair. He, at least, looked like a person.

The Doctor's calculated smile faded into a calculated frown. "I apologize again for this inconvenience, Ms. Linske. It was not my intention to bring you here. I'm afraid my colleagues"— Amanda heard *minions* in the way he said *colleagues*—"just panicked when . . . Well, you were there."

"Yeah, I was," she snapped. "I was there when your gang broke into my house and threatened me and my brother."

The Doctor raised an eyebrow. "I was under the impression that you had given them permission to enter."

"Not through my windows," she said.

"Ah," he intoned. "We shall pay for any damages to your home or property. In fairness, we were in pursuit of a very dangerous creature at the time."

Amanda scoffed at him.

"Oh, come now. You can hardly blame us," said the Doctor very calmly. "After what happened in New York? After we learned he had attacked patients at your hospital?"

She gave him the steely glare reserved for when you don't want to admit someone has a point.

"Naturally, we assumed you and your brother were enthralled or otherwise endangered by the creature you unleashed and thought it best to intervene before *it* could do any more damage."

"Wait, who said I unleashed him?" Amanda asked, taken aback.

"Didn't you?" replied the Doctor. Amanda said nothing. "I'll take that as a yes?"

"How did you know?" she said quietly.

"Retrospection," he explained. "Since we now know you weren't under his control, the only reason I can think of for why you would allow such a monstrosity to stay in your home is out of some misguided feeling of responsibility. Ergo, you must have released him. Simple. Incidentally, I am curious how you discovered the whereabouts of our Mr. Bile. I was unaware of his existence, and I do keep an eye out for that sort of thing."

Amanda thought long and hard before answering. In the end, she thought telling the truth couldn't do her any harm, but it might buy her some goodwill, or at least, some quid pro quo. "My brother."

"Ah yes, your brother. Very . . . thorough little lad, I hear." The Doctor's smile faltered. Just for a second, and ever so slightly, but it did.

"Yeah, he is," she agreed, pleased to finally see a flaw in his infuriating calm. "He had a book. Something he 'borrowed' from the historical society."

"*The Journal of Erasmus Martin*," the Doctor said, finishing her thought. It was not a question. He knew.

"Yes," Amanda confirmed.

There had been a slight hesitation that held in it the question, how do you know that? He smiled, picking up on that. "I have been looking into the history of Mr. Bile since the incident in New York. The history of your whole town, in fact. Quite fascinating," he explained. He left out the part about searching the Internet for the Shepherd's Crook Historical Society's website. Best to keep the mystery and awe.

"So," he continued, "you discovered the resting place of an ancient and evil vampire and decided to dig him up in the hopes he would turn you. I must say, Amanda, while your actions are incredibly foolish, they do boast of initiative."

Amanda gaped, dumbstruck. She hadn't told *anyone* about that. Well, except a coma patient, but who was she going to tell?

"Why so surprised?" the Doctor asked. "You've been camping out at our clubs for over a year now, trying to get our attention."

"I—I thought you hadn't noticed," she said, her brain bogged down by this sudden influx of information.

"My dear Amanda," he said, getting up and striding over to his desk, "we notice everyone. Even those who don't know they want to be noticed yet. Now, where is your file? Ah, here we are."

He picked up one of the folders from his desk and opened it. Had Amanda's brain been working properly, it would have alerted her to the fact that he had quite obviously taken her record from the top of the stack. However, the logical and cynical parts of her brain were currently closed due to revelations, and any and all thoughts were being rerouted directly through emotions, just as The Doctor Lord Talby had intended.

"You're parents died two years ago?" he asked, intentionally getting it wrong.

"Three," she said in a monotone.

"Ah yes," he replied. He pretended to correct the paper in front of him. "Yes, three years. The death of any parent is quite sad, but both at the same time . . . A car accident, it says here."

She nodded.

"Nineteen, and both parents dead. That must have been very hard for you," said the Doctor. Amanda did not reply. "At that age, you should think yourself immortal. That way you can do great and impossible things. Or at least, very unwise things. To be so suddenly and rudely awakened to the reality of one's mortality . . ."

He faded out, letting his words hang in the air for a moment before giving a shrewd, knowing smile. "But that wasn't it, was it? No, you also have that brother of yours to take care of. What would become of him if something happened to you? Who would take him in? Keep him in check? Care for him? I doubt very much any family would adopt such a strange little boy with all those potential serial-killer interests?"

"I can't die!" she blurted out, the dam of emotion finally breaking. "I see it every day, car accidents, cancers. Three months ago, a kid younger than me fell down dead from an aneurism. Out of the blue, he was dead.

"It can happen just like that. It did happen. Our parents were fine—happy, healthy. Then they left for a John Mellencamp concert, and we were alone. If something happens to me . . ." Amanda had wanted this meeting for so long, to plead her case to the vampires, and now, she found all her reasons, all her well-thought-out arguments were gone, replaced simply by the core of her need. "I can't die. I just can't."

Perched on the edge of his desk, he leaned forward, and in his most sickeningly empathetic tone said, "What you've done, everything you've done, is quite admirable. Really, it is. You should be commended."

He paused, relishing the opportunity to use his favorite word.

"However . . . I'm afraid it's really not that simple. You see, you are already so . . ." He paused. He had almost gone too far. He backed off what he had been about to say and tried a new tact. "Becoming a vampire is a transformation in spirit, which you have in spades, and also of body. We take what we are—blemished, imperfect, human—and we change. We become perfect. We become beautiful. But the transformation between the two states is important. It gives us strength. Tests our resolve and our dedication."

"I will do anything," she told him.

"The transformation I speak of is not just physical. It is not just about good looks and supernatural powers. It is also a transition between two states—life and unlife. You must fully surrender one to enter into the other. You must sacrifice."

"I've given up everything—my friends, my future, everything," Amanda argued. "There's nothing left."

"Except your brother," he said.

Amanda's heart sank.

"He is a part of your mortal life and, as such, would need to be shed before beginning your immortal existence. Now, I'm not infallible. I've been wrong before. You might be splendidly suited for vampirism, in which case, I would be more than willing to turn you, right here, right now. You would just have to agree never to see your brother ever again."

It was tempting. To be a vampire. To live forever. To join the young and beautiful creatures of the night in their carefree world of adventure and romance. However awful a person it may have made her, she considered it.

But . . . Simon.

"No." It was all she could bring herself to say, and even then, it was a barely audible croak.

Talby smiled. "I understand. But you see now, don't you? Your reason for wanting to become a vampire is the very reason you cannot be one."

Amanda couldn't respond. The flood of grief and despair she'd been holding back for three years, with plans and work and responsibilities, was finally overwhelming her. She could not move. She could not think. She could not even muster up the energy to cry.

The Doctor thought it glorious.

"We will keep you no longer than is necessary." He gently ushered her toward the door. "I promise, once the creature Bile arrives, you will be free to return to your life."

There was the merest hint at the phrase "such as it is," at the end of his sentence. Amanda's sass pushed its way up through the numbness she displayed. "So I'm bait, then?" she retorted in a monotone. "That's ever so polite."

"There's the fierce and independent woman we all want to see," the Doctor replied, giving her a condescending little punch on the chin. "You just go back to your room and have a good cry. I'm sure you'll feel better afterward. Maybe with the help of some chocolates or some alcohol. Or some combination thereof."

At the door, he handed her off to Nora, who gently embraced her new friend. She'd obviously been eavesdropping.

"Nora, see that she has some of the chocolate liqueurs," he instructed. The Doctor Lord Talby watched them go before shutting his door. He abhorred having to lie. It wasn't the sort of thing a gentleman should do but, in this case, was necessary. After all, how could he explain to the girl that the only reason he didn't want to change her was because she was already beautiful? Even thinking it sounded callous.

You see, The Doctor Lord Talby had two secrets.

One was that he actually hated beautiful people. He chose not to think of the reason, though if you were able to see his thoughts, every so often you would glimpse it in flashes: a beautiful woman, an empty altar, and his more handsome and sexually voracious brother. Make of it what you will, but the result was that he jealously despised those who were naturally very attractive.

His second secret was that most of the surgeries he performed on his would-be vampires were completely unnecessary. He just enjoyed causing pain.

Chapter 20

Baghdad was dangerous. Everyone said so: Catherine, Simon, the travel advisory they'd received upon booking their plane tickets. Everyone. It seemed there had been a war,[51] and while order had been restored, violence still flared up periodically, making the city dangerous. Of course, the people of Baghdad weren't aware that beneath their ancient city, an even greater danger slept: one that made the brutal Mongol invasion look like a game of touch football.[52]

Deep within the earth, Yulric journeyed through an old, unknown tunnel filled with remnants of Baghdad's past. The walls were lined with a thousand years of history—artifacts, buildings, skeletal remains—that had been buried, burned, and built over. It was hours before the vampire passed into a

---

51. Not that one. The other one.

52. And Yulric would know, having been carted back to China as a curiosity for the Khan's collection.

properly ancient era, and it was several more before he came
to the great stone wall with a hole in its center. Yulric climbed
through, aware as he did so that the wall had been broken out
of, not into.

Within the cavern on the other side lay a large, ancient city.
Stone and mud structures rose out of the sand—some intact,
others in ruins—but all showing the unmistakable ravages of
age. Streets littered with the detritus of everyday lives led to
dunes so high, they nearly touched the stone overhead. Farther
in, the damage became less random and indistinct. Signs of fire
could be seen, accompanied by the occasional arrow. Pieces
of pottery lay broken across the floors of ransacked buildings.
The gates to food stores hung awkwardly off their hinges, open
to the world they'd unsuccessfully tried to keep out.

And scribbled everywhere were messages from the long
dead. Warnings pocked the walls, some informing desperate
neighbors to keep away, others to prevent future travelers like
himself from venturing farther. Pleas marked those inches that
warnings did not scar. The people in their final days, begging
their gods for food, for rain, for deliverance. Then every so
often, though more frequently as you approached the center of
the city, carved onto the doors was the same message over and
over again. Part curse, part denouncement, what it actually
said was eloquent and terrible, but what it amounted to was
quite simple: *I ate my neighbor.* It never failed to make Yulric
smile.

After this entertaining walk down memory lane, Yulric
reached the empty space of the center square. In front of him
stood a ziggurat in all its glory. Before a woman considered
naming her baby Jesus, priests had worshipped and sacrificed
here. Before one god decided to free his people from Egypt,
many gods watched their followers from its summit. Yulric

ascended hundreds of stone steps to reach the shrine at the top of this half pyramid.

The entrance to this former sanctuary was darker than the impenetrable blackness of the underground cavern. It was so dark, in fact, that neither Yulric's mortal nor his immortal eye could make out what lay beyond. As it wouldn't do for him to be tripping over his own two feet, he picked up a femur from a nearby pile of sacrifice victims and, using a "borrowed" T-shirt from Amanda's wardrobe, set it ablaze.[53] He had no intention of ever telling her what had happened to it.

Holding his light aloft, he took a moment to peer into its dancing flames. This was right. This was proper. Journeying into the depths of a cursed and ancient temple mired in darkness, led only by a torch made from a human leg. And the boy had tried to convince him to take a flashlight.

The vampire passed through the shrine's archway and again found himself walking down a sloping passageway. As he went, his torchlight revealed the story of Akkad etched into the stones of the corridor. The walls spoke of the city's founding, both the story where the gods built a kingdom in the desert for the greatest race of man, as well as the lesser-known tale of a beleaguered architect trying desperately to convince a group of herders that settlements were the wave of the future. It told of the oppressive rule of foreign kings, the coming of the great king Sargon, and his later rebirth in the form of his grandson Naram-Sin, who defeated the Hittite kings, the rebellious Magan, and the Lullibi leader Bruhd-wai.

Farther down, the images became darker and more varied, sometimes whispering, other times screaming the tale of the city's fall. The pictograms spoke of the god king's great sin:

---

53. Originally he'd offered the top to his new female acquaintance. "Are you sure this isn't a bra?" she had asked, throwing it back at him.

defiling the temple of Nippur. Abandoned by the gods, a great curse fell upon Akkad, devouring all life. More erratic carvings told of cannibals, of fire, of angry sands swallowing the city whole, and of a nameless thing that came out of the darkness. The scrawls petered out with final warnings for anyone who came after to flee for their lives. Yulric chuckled at the desperate concern for his soul's well-being from thousands of years ago.

At the very heart of the ziggurat was a large chamber where the high priests and priestesses had conducted the most secret rituals of the gods. It had high vaulted ceilings rising to the top of the ziggurat itself and was decorated like a bizarre and oddly fish-themed version of the Sistine Chapel.[54] In the center rose a high altar, nearly a ziggurat in its own right, fifty steps led up to its peak. And, everywhere, there were the discarded bones of sacrifices, both animal and man.

This was Yulric's destination; however, when he arrived at its entrance he found said chamber sealed. Across the opening to the great central chamber lay a huge circular stone. Emblazoned on it was a hideous human-headed spider, whose belly had become home to quite the collection of graffiti over the years.

Nearly every culture that had ever inhabited or invaded either this ancient city or the modern one above was represented. Though the highest were in languages unknown even to Yulric, the lower he read, the clearer the messages became. The last three warnings were obviously the most recent: in Arabic, MAY ALLAH PROTECT AGAINST THAT WHICH IS INSIDE AND DAMN ANY WHO OPEN IT; in English, FOR THE PRESERVATION OF THE EMPIRE, SEALED 1910 UNDER ORDERS OF HIS MAJESTY

---

54. Not that Yulric would know, but he'd heard it described from people who could actually enter a chapel. Then he'd killed them.

BY HIS HUMBLE SERVANT SIR HENRY CALIBREY. MAY GOD PRESERVE US; and in American, NO SERIOUSLY. DON'T FUCK-ING OPEN.

All that was of no concern to Yulric. What vexed him was the combination of cross and crescent moon that the previous Christians and Muslims had etched onto the surface. Even from across this antechamber, the vampire's newly formed skin blistered within the presence of the dual holy symbols. He had little hope of getting any closer. Fortunately, he did not have to.

From within his robes, he pulled a small stick explosive the boy had made for him.[55] Using his torch, he lit the fuse and rolled it gently to the foot of the seal. He took a few steps back into the passage to avoid any cross-laden debris. A moment later, there was an explosion that rocked the entire temple. Dust and small stones fell around him, but overall, the structure held.

The same could not be said of the room he had just left, however. The ceiling and far wall had partially collapsed, leaving piles of heavy stone rubble. Yulric did not mind. The seal, while not destroyed, had been damaged by the blast. The image of the spider woman now consisted of her head above the nose and a few lines, which might be legs, on the edges. The rest, including the symbols of Christ and Allah, had been entirely excised by the fire stick. An impassable cave-in was barely a hindrance.

The sound of tiny spider legs clattering against stone echoed into the empty temple chamber as tiny white arachnids flooded out of cracks in the debris. After a moment,

---

55. When asked how he had created an explosive when local Authorities were on the lookout for someone doing exactly that, Simon shrugged and said, "Nobody expects an American to make a bomb in Iraq."

they swarmed together into a mound, which slowly rose and became Yulric once more.

"I see you learned your lessons well, young Yulric?" The voice echoed out of the darkness, speaking a language that had died with the arrival of the Common Era. Yulric moved toward the high altar; ancient bones cracked and splintered beneath his feet with each step. Huge webs lined the room; the most significant of them ran from the central platform. Suspended within them were dozens of mummified remains, cocooned in gossamer wrappings, their final, terrible expressions perfectly preserved.

Yulric knelt before the altar and in very basic Akkadian replied, "I have freed you from your imprisonment, my lady."

One of the desiccated corpses in the web unfurled itself. It silently skittered down the web until it hung just above the English vampire, peering at him with empty eye sockets. "I did not expect you back so soon, my pupil."

"It has been over seven hundred years."

"Has it? How time flies." Her voice rasped with centuries of disuse. "And why have you sought me out this time? More forbidden knowledge?"

Yulric remained bowed. "I seek your aid against an enemy."

"You wish me to follow you, you mean?" Arru chuckled mirthlessly. "And why, *young* Yulric, would I do that?"

From within his robes, Yulric removed the portable DVD player he had brought. "Let me tell you of the modern vampyr . . ."

Chapter 21

Amanda managed to get out of her room fairly easily. Thanks to her brother's many attempts to hide weapons from her, she knew how to pick a lock. Once through the door, she found she had not warranted a guard. She tiptoed down the hall as quietly as she could, hoping that whatever vampires might be nearby weren't paying attention.

The corridor turned and then came to a junction. The passageway to her left ended in a railed balcony overlooking what she assumed, based on the spacious floor plan and the gurgling of a fountain, was the lobby of the building she was in. She could clearly see the aperture for a set of stairs, stairs she could use to escape if not for the fact she would be in plain sight of anyone entering or leaving. Straight ahead was an endless maze of doors and offices. Somewhere in that mess would be the discreet stairwell required by law in case of an emergency. However, each step farther into the belly of the beast increased the likelihood of being spotted by someone. Finally, to her right was an elevator, an enclosed space from which she could not escape and which held a fifty-fifty chance of discovery every time the doors opened.

The sound of voices from the lobby pushed her toward the elevator. She hit the button and listened hard. She could not quite make out what was being said, but the chatter was definitely getting closer. She pointlessly hit the button two or three more times. The doors dinged and slid apart. Amanda flattened herself against the wall, but much to her relief, it was empty. She hurried inside and hit the first-level button. Just as the doors shut, she thought she saw a pair of heads cresting the stairs.

The car began to move. Amanda looked around the box for somewhere to hide. Impulsively, she climbed onto the railing that stretched waist high around the walls and tried to push up a ceiling panel so she could conceal herself on the roof of the elevator.

This is how Nora found her on the first floor.

"Um, hi?" uttered the bemused vampire.

"Hi," Amanda answered. She did not move from her uncomfortably precarious position. Nora likewise stood motionless, only holding out a hand to stop the doors when they began to close.

"I don't suppose I can convince you to forget what you're seeing and let me go," Amanda wondered.

"Probably not," Nora replied.

Amanda sighed. "I didn't think so." She hopped down. "Take me back."

Nora escorted Amanda to her room. After that, a vampire was always on guard outside in the hallway.

That was her first escape attempt.

Chapter 22

"Why exactly are we here?" Catherine asked as she trudged along a forested riverbank in the middle of the night. She was entirely too well dressed to be trudging anywhere. The khaki capris she was wearing were no longer khaki, and her silk blouse from Nanning had ripped in three places. Her foot slipped off a wet rock, and a nearby branch snagged her sleeve, making it four.

"We have need of you," Yulric answered from up ahead. He did not notice the mud and muck that clung to his ragged robes. Neither did the leathery, eyeless hag who followed in his wake, though she had no clothes to ruin. Not even Simon complained during this jungle trek. In fact, he seemed unnervingly well prepared as he lit their way with a flashlight and hacked away foliage with a hatchet. Catherine wasn't sure where he'd gotten the small ax from but found herself too busy cursing the increasing squish between her toes to care.

"If this cave isn't our destination, we're turning back," Catherine called out.

Simon turned back to her, puzzled. "What cave?"

"This cave," Yulric answered. Twenty feet ahead of the mortals, he pulled aside a tangle of vines, revealing a partially submerged cave on the far side of the river bend. Catherine pushed forward, passing Simon, who watched her with concern.

"You want us to go in there?" Catherine asked incredulously.

"We cannot," hissed Arru. She pointed to the rock wall above the opening.

Catherine squinted, and though her left eye teared up quite a bit, she could just make out the worn etchings in the stone. "The yin-yang?"

"Bagua," Simon corrected. He was examining them through a pair of binoculars. When had he had time to pick those up, or had he been carrying them with him this whole time? He turned to Yulric. "You have been here before?"

"Yes," Yulric nodded.

"How did you get in back then?" asked the boy, taking off his shoes and socks.

Yulric pointed toward the opening. "The way was not barred when last I was here."

Simon snorted as he picked up a stick off the ground and stuck it in the water, feeling for the ground. It did not hit resistance. "We swim," he told Catherine as he set down his flashlight, its beam directed at the cave.

"Great," Catherine sighed. Her hands moved toward the buttons on her blouse instinctively. She then remembered she would be undressing in front of two horrible monsters and a small child and decided that she might as well completely ruin her clothes.

The two humans waded into the water. The water was just cool enough to be uncomfortable, especially in the night air. As the pair swam forward, a thousand concerns filled Catherine's mind. Would the river current pull them under? Could there be crocodiles nearby? Did China have crocodiles? What about those parasites that swim up your pee? She'd only heard those horror stories involving men, but what if she peed and they got inside her? *Just don't pee,* she told herself, though suddenly it felt urgent.

Seemingly an eternity later, they found themselves paddling through the cave entrance. Simon cracked a Halloween glow stick to better illuminate their surroundings, which they discovered were mostly just more water. Something fluttered near the ceiling, causing Catherine to wonder about bats and how up-to-date her rabies shots were. A few strokes later, she felt the stone floor brushing against her feet, and she stood. A little ways on, the small boy did the same, and they waded toward a central, raised platform of stone.

A body lay within a circle surrounded by Chinese characters. Through the faint green glow, Catherine could make out the tattered remains of a silk dress. Long, scraggly black hair splayed out in every direction. She, Catherine assumed it was a woman, lay faceup, her white eyes staring at an identical configuration of symbols on the roof of the cavern. Her skin glistened in a sickly way that reminded Catherine of wet cheese. Her hands, which had horribly long and sharp black nails, were folded on her chest, wrapped around one of twelve jade pins that protruded from her body.

Catherine and Simon pulled themselves out of the water. After giving the pattern of symbols carved into the rock a cursory glance, the boy moved to the woman, whom he examined more carefully. Catherine watched through her right eye, as her left had become unbearably itchy. Simon went from needle to needle, reading the symbol on each. It made Catherine feel like a bit of a slouch. She had taken four years of high school

French and another three in college, and she could barely remember any of it.

Finally, the boy put on a pair of gloves. "We need to remove the needles."

"I kind of figured," Catherine said, reaching out. Simon made to stop her but was too late. She pulled out the most central needle.

The body came to life. It did not rise but began snarling and writhing on the ground. Catherine screamed, dropping the needle. Simon sprinted over, swept up the pin, and plunged it back into the creature's chest. The woman fell motionless.

"We remove the heart pin last," he cautioned.

"Y-yes," she agreed, shaken by the ordeal. Simon moved to the opposite side and, with a slow reverence, slid a needle out of the lower abdomen. It was longer and thicker than a normal acupuncture pin and covered in an unidentifiable brown substance Catherine didn't even want to think about.

Hesitantly, she moved to the side and gripped another "low" needle. She looked to Simon for confirmation that this was all right. He nodded, and with a yelp of disgust, she pulled it free, releasing an uncomfortable chemical stench, like antiseptic. They continued this way for a while, removing all the needles individually, always steering clear of the most prominent one until it stood alone.

"So, now what?" Catherine asked.

Simon reached into his pocket and removed two items, a small Ziploc bag, which held a yellow piece of paper covered in Chinese characters, written in what Catherine hoped but assumed was not red ink. The other was a thumbtack. The eight-year-old carefully removed the piece of paper from the bag and then thumbtacked it to the creature's forehead.

"Don't breathe," Simon instructed. Then, holding his own breath, he removed the final pin.

The creature jumped up and then . . . stood there, unmoving. The humans watched it, also not moving. Catherine's lungs began to burn with the effort and finally let out an audible exhale. Simon tensed, ready for the creature to attack, but nothing happened. Only then did he, too, begin breathing.

Simon barked something in Cantonese and pointed toward the cave entrance. The woman turned and, with her arms outstretched, hopped, literally hopped, into the water. Catherine could not help but laugh.

"Don't get too excited," the boy told her. "I doubt the chicken blood will survive the river." They stood and watched as the head of the creature went up and down in the water, until it disappeared completely.

"Let's go," Simon said finally. Catherine noticed he pocketed all twelve needles on his way out.

When the pair returned to the shoreline, they found Yulric in deep conversation with the creature, now free from thumbtack and paper. All three vampires turned to them as they climbed up the bank.

"This is Xie Yu Mei," Yulric said. "The only intelligent jiangshi I have encountered in my time."

The woman, whose skin they could now see was pale and green, uttered something Catherine did not understand. Beside her, Simon responded, and while she could not understand the words, the way he was fingering his small hatchet made it clear that threats were being exchanged. Before they could come to blows, though, Yulric stepped between them and rattled away in Cantonese. Reluctantly, the Chinese vampire nodded and rather than attack outright, she flung the thumbtack at Simon's feet. Clearly, this was not over.

"Let us return," Yulric said. The vampires began to walk away, or hop away in the case of Yu Mei.

"One second," Catherine called. The group halted, annoyed.

"I'll be right back," she told them and ducked into the dense foliage. She *really* had to go.

Chapter 23

Amanda wasn't really sure where she stood on the subject of heaven. Her parents had never been religious, and while she had clearly discovered supernatural forces at play in the world, somehow she had never given much thought to the possible positive implications of this fact. Of course she told her brother that their parents were in heaven looking down on them, but that was just what you tell kids, even ones as naturally cynical as Simon. Whether such a place was real, she more wanted to believe it was true than actually felt it was.

That said, if heaven did exist, she imagined it looked exactly like the set of *The Phantom Vampire Mysteries*.

"I can't believe I'm here." Amanda giggled as she stood within a row of back-lot buildings that made up the small town of Devil's Cross.

"You can go anywhere you want," Nora told her. "Just . . . not too far."

"Oh my God! That's Sandhya Amavasya's shop," the human turned to her guard/guide. "Is she really a ten-thousand-year-old alchemist, like on the show?"

"Sandhya? No, she's just a vampire," Nora replied.

"Huh. Oh! Is that—" Amanda ran across the empty street. Nora walked behind her, an amused smile on her face. This was the first time she'd seen their guest happy about anything since her meeting with the Doctor.

Amanda danced around a twisted willow. "It's the tree. *The tree!*"

"Yes, it is," Nora agreed.

"Take my picture. Take my picture." Amanda posed against the side of the trunk while the vampire took a photograph with her phone.

"Can you send that to me?" Amanda requested.

"Already done," Nora replied, hitting a few buttons. She didn't put the phone away, assuming there would be more pictures to come. "Where to now?"

"Where's the graveyard? I want to visit Phantom's crypt," Amanda answered.

"That's actually inside the soundstage," Nora said. "This way."

She led her friend back through the streets, stopping for more photos in front of Berwyn's motorcycle and the petrified statue of Carmilla. Finally, they turned at the bend in the road, where, behind some matting and a thick copse of pines, one of the studio buildings hid. Nora ushered Amanda inside the soundstage where most of the interior sets were housed. They passed through Sasha's bedroom, which held no interest for Amanda, and the Sanguine Noir bar, whose operational beer taps the pair indulged in, until they came to the residence of everyone's favorite fictional vampire ghost.

It, however, was not empty.

"Oh!" cried an African American woman in a bra, who rolled over and fell behind the sarcophagus in the middle of the room.

"Haha! Hey, Nora. Amanda," greeted a shirtless and abashed Phantom, sitting up from the same plinth.

Nora fumed. "Interrupting. Something. Are we?"

"What? Of course not, I was just running lines with . . ." Phantom trailed off, obviously having forgotten the name the girl had given him. "What are you doing here?"

"I wanted to see the crypt," Amanda admitted, apparently caught between the mesmerizing sight of Phantom's abs and the very clear distress Nora was feeling.

Phantom brushed his long hair back from his face. "Well, here, let me give you the grand tour."

The girl reappeared on the far side of the room. "Sorry about that," she said nervously. She had just managed to get her shirt back on, and it was inside out.

"Thanks for helping me, uh, run lines," Phantom said.

"Yeah, no problem," she replied, making a hasty retreat from the set. "I'll see you on the set, er, Nora."

Nora glared at the woman until she disappeared through the door.

"So, a tour . . . ," Phantom began.

Nora spun on him. "Who was that?"

Phantom shrugged. "Just a PA. We were going over notes."

"What notes? We're not in production," she spat at him. "Ugh. And on the set, no less."

"Please," he whined. "Like you've never got it on on the set."

"Ew. No," Nora replied. She turned away, trying to control herself. "I can't believe you."

"What? What can't you believe?" Phantom retorted. "What's your problem?"

"My problem? *My* problem?" Nora was now in his face.

"Yes, Nora," said Phantom. "Your problem. After all, it's not like we're together . . ."

Anymore. The word hung there in front of the pair of them. Again, a moment passed between them as they stood far too close to each other, their fiery words urging them toward the fiery passions. Phantom leaned in, ready to give in to this desire. Nora, however, rocked backward. She had been down this road with him one time too many.

"Come on, Amanda. Let's go," she said.

There was no reply.

"Amanda?"

The vampires glanced around the crypt set. They were completely alone.

"Dammit!" Nora cursed. She sprinted off at an unnatural pace. Within seconds, she was outside the building, searching the grounds. She managed to catch up to Amanda, chatting with the PA, trying to follow her out.

"Amanda," she said, appearing in a blur in front of the human. "Going somewhere?"

"Oh hi." Amanda smiled. She made a big show of being surprised to find herself almost off the studio grounds. "Sorry. Katie and I were talking about her job, and I guess I lost track of where we were going."

Nora gestured back toward the main building. "After you."

"Bye, Katie." The human waved. "Her name's Katie by the way. So, did you and Phantom have it out?"

"I don't want to talk about it," Nora replied.

"Well, of course not." Amanda laughed. "You're sober. But of course we can fix that."

"I'm not sure that's such a good idea," Nora said, eyeing the gate.

"Put someone else on the door if you like," Amanda suggested as they walked back to her apartment. "But honestly, there's no point. I wouldn't miss hearing this for the world."

That was her fifth escape attempt.

Chapter 24

"So what brings you to Ghana?" asked Raquel Gutierrez, the American doctor with the impossibly gorgeous smile.

"We're collecting stories," Catherine answered as she followed the woman through the small village to the huts where she and her fellow Peace Corps volunteers were staying.

"Stories?"

"Folklore," Catherine responded.

"Mommy is the preeminent folklorist for the Miskatonic University," Simon said, trying very hard to sound like a normal child, despite his use of the word *preeminent*.

"I'm compiling folktales from all over the world," Catherine explained. "Iraq, China, Tibet, India . . ."

"Sounds like you've been productive," said the aid worker.

"Actually, we've run into a bit of bad luck lately." Catherine laughed. Their last two trips had come up empty. Tibet, especially, had been frustrating for their undead companions. At least in India, the Brahmarakshas had been slain proper, like a vampire should be. The Preta, though, had merely refused on moral grounds and disappeared in a puff of karmic redemption.[56]

"Well, I hope you have more luck here in Ghana." Dr. Raquel smiled.

"I'm sure we will," Catherine said, admiring her dimples. "You haven't heard of something called an Adze, have you?"

"Ugh, the Adze," the doctor groaned. "My older patients won't shut up about it. They go on and on about how it's feeding on the children, making them sick. You try and tell them that it's just malaria, but you're only a doctor and they heard it from their great-grandmother, who saw one once." A heavy sigh managed to wipe away much of her frustration, returning most of her smile. "Still, good for you. I'm sure they'll enjoy having a willing audience."

There was a clatter from behind them as a pair of volunteers dropped the heavy wooden box they were carrying.

"Careful with those," Catherine called back. The volunteers looked back at her glumly, having carried the heavy container all the way from the bus.

"Do you always travel with so much gear?" Raquel asked, glancing at the three long boxes.

Catherine shrugged. "I've collected a lot of stories."

"If that's what failure looks like, I'm not sure you can afford much more success," the doctor joked.

"Not without a forklift," Catherine quipped back.

She and the doctor shared a good laugh. She saw Simon cringe, then he returned his gaze to the local villagers; all were staring at him, the only child to be seen.

"This is where you'll be staying," announced Dr. Raquel as they came to a small two-room hut.

---

56. Elsewhere in the world, a very happy sea sponge was born.

Catherine took off her sunglasses, revealing her dead eye with its small black pupil. The aid worker, catching sight of it, visibly flinched and turned away, toward the village. "I know it isn't much, but out here, it's all there is."

"That's okay," Catherine assured her. "I've been promised a Spanish villa next." When she emerged, she'd put on her sunglasses again. She saw the doctor's relief. "Bring the boxes inside."

The American college students lugged the three sealed boxes into the small wooden structure and then fled before being asked to do anything else. After all, they'd come to Africa to help *real* people, not other Americans.

"Well, thank you, Dr. Gutierrez, for all your help," said Catherine.

"Raquel, please," the doctor insisted. "If there's anything you need, please, let me know."

"I definitely will," Catherine replied.

◆　◆

The night was dark in the village, which occupied a small clearing cut out of the forest, always on the verge of being reclaimed. Small windmills provided electricity, but mostly that was used to power small refrigerators and televisions. Charcoal lamps and candles lit homes, but times being what they were, shutters were kept closed despite the heat. And so the only light one could count on was what little moonlight made it through the canopy, and the occasional firefly.

Blink and flash. Blink and flash. The small insect lazily flew through the still air. Blink and flash. Blink and flash. Its progress was slow, but fireflies aren't known for being in a hurry. Blink and flash. Blink. It landed on the sill of the only open window in the village, that of the new arrivals, the folklorist and her son. Without any seeming purpose, it crawled inside.

On the far side of the room, the small boy slept, despite several hours of careful instruction on proper slumbering technique. Around him hung several layers of mosquito netting. The firefly let out a barely audible chirp that amounted to a chuckle. It used its head to lift the nets and ducked inside. It crawled up the leg of the cot, across the legs of the boy, and over the legs of an illustrated Buddha on the reincarnation book that lay open on the bed,[57] until finally it arrived at its ultimate destination, the boy's outstretched thumb. With fiendish relish, the small insect cleaned its mandibles in preparation for its sanguine meal. Thus distracted, it did not notice the forefinger coil up beside it.

A flick sent the surprised bug reeling onto the dirt floor of the hut. It fluttered its wings to right itself just as a jar came crashing down around it. The firefly's glow began to pulse. It became brighter and brighter. Then, the room flared white. The jar shattered with a tremendous *crack!* Simon reeled back, shielding his eyes. When the radiance subsided, he was faced with an elderly, feral, hunchbacked man with black chitinous claws.

"You should have let it alone, little boy," the creature growled with a smile. "Now I will eat your heart and liver while you watch."

Simon took out two specially prepared syringes from beneath his pillow. One was filled with DDT; the other with antivirals. "Try."

The door to the next room swung open.

---

57. A gift to Simon from some very excited Tibetan lamas.

"That will not be necessary." Yulric motioned for the hunch-back to join him. "Adze, it's been too long. We have much to discuss."

Chapter 25

Phantom Studios offered tours to the public four times a day, every day. Tourists, mostly black-clad teenagers with their embarrassingly normal Midwestern parents, came through on a bus that ushered them around various points of interest, including the Devil's Cross back lot, the sets, the production building, the writers' shed, and the actors' apartments. On an alternating basis, one of the actors came out, under an awning that protected him or her from the sun, and took pictures with his or her adoring public. Then the bus took the visitors back through the main gate, where they departed and, with their unnecessarily angst-ridden teens mollified, continued with their vacation.

The entire thing moved like clockwork. You could set your watch by it, which, incidentally, Amanda had done.

"Five, four, three, two . . ." She took off running across the floor of the spacious apartment. It took her several seconds to cover the ground, which, fortunately, she had accounted for. She sprinted full steam through the already open balcony doors, stepped once onto the ottoman she had set out there, stepped another time onto the railing and leapt. There she hung, in midair, staring at the bus, which—thank God—was underneath her, and waiting for gravity to do its thing.

This was so stupid, she thought as eyelined eyes went wide and camera phones flashed. Then she came crashing down into the aisle of the double-decker tour bus.

The riders erupted into applause.

"I didn't know there was going to be a stunt show," said a mother in a Minnesota Twins hat. The black-haired boy next to her rolled his eyes with the practiced motion of adolescence.

Amanda waved and posed and took pictures with reluctant Goths, who secretly wanted to have their picture taken with her but would never admit it, until the tour came to an end outside the gates. Then she exited with the rest of them and faded into the obscurity of Los Angeles.

She didn't have any money; that was her main problem. When the vampires had taken her from home, they had neglected to grab her purse on their way out. So before she could buy a plane, train, or, most likely, bus ticket that would take her back, she had to come up with cash. She had considered grabbing one or two things from her room to pawn, but they might have thrown off her balance on her run. This led her to her current course of action—looking for a nightclub.

It was Tuesday, not the best night for clubbing, but this was Los Angeles; there was always someone with money who wanted to get drunk and dance. Amanda followed the streets, listening for the telltale thump of dance music, watching for the understated blacklit signs, which heralded the abundant use of strobes within. It wasn't that difficult. Once she ended up on Hollywood Boulevard, she found several within walking distance of each other to choose from.

The club she settled on was called Bastion, strictly because it was the kind of insufferable establishment that went out of its way to make sure you didn't know it was called Bastion. The sign out front was black with a thin black scrawl that presumably spelled the club's name. The cards handed out by the staff were also black with the thinnest outline of a chess castle in purple—no name, no address, no phone number. If you didn't already know how to find Bastion, you shouldn't be anywhere near Bastion. If you came up to Bastion and called it Rook or Castle or Chess Piece, you shouldn't be anywhere near Bastion. The club was exclusive and the guest list at the front had only three names: a dollar sign, sunglasses, and the number ten. If a man or woman wasn't rich, famous, or smoking hot, they were not Bastion material.

Amanda ducked into an alley a few blocks away so that she could partially undress. Underneath the T-shirt and sweats she had worn for maneuverability during her jump was a cute number she had borrowed from the apartment's nicely stocked guest closet, a little black dress. Very little. It actually didn't fit very well, but that was kind of the point. There was going to be too much leg and too much cleavage to turn away. She pulled her hair out of its ponytail and gave it a bit of a tussle. Taking a few makeup necessities out of the pockets of her sweatpants, she did a quick and serviceable makeup job. She wished she could have found a way to carry some high heels out with her but decided flats would be fine. Nobody would be looking at her feet.

She worked up a confident strut on the way back to Bastion, building up significant steam so that by the time she arrived at the door, she was working *everything*. She didn't even bother waiting in line; she just went straight for the man at the rope, who let her in with barely a once-over.

The club inside was a rather tame version of those she was used to. Everything was more expensive, and because of that, everyone was on slightly better behavior. The mass of dancers could actually be said to be dancing rather than just rhythmically grinding up against each other. The fixtures on the wall, the furniture, and the decorations were extravagantly minimalist. The entire club was lit by pink, purple, and black lights, and they were everywhere, from underneath the floor to underneath the bar.

Amanda spent her first twenty minutes among the dancers, partially because "Hey, why not have some fun," but mostly so she could paint a great big target on herself. When she felt she had allowed enough time for the true players[58] in the crowd to spot her, she made her way to the bar. Sensing movement on either side of her, as young men with trust funds and venture capital made a dash to get to the bar ahead of her, she slowed her pace, taking a moment to fix her dress and admire her surroundings.

"Son of a . . . ," she mouthed.

Nora was sitting in a booth across from her. Amanda changed direction and made for the vampire.

"Seriously?" she exclaimed as she stormed up to the table. "Seriously? How did you find me?"

Nora choked on her martini at Amanda's sudden appearance. Unable to speak, she gave a little shrug. The truth was she had just come out tonight to enjoy herself. The fact that they had both chosen Bastion was mere coincidence. But of course, she wasn't about to admit that. One of The Doctor Lord Talby's rules was never admit to the mundane truth when people were willing to chalk something up to your supernatural prowess. So it was here.

---

58. Translation: douche bags.

Nora stretched out her arm, offering Amanda a seat and, once she'd found her voice again, croaked, "Drink?"

Amanda sat down and ordered a glass of wine, which miraculously appeared within a minute, courtesy of "the gentleman at the bar." There were twelve of them standing where the server pointed, and it was impossible to tell which was *the* gentleman, because they all winked when she glanced over.

"Why did you come to a club?" Nora asked, sipping her drink.

"I was going to pick a pocket," Amanda answered, giving a nod to the men waiting for her to finish so they could buy her another.

"But why here?" the vampire continued. "Why not just hit someone on the street?"

"I'm not going to steal from someone who needs the money," she sneered indignantly. "If I'm going to take advantage of someone, (a) they're not going to miss it, and (b) they are going to have it coming."

"Well, you certainly came to the right place for that," Nora muttered, downing the rest of her martini. Two more arrived via waiter to replace it. Both women stared at them incredulously. "Our powers combined," Nora marveled. They both laughed.

"So, I guess you'll be taking me back?" Amanda said finally.

"No rush," replied Nora, taking a drink in hand.

Amanda's eyebrow went up. "Really?"

Nora shrugged. "I need a night away from . . . things."

Amanda gave a knowing nod. "Well, this certainly is a place for that. Plenty of 'things' to go around." She leaned across the table. "How much damage do you think we could do to their wallets?"

Nora smiled conspiratorially. "Only one way to find out."

It was her eleventh escape attempt.

Chapter 26

Catherine had always thought her first stay in a honeymoon suite would go a little differently. Oh sure, she'd pictured the spaciousness, the fireplace, the rugs designed to hug naked flesh, the complimentary champagne with every room service order, the en suite Jacuzzi, the heart-shaped bed with red satin sheets, the trail of rose petals leading to locations of potential lovemaking, all of it. She'd just imagined she'd be sharing said den of copulation with a partner or girlfriend or Dana Scully,[59] not an eight-year-old and a gaggle of vampires.[60]

Currently, all the vampires were gathered around the heart-shaped love seat, watching a Spanish-dubbed episode of *The Phantom Vampire Mysteries*. This included the new arrivals they'd found here in Mexico. Sealed within a temple to

---

59. Not Gillian Anderson, the actress, but the actual fictional character Dana Scully. This had been when she was in high school. Mostly.

60. A group of vampires is actually called an AAAAAAAAAAAAAH!

Quetzalcoatl they had unearthed the one they'd come to find, Spanish inquisitor turned conquistador Cebrian d'Oviedo. Unexpectedly, though, he hadn't been alone. For the past five hundred years, Cebrian had been arguing with a vampire none of them had ever heard of before. This Tezcatlipoca, as the Spaniard called him between angry mutterings, had a jaguar's head, feathers, a leg made out of obsidian, and was, by all accounts, the most ruthless and bloodthirsty god in the Aztec pantheon.

Vampires. Just when you thought you'd seen the most disturbing variation, the next popped up, worse than all the rest.

"I don't see how this is helpful," Simon grumbled. The two humans had taken refuge in the kitchenette. He was currently taking a break from researching Mesoamerican mythology to shoot angry glares over at the vampires.

"He's giving them a reason to follow them," Catherine replied. She finished dipping a strawberry into the chocolate fondue. "Mmm."

"One would think releasing them all would be reason enough," said Simon.

"That just makes them resentful," she explained.

"We saved you and you aren't resentful," Simon countered.

"I'm not a raging psychopath." She lovingly placed another chocolate-dipped strawberry into her mouth. "Oh, that's good."

"Still, Yulric is the logical choice to lead. He brought them all together, he speaks all of their languages—"

"Not Tezzie's," Catherine interrupted.

"Except Tezcatlipoca's, yes." Simon glared at her. "Still, he's the one with the plan. Why wouldn't they follow him for the duration?"

"Because they're afraid of him," Catherine answered.

"How do you know that?" Simon asked.

Catherine paused. She didn't know how she knew what the other vampires thought, but she did. And there was more, right on the tip of her tongue, slowly materializing. "Something, I think, something about his resurrection." Her mind flashed. In a single moment, she witnessed the origins of each of the vampires . . .

In a desert land, a curse descended upon a mighty city, taking up residence in its temple and draining the area of all life . . .

In a dense tropical forest, a plague, taken form, hunted for prey as an inconspicuous insect . . .

Under the steps of a mighty pyramid, a god drank the blood pouring down from a hundred sacrifices . . .

Deep within the earth, a crying Chinese woman stopped clawing at the roof of her coffin and breathed her last . . .

And somewhere in Spain, an otherwise serene funeral procession was interrupted by an errant hen . . .

Still, as Catherine's psyche was assaulted by other times and places, she sensed something looming over all the rest. She pushed past the other visions and literally fell into one that was hidden. She braced herself for impact, but her descent was halted abruptly. When she opened her eyes, she was hovering in the dark over the supine form of Yulric Bile. His arms were crossed over his chest, his hands clasped around an ancient battle-ax. At his side rested a full helmet, complete with an image of his face etched onto the front. Behind his head was a large leather-bound book the size and weight of a small child. This was the barrow of Yulric Bile, his final resting place. Here he was buried, with all rites and honors by people who feared what might happen if they dared neglect them.

But there was something wrong. Even as this thought floated before her, she could feel malevolence oozing around her, contaminating everything it touched. There was nothing amiss: no curse, no bite, no sign of disrespect. This was no out-side eldritch force; this vile aura emanated from the body itself.

The eyes sprang open, and in the dark of the grave, she saw Yulric smile. Suddenly, she was no longer floating above the body; she was the body. She peered up at the image of herself looking down, and this time, it was she who smiled.

And then . . . agony, fiery and unbearable. The images dis-solved around her as she let loose a bloodcurdling scream.

◆   ◆

A sharp pain split Yulric's skull. It was as if someone had taken a red-hot acupuncture needle and shoved it through his left eye, into his brain.[61] Involuntarily, he hissed in a breath and brought up a hand to cover it.

A cry rang out in the hotel suite. Yulric removed his gaze from the television to see Catherine in the kitchenette, howl-ing in pain. The boy was holding something to her face. The vampire was about to dismiss it as a helpful ice pack when he caught a familiar flash of silver, which made him wince. A moment later, the screaming died out, replaced by heavy, steadying breaths. The boy pulled away, and Yulric saw clearly the large silver cross in his hand.

Yulric's mind raced. Why would she have such a violent reaction to the cross? Was it coincidence that he'd been in pain at the very moment she'd cried out or something more? What exactly had happened? He was about to investigate the inci-dent when he was interrupted by Arru.

"What is the tiny man in the box saying now?" she asked. On the screen, Phantom and Sasha were standing close to one another in the rain.

---

61. And he would know.

Yulric's suspicions evaporated as he was returned to his immediate purpose. Processing what he'd just heard, he translated Spanish into the most common language between them, Latin. "He said"—Yulric nearly vomited in his mouth having to repeat it—"I love you."

There was a round of disgusted hisses from those who understood.

"Love, bah!" spat Cebrian.

"What does love have to do with anything?" Adze grimaced.

Tezcatlipoca growled something in Nahuatl. The other monsters gave him a mystified look, then turned back just in time to witness Phantom and Sasha kissing. The group erupted into jeers. Bits of popcorn, which Catherine had insisted on making them, were hurled at the screen, along with a glowing green energy that caused it to spark, smoke, and melt.

"I have seen enough," Arru said. "You were right to summon us."

"How could this have happened?" asked Yu Mei. The vampires turned to Adze, the only one of them who had not been imprisoned.

"Don't look at me," he told them. "I am still feared in my lands."

Yulric shook his head. "I do not believe anyone here would be so careless. Only a fool would . . ." The English vampire trailed off as mental calculations were made. In a flash, he was in the kitchenette across from the two mortals. "We need to go to Tuscany."

Even through the dull ache in her left eye, Catherine smiled. This was, by far, the best vacation ever.

Chapter 27

It had long been understood by the vampires of Europe that it was only a matter of time before a member of the great families—the Hapsburgs, the Medicis, the Borgias—was to join their ranks. With the kind of power these dynasties wielded for centuries, it was impossible to imagine one of them wouldn't seek to extend their influence beyond life. The only question was which of the many ruthless, cutthroat members would carry their names into eternity.

Sadly for the pride and honor of both the Medici family and vampires as a whole, the person who had finally achieved immortality was Cosimo II de' Medici, an overweight and underambitious member of the family, who'd been perfectly content as a footnote in the future biography of Galileo. But he'd found himself gifted with immortality, thanks to an ancestor's botched Satanic pact. Now the possessor of a host of supernatural abilities and a thirst for blood, Cosimo had taken to vampirism like a theater person takes to sports—badly.

And so it came as no surprise to anyone that, when Yulric Bile dragged the Italian vampire out of his ornately decorated sarcophagus in the private, unsanctified Italian chapel he'd had built, the first words out of his mouth were cries of "It wasn't me!"

"What wasn't you?" Yulric growled, throwing him to the tiled floor in front of the five other vampires.

The Italian vampire gulped. "Whatever it was you think I did?" His gaze darted around, apparently searching for an alibi. He pointed to his box. "I've been in a sarcophagus. See?"

Arru took a step forward. "In Latin, if you please, so we can all understand."

Tezcatlipoca grumbled something in Nahuatl.

"So most of us can understand anyway," Arru corrected herself.

Switching to the dead language most of them spoke, Yulric uttered only two words: "Proper vampyrs."

"Oh," Cosimo uttered.

"Yes," agreed Yulric. "Oh."

"So you read Douglas's pamphlet then?" Cosimo's eyes lit up. "Do you have it with you? Can I see? I'd love to know what changes he's made since—"

Yulric held up his hand, and the Italian vampire fell silent.

"I want to know how," Yulric bellowed, his voice echoed around the chamber, which, despite its Renaissance trappings, managed to avoid any actual Christian iconography.

"Well, you see, I was bored, and there weren't any good operas, and there was this man named Darwin, who through a series of observations on the Galápagos Islands . . ."

The vampires listened intently as Cosimo began to ramble about finches and niches and the bizarre belief that animals change over time. A few of them tried to interrupt but to no avail. Even Tezcatlipoca's rumbling jaguar growl only excited the little Italian, who went on to explain how this *evolution* had affected big cats in general and the jaguar specifically. In the end, there was nothing to do except wait for him to run out of steam. As his main claim to fame was a friendship with a famous astronomer, this took quite a while.

"And that's why I say a leopard can change its spots. It just takes a million years," he finally finished with a bit too much laughter. Once he had composed himself, Cosimo went back to his original point. "And I thought, well, if it works on finches, why couldn't it work on vampires, too?"

"You tried this evolution on vampires?" spat Cebrian.

"What? No. No, no, no," cried Cosimo. "I would never dream. I'm just a layman. I don't have the skills. No, I found a proper scientist to do it for me."

"The Doctor Lord Talby," Yulric answered for him.

"Douglas was very keen on my 'dea,'" said Cosimo. "He had all sorts of marvelous thoughts. It was his idea to attempt a kind of social evolution to the vampire, as well. A perception change. We commissioned writers and painters and . . ." He trailed off as Yulric walked past him to stare at a fresco of Orpheus descending into the underworld.

"How did you conduct this experiment?" the English vampire hissed.

Cosimo, unwisely, took a few steps toward him. "Do you want to see the data? I'm sure I have my notebooks around here somewhere."

"How did you make the vampyrs?" Yulric clarified, oozing contempt with every syllable.

"Oh, well"—Cosimo chuckled—"that took quite a bit of trial and error, let me tell you. Some of the results we ended up with—ha. In hindsight, it seems so obvious that the mingling of blood would do it. Take my blood, drink it, everlasting life, you know."

The vampires clearly did not know. Except for Cebrian, who quietly explained, "It's a Christian thing."

"Can I ask a question?" Cosimo pleaded. With a wave of his hand and a glower, Yulric gave him leave. "I guess I don't really understand, well, what the problem is?"

One of Yulric's eyes blazed with anger. The other remained fairly pretty.

"You don't understand?" he snarled. "You don't realize what you've done to us?"

"No?" the Italian squeaked.

In a flash, Yulric had him pressed up against the wall. The marble behind him cracked under the pressure.

"We have become shadows of our true selves. Defenseless, nearly powerless. Killed with a mere stake through the heart and turned to dust."

"True, we never did figure out why that happens," the Italian rambled. "I suppose it's a result of the weakening of the curse. Though, personally, I've always wondered if it could be a psychosomatic reaction caused by . . . Ack!"

Yulric's grip on the man's throat had tightened. "You have traded our power and reputation for mere beauty. Do you not realize that vampyrs are now seen as . . . good?"

Cosimo pulled Yulric's fingers away, just enough to croak, "What's so wrong about a good vampire?"

◆　◆

The next morning, the residents of Tuscany awoke to find the small Medici chapel on the far side of town was gone. Where once it stood was a pile of oddly rounded marble and gold-leaf pebbles, each no bigger than a fingernail. Those who lived nearby remembered being awakened by a horrible clap of thunder in the middle of the night, which was odd, because it hadn't rained. The police and AISE investigated the possibility of a terrorist attack, but no one ever claimed responsibility and there was no evidence of an explosive device. In the end, it was labeled a gas explosion, and everyone involved went to lunch.

The same morning that the chapel disappeared, Catherine Dorset left Italy with a wonderful tan, a little boy, and six caskets in tow.

Chapter 28

The Doctor Lord Talby sat at his desk, casually flipping through the files of future vampire candidates. "And how is Vermillion working out?" he asked the speaker on his desk.

"It took a while, but we figured out where to pose him," replied a voice that remained deep and sultry despite the phone's added tinniness.

"Good, good." Talby set aside a file on *Johnson, Janelle*. "Any sign that he might be falling into old habits?"

The voice laughed. "None. The look he gave those wannabes last week made the fat girl cry. It was hilarious." Quickly, the voice composed itself with proper vampiric dignity. "It was tolerable."

There was a slow, deliberate, and oddly sensual knock outside his office.

"Thank you for the update, Karos. Please keep me informed." The Doctor ended the call and turned his attention to the door. "Come in, Phantom."

Phantom entered sullenly. Phantom did everything sullenly. Back before, when he'd still been Bobby Samuels, he'd been a very upbeat, chipper person. They'd had to break him of that.

"Women," he'd told the clay that would become a sex symbol, "don't want happy. Happiness only comes at the end of a story, and do you know why that is?"

Bobby had shaken his head.

"Because there's no more story to tell," he had answered. "Until then, they want mystery and danger and lots and lots of brooding. So if it's women you want . . . ?"

Bobby had nodded.

"Then, wipe that grin off your face," he'd instructed.

Bobby had and had never looked back.

"Doctor?" Phantom called, rousing Talby from his nostalgia.

"Yes, Phantom, I'm sorry. What is it?"

"It's our, er, guest. She's gone."

The Doctor chuckled. "There's no need to be concerned, Phantom. Nora's with her."

"Are you sure?" Phantom questioned. "Because those other times . . ."

"Nora explained the situation to me herself," Talby replied. "Ms. Linske is convinced that there is no escape from us, and the two of them would like some—how did she put it?—girl time. They'll be back in the morning. Frankly, I'm surprised you even noticed with all the time you've been spending on the set."

Phantom turned paler than normal. "You heard about that?"

Again, the Doctor laughed. "Phantom, this is a television studio. We have cameras, everywhere."

The younger vampire shifted uncomfortably. "I'm sorry, Doctor."

"Nothing to be sorry about, Phantom." He rose from his desk and patted his protégé on the back. "It all adds to the mystique of the vampire."

"I still don't like it," Phantom muttered.

"Phantom. Muttering," Talby corrected.

"Sorry, Doctor," Phantom let his hair fall in front of his face and squinted. "I still don't like it."

"You don't like that Nora's attention is somewhere other than on you, you mean?" The Doctor posed the question with a fair amount of insight.

The younger vampire coughed, but said nothing.

"Ah, Phantom." Talby sighed, walking back to his chair. "We always want most what we can no longer have."

The door to the office opened and Berwyn stepped in. "Excuse me, Doctor Lord Talby?"

The Doctor gave a pained smile. He made a note that they would need to have a talk later about entering without knocking first. "Yes, Berwyn, what is it?"

"Remember how you told me to keep an eye on the airports for anything unusual?" Berwyn said.

"No," replied the Doctor.

"Oh." Berwyn tried again. "Well, remember how you told Cassan to keep an eye on the airports for anything unusual?"

"Yes," the Doctor answered.

"Well, with Cassan being a bit . . ." Berwyn searched for the right words.

"Preoccupied," said Phantom.

"Preoccupied, yes." Berwyn continued, "I kept my eye on the airports and—"

"Why is Cassan not seeing to the task I gave him?" the Doctor asked tersely. He did not like to think himself a tyrant. In many respects, he was as laid-back as you could hope a two-hundred-year-old Victorian gentleman to be. Why, just last year, he had instituted a casual-dress day. Still, when he gave an order as important as "Watch for an enemy bent on destroying us all," he expected it to be followed.

"Well," Phantom said finally, "he's in mourning."

"Still?"

"It's only been a few months, Doctor," said Berwyn.

"Exactly." The two younger vampires shared a sideways glance. Talby sighed. There were times when The Doctor Lord Talby regretted focusing on the outcast demographic for this experiment of his. Granted, there was no limit to what an outsider would do for the promise of "love," but they were all so sensitive about it. Say what you will about the rich and beautiful, but at least they got over it.

"Tell Cassan that Victoria will be avenged. Scratch that, don't say her name. Say 'his love' shall be avenged, but that it can only happen with his help. Otherwise, the monster goes free and her soul will be lost to . . . etcetera. Have one of the new writers pad it for you, but get Cassan back to his post."

"But that's just it, Doctor. I don't think he's needed there anymore," Berwyn said, again cutting across his master. "I think—I think they're here."

The Doctor's heart had been skipping its beats for over a hundred years. Even so, it skipped a skip. "Do you?" he asked, trying with difficulty to stay calm.

"Amanda's brother just flew into LAX with another woman. They . . ." Berwyn steadied himself. "They had six caskets with them."

"Six?" uttered the Doctor in a state of shock.

"Is that all?" Phantom jeered.

"Six?" Talby repeated more frantically.

"Uh, yeah. Yes." Berwyn consulted the printout he'd charmed off the handsome customs official. "The woman said they were her brothers, who'd died in a mountaineering accident, but . . . that's just what she said."

"What's the big deal?" Phantom questioned, a little nervous at his mentor's reaction. "We have at least twenty vampires here in the building."

Talby was not listening.

He'd known they were out there, the old vampires. Cosimo had told him so. He'd always suspected they might rise eventually, and they'd have to be dealt with, but that day had always been far off, in the future. And with every decade that passed Old One–free, he could delude himself into thinking that maybe it would never come. Now the day was here, and rather than facing a single vampire, or two or three, which he could just dispose of and then go back to his business, a half dozen. All much stronger, all more powerful, all infinitely more clever than any modern vampire.

Except myself, thought The Doctor Lord Talby. *You have planned for this. It will work. Let them come.*

His doubt continued to shout inside his psyche, but the Doctor's ego had taken hold once more. Confidence and self-assurance flooded back into him, and suddenly, everything was much easier to see.

"When did they get in?" he asked, his voice returning to calm.

"An hour ago," replied Berwyn from behind him.

"Gentlemen, company will be arriving shortly." Talby turned back to the pair standing before his desk. Upon seeing the knowing smile on his lips, both visibly breathed a sigh of relief, as he'd known they would.

"We'll need Nora and our guest to return," he continued.

"I'll call her," Phantom offered.

"No, I had better do it," said the Doctor. "A call from you might be 'accidentally' missed. It's important she knows how serious this is. Berwyn, if you could talk to Cassan. We'll need him, as well."

Berwyn nodded and ran from the room.

"What about me?" asked Phantom, miffed that the Doctor knew that Nora was ignoring his calls.

"You, Phantom, have the most important job of all," the Doctor told him, soothing the young man's pride. "I need you to get a hold of every coven in Los Angeles. We need them here right away."

"What about San Francisco?" Phantom suggested. "There are a half-dozen covens there we could use."

"No time," answered the Doctor. "No, Los Angeles will have to do."

"Yes, sir," said Phantom, his spirit renewed. "Then what?"

We use them as cannon fodder, thought the Doctor. What he said was much more judicious. "You delay the monsters."

"Delay them?" Phantom repeated incredulously.

"As best you can," said the Doctor. Seeing the look on Phantom's face, halfway between insulted and fearful, he added, "It's all part of the plan."

The young vampire didn't understand but, like a good soldier, nodded as if he did.

"Go now," the Doctor commanded. Phantom obeyed, leaving The Doctor Lord Talby alone to prepare for the fight of his existence. He picked up his phone and dialed.

"Hello, Legal? It's The Doctor Lord Talby. I require seven copies of form 27C."

Chapter 29

"Here, take a look," said Simon, offering his binoculars.

"I can see perfectly well without those," replied Yulric.

"Even with the new—" began Simon.

"Yes, even with the new," Yulric cut him off. He'd recently found out his left eyeball had something called astigmatism, and he could be a bit testy about it. Also, people would not stop calling it *cute*.

"Suit yourself," said Simon, who had no sympathy for those too proud to help themselves. He went back to peering through his binoculars. They were a homemade set. Because he was a child, they were made from used toilet-paper rolls. Because he was Simon, he'd ground his own lenses.

A sound best described as scuttling made both boy and vampire turn. A score of rat-sized spiders was scurrying out of the underbrush where they'd hunkered down to keep watch. Before their three mortal and one vampiric eyes, the giant arachnids piled on top of each other, bending and fusing, to form odd, almost humanlike shapes. In no time at all, the spiders were gone and Arru of Akkad crouched beside them.

"There are fifty patrolling the outside of the fortress," she said. The vampires were either unable to grasp the term *studio* or just found it highly undignified to be storming one.

The shadows lengthened and shifted, and, rising out of them, as if they were water, came Tezcatlipoca. He said something in Nahuatl.

"Sixty-seven inside, including he who you seek," Cebrian translated.

"You do not say," Yulric replied with a slight smirk. He'd been slowly deciphering the Aztec's language, but wasn't in a rush to let on. Knowledge, after all, was power.

A loud thud from behind alerted them of another arrival.

"I found none transformed," reported Yu Mei in Cantonese. "Not as animals, mist, nor shadow."

"I told you they would not be," he shot back at her.

"But now we know for sure," she said sullenly. Being pale green and able to move only by hopping, she had naturally been left out of the reconnaissance assignments. She'd gone off anyway, if only to prove she, too, could be covert when the need arose.[62]

Finally, a small lightning bug floated gently out of the sky, the glow of its thorax rhythmically pulsing. Just as it reached their position, the light flashed and the hunched figure of the Adze took its place.

"The girl is there," said Adze, joining the squatting figures.

"In the tallest tower?" asked Cebrian.

"Chained in a dungeon?" asked Arru.

---

62. The area police received several reports of a green Martian female hopping around the area. Units were immediately dispatched for some drug busts.

"On the sacrificial wheel of time, ready to plunge the world into infinite darkness?" asked Tezcatlipoca after much translation.

Everyone stared at him, mostly because it had been an awfully specific question. Simon, Yulric, and Cebrian, however, had all noticed that the former Aztec god had understood what Adze had said.

"Actually," answered Adze, "I think she's in a guest room."

The vampires all gave a disappointed sigh. There were mutterings in half a dozen languages, which all roughly translated to "no sense of tradition."

"How many guards?" asked Simon, looking back into his binoculars.

"Two," Adze told him. "The black man and white woman with blond hair from the show. They were arguing."

"Excellent." Simon smiled. He looked up to find the angry face of Yulric Bile an inch away from him. Anyone else would have flinched at the sight. Anyone else would have moved back from an invasion of space. Anyone else would not be Simon.

"What?" asked the small boy, meeting the vampire's gaze.

"That is Cassan and Nora," said Yulric.

"It's likely, yes."

"You cannot kill them," said Yulric.

"Can't I?" said Simon, his eyebrow raised. It was more of a challenge than a question.

"No, you cannot," hissed Yulric. Simon had already killed half the cast of *The Phantom Vampire Mysteries*. He'd be saved if he was going to let the boy destroy the rest of the show.

"Very well," said the boy, bowing his head slightly. "I promise not to kill Cassan and Nora, except as a last resort."

"And to make sure it truly is a last resort, she is going with you." Yulric pointed at their rental bus, where Catherine was sitting, reading. Simon's eyes grew squinty and shrewd and very "eight-year-old who hasn't gotten his way."

"Is that why you brought her along?" asked the boy. Yulric just smiled. The truth was, he wasn't quite sure why she was still there. She had played her part. And while, annoyingly, the boy had taught her enough tricks that he was unable to retrieve his eye from her, she was free to leave now that their bargain had been fulfilled. But she didn't. She insisted on staying. And he had not said no.

"Very well." Simon sneered. He took up a stick and began drawing in the dirt. "You all will go through the front, distracting the vampire guards. I will"—he shot an annoyed look at Catherine on the bus—"*we* will sneak around the side and release my sister."

Yulric cleared his throat.

Simon rolled his eyes. "And we'll do it without killing Cassan and Nora." The boy continued, "Everyone will converge in the lobby. Once your group has cleared the way, mine will make our escape. After that, you are free to do what you like. But not before. *Is that understood?*"

The small boy looked around the circle at the angry, defiant, and terrible faces of the assembled vampires: the Saxon sorcerer, the Akkadian curse, the African plague-bringer, the Chinese life-drinker, the Spanish inquisitor, and the Aztec god. None of them said a word.

"Good," Simon said. He took out a pocket watch. "Give us ten minutes to get in position." He went to get Catherine. The elder vampires followed him with their eyes and then turned aside, pretending they hadn't just been told what to do by a small child. All, save Yulric.

Vampires don't believe in reincarnation. As a rule, they try not to think about any sort of afterlife too much. That being said, when you live for hundreds of years, you can't help but notice that you keep running into the same people over and over again, following you across the centuries, haunting your steps.

Yulric Bile may have *watched* Simon Linske leave, but who he *saw* was Erasmus Martin.

Chapter 30

A bus pulled up outside the Phantom Studios lot. The vampires on guard paid it no mind. Living in LA, they knew the only creature on this earth more pathetic than a tourist was a lost tourist. And the only thing more pathetic than a lost tourist was a tourist who had to be told that the attraction they'd come to see was closed. None of them wanted to deal with that, and all but one didn't have to.

Gwendolyn the Black (née Jenny Svenson) had unfortunately drawn the short straw and been given the job of official guard duty. She had to wear a uniform (one very unflattering to her figure by the way), man the entrance checkpoint (a phrase she found immensely sexist and decided to change to *woman* the entrance checkpoint), and keep up the appearance that this was just your average television studio. Of course, she had asked the Doctor why the mortals who usually *womanned* the checkpoint could not do the job.

"They have a union," he'd said, "and slaughter by vampires is not covered by their insurance."

So here she was, Gwendolyn the Black, sitting in a tiny little box, watching a tiny little TV that didn't have cable, and wearing a security-guard costume that wasn't tiny or little enough to be sexy. Now, to make matters even worse, she actually had to do her job.

Gwendolyn slid the window open. "We're closed," she yelled at the bus. The driver didn't open the window. Gwendolyn leaned over and tapped on the glass. "Hey. Hey, we're not open."

The bus did not move. The shape of the driver did not move. The door on the other side did move. It opened.

"For the love of . . . ," Gwendolyn muttered as she stepped out of the guardhouse. She continued muttering to herself all the way around to the front of the bus, until she reached the door. "We're closed," she repeated.

"And we were so hoping to see some vampires." The darkened bus was abruptly illuminated by an eerie light. Gwendolyn's eyes went wide as they met the gaze of a hideous female corpse with empty eye sockets. In the crone's right hand burned a fire of deepest black.

Gwendolyn managed a quiet gasp of "crap" before her entire head was engulfed by the dark flames.

◆　◆

"I don't see why I can't guard her!" Nora shouted. Her hands were on her hips. Anyone who knew Nora knew that hands on hips would likely be hands punching your face in very short order.

"Because when you watch her, she gets out," Cassan retorted. He did know Nora, but he was in a bad way right now, almost beyond the ability to function. He couldn't eat.

He couldn't sleep. He couldn't even really be angry. He was just sort of numb all over. And so he found that he did not care if Nora beat the crap out of him. At least, then, he might feel something again.

"It's her first trip to LA," Nora shouted back.

"Well, the Doctor said you should go downstairs and assist Phantom," said Cassan.

"Assist him with what? Waiting?" she said sarcastically. "There are a load of other vampires down there, doing just that. But not one of them can tell you how Amanda will react to the arrival of her rescue party. I can."

The argument was interrupted by a knock from the door they were supposed to be guarding. With a bit of trepidation, Nora unlocked and opened it. Amanda stood there, still in the slinky dress she'd worn to the club earlier, though now paired with a pair of comfy sweatpants, which she'd clearly just put on underneath. Her hair was down, and her contacts were out, but she still had all her makeup on. In essence, she was the epitome of relaxed sexiness.

"You guys should probably come see this," she said, motioning for them both to enter.

Cassan gave her a stoic look of disbelief and even Nora couldn't help being a bit suspicious, but Amanda moved away from the door, evidently intending to go change out of her "evening wear" and into her evening wear. Feeling it a safe bet their charge was not going to run off without first putting on a shirt, the two vampires entered the room.

"Out there." Amanda motioned to the balcony.

The vampires passed the piano, the tasteful couch-and-love-seat combo, the art, the modern art, the home entertainment system, the bookshelf of autographed first editions, the fully stocked bar, the dance floor, and the daybed before they reached the open balcony window.

Calling the sight that greeted them a fight was very much like calling the expanse of tastefully decorated comfort behind them a room. In the partial illumination of the street lamps from the lot below, they could see fifty of their fellows. Fifty strong young immortals armed with crosses, holy water, and stakes were standing up against six elder vampires. Rather, forty-eight were standing. Now forty-seven. Forty-four.

The two on the balcony looked on as the beautiful undead were mowed down. They watched as a green-skinned woman flipped over a man in a fashionable black trench coat and used her long nails to slice his head clean off. They stood witness as an eyeless mummy ripped the arms off a woman, then watched her writhe in pain, as if she were a fascinating insect. A jaguar-headed creature flew out of the sky and ate the face off a screaming vampire. A rotted priest pulled the skin off another with torturous precision. A hunchback sat atop a man's chest, eating his heart as the corpse crumbled to ash beneath him.

The air was filled with screams and dust and death. It was horrible, monstrous.

In the midst of the carnage stood Yulric Bile, eyes alight, laughing ecstatically. The ancient vampire waded into the fray, one hand grabbing and slashing with brutal strength, the other wielding, for no vampiric reason, an old, well-used ax. Not the kind you picture a fireman with, nor the tool for chopping lumber, this was an ax you find in a museum next to a set of armor labeled THE HUNS 500 CE or THE VIKINGS CIRCA 854 AD. Yulric's, however, was not gathering dust behind glass but being used to separate heads from bodies.

He saw Nora watching him from the balcony. A malicious wide smile spread across his face. Nora was suddenly filled with a terrible realization, one that few others would ever know: while many were the paths to vampirism, the oldest and foulest was simply being too evil to stay dead.

A movement to her right drew Nora's attention just in time. Cassan was scrambling over the balcony to join the fight.

"Cassan, no!" She grabbed his arms and pulled hard. As the strongest of their coven, normally, she could have dragged him back, no problem. Right now, however, she was having trouble.

"Let. Me. Go," he bellowed as he fought against her.

"You'll be killed." As she said it, black flame shot from the hands of the eyeless hag, further reducing their side from thirty down to twenty-two.

"I don't care," he snarled. A quick head movement put Nora in fear that Cassan might try to gnaw his arm off if she didn't let go. Or worse, her arm.

"You were told to stay here," she said, now appealing to the sense of duty he'd always enjoyed. "You were ordered to guard this room."

"He killed Victoria!" the man screamed, tears of sadness and rage filling his eyes.

"No, he didn't," said a voice far behind them. Nora's grip loosened, but it didn't matter because Cassan had stopped struggling. Both of them were now staring into the room.

Standing about ten feet from the door were three people. There was a short brunette in sunglasses, frozen in the manner of someone caught in wrongdoing. There was Amanda, holding a packed bag and shaking her head in annoyance. And, there in front, was a young boy, dressed all in black.

"Why? Why?" asked Amanda. "We were almost gone."

"He shouldn't be given credit for something I did," said Simon in the same tone most boys would use to complain about Little League MVP trophies.

"Credit? *Credit?*" screamed Cassan, stepping back over the balcony rail and into the room. Nora followed, though more cautiously. She'd already seen what this little boy was capable of and didn't like the idea of being within shuriken-throwing distance. Or crossbow-bolt shooting distance. Or halberd-spearing distance. Or—

"Yes," the boy said calmly. His voice held no malice nor any trace of mocking. It was as if he was giving an answer in school. "It's a matter of fact. He did not kill the vampires at our house; I did."

Cassan twitched. Every fiber of his being was screaming for bloody vengeance, but tearing a child limb from limb was not okay. He may have been mad with rage, but he wasn't a monster.

Simon glanced at his pocket watch. "Time to go."

"Wait," cautioned the woman in the sunglasses.

"Wait for what?" asked Amanda.

The woman held up her hand. Ten seconds later there was a tremendous explosion from below them. Not that they felt it, the room being so large and earthquake ready. They heard it, though, echoing up through the still-open balcony door. The woman smiled. "Now we can go."

"*AAAAH!*"

The blast seemed to have settled Cassan's inner turmoil. He let out a wail of pain that foretold imminent violence.

"Cassan, don't," pleaded Nora.

"No!" Amanda shouted.

Cassan charged. He raced toward the door behind the escapees. However, there seemed little doubt that he was intent on killing anyone in his way. Nora ran after, hoping against hope that she could get a step or two ahead of him. The boy just stood there, waiting. Clearly, he was aching for a fight. Unfortunately, he didn't get one.

Nora slid to a halt as Cassan exploded into dust in front of her. The powder was slow to dissipate, but when it did, Amanda was standing on the other side, having stepped in front of her brother, stake in hand.

Nora fell to her knees amid growing piles of her former friend and cast mate. "You—you killed him."

Amanda joined her on the ground. "I am so sorry," she said. "I couldn't—he was going to hurt Simon. I am so, so sorry."

Nora caught Amanda's gaze and turned furious. "The Doctor was right about you. You could never be a vampire."

"I guess not." Amanda stood. "Will you try to stop us?"

Nora considered it for a minute. She considered killing them all where they stood for what they had done to her friends. But in the end, she couldn't. "Go."

Amanda gave a small nod of thanks and left her friend to grieve.

"Well, that could have gone better," remarked Catherine.

"I'm sorry. Who are you, exactly?" Amanda replied.

Chapter 31

The elders burst into the lobby of Phantom Studios, an impressive, airy space large enough that sixty-eight well-coifed, well-groomed modern vampires could lie in wait on three sides, and six supernaturally superior ones could face them on the other. A second floor, lined with eternal twenty-somethings, wrapped around the sides of the lobby, ending in spiral staircases to the immediate right and left of Yulric's AAAAAAAAAAAAAAH! of vampires. There was even a hole in the middle of the floor, with a pool of multicolored koi swimming about, so oblivious to what was going on that a few poked their heads up with the hope of being fed.

Stoic, determined expressions looked down upon the invaders from symmetrical facial features on ones who had refused to do battle without their makeup. Fashion varied greatly among the young vampires, from ridiculous frilly shirts and black velvet to the more common designer jeans and silk tops, with a stop here and there at "how does that stay on?" Not that the older vampires were necessarily any better. Only three of them were properly dressed, and at least one of them was completely naked. The difference was you didn't want to see what Yulric's cadre had.[63]

"They seem confident," Arru said quietly as she glanced from one stony face to another.

Yulric's eyes darted around the lobby. "This is their place of power. What could possibly harm them here?"

"Maybe someone should show them what we did to their friends outside." Cebrian laughed, his red-and-white robes now just red.

"It would make no difference," Adze said conversationally, though he too was taking in each and every body before him. "They think themselves immune to death."

"Because they are vampires?" Yu Mei snorted.

"Because they are young," replied Adze.

"Shall we kill them now?" asked Tezcatlipoca in his own language.

"He wants to know if we are going to kill them," repeated Cebrian.

"Did he now?" replied Yulric, enjoying his private secret. "What do we think?"

"Perhaps we should give them a chance to surrender," said Yu Mei.

Cebrian let out a hiss of disgust. "Let them surrender? Spare them? Please, tell me you jest."

"Oh, we will kill them anyway," she clarified. "But we should still let them surrender. To be polite."

---

63. Especially in the case of Tezcatlipoca. Having both the head of a jaguar and quite a few feathers, there was no way of telling what was under that loincloth.

Cebrian laughed. The other vampires nodded their approval, even Tezcatlipoca, which made Yulric more certain that he wasn't the sole one keeping secrets.

Before any of them could act, though, a voice rang from the center of the balcony. A deep, brooding, tender voice that any girl between the ages of ten and thirty-five would kill to hear on a daily basis, if only on her voice mail.

"If you'd like to surrender, now is the time," it boomed across the lobby.

Several vampires on the balcony parted as Phantom and Berwyn stepped forward from the crowd. Moving with a confident grace, the pair leapt over the railing and landed lightly on the floor below. Neither showed any concern. After all, they had played this scene often enough to know how it would end.

"You're surrounded, outnumbered." Phantom gestured to the vampires all around him. "But we don't have to do this. Just lay down your arms, and I'll take you to see The Doctor Lord Talby. No one gets hurt."

"What's he saying?" asked Cebrian and Yu Mei at the same time.

As the only English speakers, Adze, Arru, and Yulric looked at each other. After that, none of them could stop laughing, for a full minute. All around the room there was a low level of uncomfortable shifting. Even Phantom, who had been scoffed at by several evil beings,[64] looked confused. This was not how it was supposed to go, his expression said. A villain's laughter was supposed to be cold and maniacal. They weren't supposed to find something you said actually funny.

After Yulric had composed himself enough to explain what Phantom had said to the others, and after *they* had stopped laughing in turn, Yulric finally faced Phantom. "Leave."

---

64. In fiction.

"That's it?" Phantom blurted out, having expected a lengthy monologue worthy of a Saturn Award.

"Leave now," Yulric added.

"You can't have the Doctor," Berwyn shouted, with a look to his fellow actor. Improvising was not his strong suit. "You'll have to kill us all to get to him."

There was a hesitant murmur of agreement. The assembled vampires were not quite ready to die for any reason. But they agreed anyway, hoping it might impress that hot female ten feet away whom they hadn't slept with yet.

Phantom stepped forward. "You see, together we are strong. Together we can do anything. Together we—"

Painful cries cut him off. The older vampires had gotten bored, and having a rather cruel sense of irony, were using a monologue about the strength of the collective to destroy the army of youths, utterly, completely, and irrevocably. Dark tendrils of energy were pulling the vampires on Phantom's right into the air, drawing out their essence and feeding it to Yu Mei. Those on his left were screaming in pain and falling to ash as Arru's black flame burned them from the inside out. On the balcony, the laws of physics had been completely overturned, causing many of them to uncontrollably float through the ceiling and up into the sky, courtesy of Tezcatlipoca, to which Cebrian harrumphed, "Show off." In a matter of only moments, seventy vampires were reduced to two.

"Sorry. Please, go on. You were saying how strong you were together," said Yulric, a mocking smile upon his face.

The standoff was undercut by the loud clump of footsteps on metal stairs. Down the stairwell to the side, a caravan proceeded, consisting of the strange little killer boy, a short woman with sunglasses, and the reason all these people were here.

"Ha!" Phantom cried. In an instant, he had Amanda grasped tightly. Berwyn followed suit, though he seemed hesitant to approach the kid.

"It seems the tables have turned," Phantom challenged. "What do you—"

"Ahem." Phantom looked down to see Simon holding a silver cross in his hand. "Please let go of my sister."

Phantom laughed and pulled a necklace with a cross on it from under his shirt. "Crosses don't work on me."

"I know, but she took my crossbow," the eight-year-old replied. Phantom felt the tip of an arrow press against his chest.

"It's not safe for a boy to handle such dangerous weapons," Amanda said pointedly.

"Indeed," agreed Simon, now holding a hatchet he definitely hadn't had a moment ago.

Phantom released Amanda and took a step back. "Please, Amanda, you have to help me," he uttered in a soothing voice. And when the dreamboat star of *The Phantom Vampire Mysteries* uses a soothing voice, you stay soothed.

Suddenly, Amanda was a lot less sure about escaping than she had been a moment ago. She took a step backward to steady herself. "We're leaving."

"Uh, Phantom," Berwyn said.

"Come on, Amanda, You don't have to do this," he said, rising slowly, his voice all kinds of comforting. It promised hours of cuddling preceded by hours of precuddling activity. "Just come back with us. This can all work out, I promise."

Mesmerized, Amanda stared into Phantom's soulful brown eyes. Her grip slackened. The crossbow lowered. Departing suddenly lost its urgency.

That was when Nora arrived and punched Phantom right across the face.

"What the hell?" he screamed from the ground. All the softness of his voice was gone. Now it was high, nasal, and *furious*.

"What are you doing?" Nora retorted, her hands on her hips.

"The Doctor said to keep her here," Phantom said, now back on his feet and suicidally within punching distance again.

"Uh, guys," Berwyn tried again. No one paid him any mind.

"Only so the other vampire would come for her. And guess what? He did. So there's no reason to keep her anymore. And there's definitely no reason for you to get your flirt on to do it," she spat back.

"Jealous, are we?" he replied.

Meanwhile, Amanda was shaking off the effects of Phantom's glamour. "There isn't a safety on this thing, is there?" she asked her brother.

"Why would I need a safety?" he replied.

"Good."

She pulled the trigger. The crossbow bolt shot out at the distracted Phantom. Fortunately for him, she hadn't bothered to raise the weapon back toward his heart. Unfortunately for him, she hadn't bothered to raise the weapon back toward his heart.

He screamed, now furious and in immense pain. "You crazy bitch!"

That word reverberated around the room. Despite being preoccupied with pulling six inches' worth of shaft from his shaft, Phantom became keenly aware of the fact that he was surrounded by women. Nora looked livid. Amanda stared daggers at him. Even the short, kind-looking woman took off her sunglasses to reveal half of the ugliest, angriest stare he had ever seen. And one cloudy pinprick eye, too.

"Simon," Amanda said too calmly, "reload this for me." Her brother took the weapon from her and immediately handed it back, magically ready again.

"You should go, Phantom," the short woman said. She was smiling now, but her smile did not reach her gaze. In fact, the murky eye looked like it had never seen a smile. Or a sunrise. Or this side of hell.

"I can't," Phantom replied through gritted teeth. With one hand, he carefully extracted the arrow without taking "the boys" with it. "I can't let you leave."

"What about the vampires?" she asked.

Phantom blinked. A few cogs clicked into place, and his attention was drawn away from Amanda and toward the very *empty* lobby. Under cover of quarreling couples and crossbow bolts, the elder vampires had sneaked away. At least, that's how Phantom would have described their loud and deliberate walk into the heart of the building.

"Son of a . . . ," he cursed, though a look at Amanda's crossbow stopped him from completing his expletive.

"That's what I was trying to tell you," Berwyn said.

"Come on," Phantom urged. They took off at full vampire speed through a set of double doors.

"Thank you," Amanda said.

"Just go," Nora replied tersely. The ashes of Cassan still clung to her pants.

"You could come with us," suggested Catherine, putting her sunglasses back on.

Nora considered it. Part of her cherished the idea of leaving Phantom to face the monsters alone. After all the frustration and heartbreak he had caused her over the years, it would serve him right. But even as she thought it, as so often happened, she thought of the boy Phantom had been when they'd met: sweet, sincere, unsure of himself. They had both of them been just beginning to explore their newfound beauty and powers. And they had started that journey together, in each other's hearts and beds. Sure he had become Grade A douche, but was that really enough justification to let him be murdered?

And, of course, there was the fact that Phantom wasn't alone. There was Berwyn to consider, the only other member of their posse left, not to mention The Doctor Lord Talby, who was in the most danger. He had chosen her. He had peered beneath the acne-scarred skin, the flat butt, and the barely visible chest and seen in her something spectacular. Could she just abandon the man who had welcomed her into his family? Who had given her everything? Who had been like a father to her? An old, breast-augmenting father?

Nora hadn't said a word, but Amanda understood. She placed a hand on her brother's shoulder and nodded to her friend.

Nora turned and sped off after the vampires.

"Damn," said Catherine, watching her leave. "I wanted to get a picture with her."

Chapter 32

No twisting dark forest nor fathomless abyss of stygian caves nor intricate system of endless crypts is quite as labyrinthine as a corporate office building. Even illuminated as it is in halogen lights, what it lacks in darkness, it more than makes up for in an exacting homogeneity, which can be achieved only by way of mass production and mediocrity. One corporate hallway looks very much like another, with doors and windows laid out in the exact same pattern. Not even the fake potted plant can appear anywhere other than the designated "fake potted plant corner." And just as in the dark forests and underground realms, some people never find their way out of this maze of hallways. These people are called office managers.

The point of all this is to explain how six vampires managed to become irrevocably lost.

At a crossroads of four halls, Yulric stood weighing his options. Thus far they had taken two rights and one left before doubling back, moving up a junction, and facing the same decisions all over again. He had already tried magic, scent, and logic to guide them, and each had failed in turn. This time, he went with random guesswork.

"This way," he called to his companions. There would have been mutinous whispers, except that none of the others could sense the correct path, either. Even Tezcatlipoca's excellent jaguar nose was thrown off by air fresheners, which puffed out the same random blasts of sweet-smelling spray each time they passed. And so they followed Yulric around the corner.

Whoosh! Something ran past, down the hallway they had just left. The collection of vampires turned as a second figure ran past. And a third. As a single entity, they glanced back at Yulric.

"That way," he growled in embarrassment. The vampires shuffled around the corner to find their way barred by an action tableau.

On the right side of the hall, Nora faced them, her eyes narrowed, her hands on her hips, the drape of her jacket baring a shoulder for a bit of sexy attitude. On the left, Berwyn faced them, cracking his knuckles as menacingly as one can when one is completely terrified. And in the center, Phantom stood, seemingly unconcerned, his hands casually stuffed in his pockets.

"No farther, monster," Phantom said, his voice now a well-practiced calm.

"I have no interest in you." Yulric took a step forward. The beautiful vampires twirled unnecessarily to counter his movement and wound up in a new tableau: Phantom, crouching, knees bent and hands clawed; Nora, a hand over her head as she leaned back on one leg and held the other outstretched; Berwyn, standing over both in anime-power-up position.

"Yulric Bile," intoned Phantom. "I challenge you for leadership of this coven by the laws set down by the united elder councils of the vampire nation."

The ancients looked to each other and then to Yulric, murmuring in a handful of dead languages. The younger immortals mistook this to be a sign of dissension or fear. Really, they were asking each other, "What did he say? Laws? Since when do we have laws?"

Yulric himself was staring down the hall, past where Phantom was standing, to the far door of what his vampire eye told him was a conference room and what his nonvampire eye told him was a blur. Then, both his eyes focused on Phantom. He raised a hand, and everyone fell silent. Since elder vampires don't like being shushed, it was a very pissed silence.

"I accept your challenge," he said, his voice filled with restrained wrath. Yulric had no intention of hurting the boy. What he had decided in that moment was to bind both Phantom and Nora with black mucus and stick them to a wall. He had not considered, however, that Phantom might have a plan, too.

As soon as the first bullet hit, Yulric knew something was wrong. He'd been shot before, by both Amanda and her brother, and by comparison to the gun they had used, Phantom's firearm looked practically demure. The pain from the actor's, however, was tenfold what the Linskes had previously managed. Combined. This bullet burned—literally burned—its way through him, even setting his robe alight as it passed.

He was struck a second time. Then a third. While he couldn't have said that the pain was like nothing he'd ever experienced, it definitely ranked in the top one hundred wounds, which, for a thousand-year-old vampire who'd been hunted, tortured, and nearly murdered more times than he could remember, was pretty good. A fourth bullet hit, and he was backing away.

A fifth, and he was kneeling on the ground. His chest heaved with pain rather than with breath. A click from above alerted him to the proximity of gun and shooter, who, distracted as he was, he had not noticed approaching. Phantom stood over him, gun pointed right between his eyes.

"Any last words?" asked the firearm-toting vampire.

Yulric spat out some blood, being sure it hit the fool's pristine and probably very expensive tennis shoes. Phantom's smile disappeared. His finger pulled the trigger. Yulric Bile, the great and dangerous vampire, fell to the ground in a heap of finality.

"I did it," cried Phantom, first in disbelief and then in rising excitement. "I did it!"

Any sort of dignity or style that a great noble hero is supposed to display upon defeating his enemy was momentarily forgotten. Phantom forgot Nora was mad at him and lifted her up in a great big spinning hug. Nora also forgot she was mad at him and let him. Berwyn, feeling left out, came over and, with his huge arms around the pair, hoisted them both in the air. They all three laughed. It was the happily-ever-after moment, where in a single action, all the wrongs of the season are set right, all the leftover bad guys melt away, all the relationship missteps are forgotten, and everything goes back to the way it was until the reveal of next season's main villain. In other words, damn fine television.

And just like on television, this perfect moment was being watched.

"Oh. Oh right," said Phantom, remembering that there were still five other hideous monsters to deal with. He raised himself impressively, and his voice deepened as he assumed what he meant to be a commanding tone. "As your new leader, I command you to leave this place. Disperse. Go back to your dark and secret places, return to the sleep of ages, and do not rise till you hear my voice or the trumpets of judgment day. Do you understand?"

It seemed they didn't. None of them moved. None of them blinked. A few turned their heads to the husk of what Phantom assumed was a woman and a hunchbacked black man.

"Well? What are you waiting for?" Phantom asked the collection of grotesques.

The stony woman's empty sockets met his soulful brown eyes. "The recommencement of battle."

"Uh, what?" he said, all dignity and command gone from his voice.

"Round two," rasped a desiccated voice behind him. Phantom's face fell, as did his stomach and his hopes. His testes, meanwhile, went up. Yulric Bile was on his feet once more.

The young vampire raised his gun to unleash a fresh volley into his eldritch opponent. His mind gave the order to pull the trigger, but nothing happened. For some reason, he could no longer use his gun. He could no longer even feel his gun. And now there was an intense pain coming from the end of his arm. Upon closer inspection, he found that both problems had the same cause—the hand holding the gun was gone.

Phantom let out a tear-filled scream of pain. He clutched at the stump, interspersing the high-pitched noise with frantic pleas of "Oh God! Oh God! My hand! My hand!"

During this din, Yulric Bile was prying the gun from Phantom's cold, severed fingers. After pressing several catches on the firearm, the part that held the bullets fell out and clattered to the floor. Everyone except Phantom leaned in to see that each and every bullet was etched with a cross. A shiver ran through the elder vampires.

Yulric approached Phantom, who was still rocking on the floor, mourning the loss of his hand, beauty, and career, though not in that order.

"You probably thought yourself wise," Yulric said, "shooting me with these. But you forgot one thing, dear boy."

He held up a lumpy, indiscernible piece of metal next to Phantom's face. "Musket balls deform when they strike." The younger vampire gulped as he stared into Yulric's eyes. Reasonable, rational, fan-of-the-show Yulric had checked out. Only the psychotic killer remained.

Phantom had less than a second's warning. One moment, the creature was kneeling down next to him, showing him the bullet, the next, he was whirling his medieval battle-ax through the air where Phantom's neck had been. Were it not for the small twinkle of warning that had appeared in the old vampire's hazel eye, he'd have been fit for only a Sleepy Hollow adaptation. Instead, he rolled out of the way and started dodging.

Yulric chased him. Not by running, the hallway was too small for that. He simply kept swinging his ax anywhere his prey landed. Phantom evaded the blade each time by smaller and smaller margins until one swipe caught a few hairs from the young vampire's head. Phantom felt his scalp, just as dismayed by the violation of his haircut as he had been for his hand. Yulric roared triumphantly, certain that his next swing would be the end of it.

In a split second, a decision was made. Yulric brought his weapon around. Phantom leapt out of the way. And Berwyn found himself pushed forward.

"No!" Nora's voice pierced the veil of rage in Yulric's mind and coming to, he was shocked to find Berwyn, not Phantom, standing in front of him. For one horribly comical moment, they were both united in gaping at the large red cut through his midsection. Then slowly, he began to tilt.

"*No!*" Yulric shouted. He dropped his ax as he reached out to grab Berwyn's upper half, but the young vampire slid through his fingers, collapsing into a cloud of dust.

"I thought we were not supposed to kill the tellers of stories," Tezcatlipoca said sarcastically.

Cebrian chuckled.

"Disgusting," said Phantom as he sputtered and spat, trying not to breathe in his friend.

"You!" Yulric cried. The TV star found himself suspended in midair by a pair of bony hands.

"Do it then. Kill me," Phantom said, closing his eyes.

Yulric scowled. Moment's ago, in his rage, he'd been more than ready to unmake the arrogant idiot. But now, his rational mind had returned and, with it, a reluctance to harm the actor. Also, a desire to get an autograph.

Phantom smiled. He knew. "You can't, can you? You're too much of a fan. Get him, Nora!"

Yulric looked over his shoulder to where the vampiress stood holding the ax that moments ago he had discarded. There was a nagging sense of familiarity about the whole thing. This had happened once before, he was sure of it. On the show. Season three, episode twenty-four. The finale. Lord Dunstan, still evil at this point, had been holding a recorporealized Phantom by the throat when Nora appeared out of nowhere and ran him through with Excalibur.

Yulric remembered. Phantom remembered. By the way she gripped the ax, Nora, too, remembered. For a moment, it looked as if life would imitate art. But then she threw the weapon.

"N-Nora?" Phantom called out, not quite believing what was going on. "What are you doing? Get him, Nora."

Nora shook her head. "You pushed him." She walked past the elder vampires and down the hall.

Phantom began to panic. "Please. Please, Nora. Nora? Where are you going?"

She turned as she reached the stairwell door. "I'm going with them. At least they look out for each other." And with that, she bumped the crash bar with her hips and exited backward. Nora was gone.

Now Phantom's cool abandoned him just as Nora had. His eyes bulged, his voice squeaked, and he began to struggle madly against the steely grip that held him. He clawed and pulled at the hand in ever-increasing desperation. Yulric let him, again enjoying the emotion of his prey. Blood may have been a vampire's food, but fear was what they truly lived on.

Yulric watched as the struggling subsided into hopeless despair. Tears welled up in Phantom's eyes, and silently he pleaded for mercy. Yulric pulled him in close so that the two were face-to-face.

"Your mistake was in believing your own fiction," Yulric whispered. "What you experienced before was a story. In a story, your friends always save you. In a story, Lord Dunstan is defeated. In a story, you never die."

Phantom mouthed the word *please.*

Yulric began increasing the pressure of his superhuman grip. "But this is reality. Your friends are not coming, I am not Lord Dunstan, and you—"

With a monumental display of strength, Yulric severed Phantom's head with his bare hands. Most of the former TV star fell to the ground and disintegrated. Yulric looked at the nine-pound head still in his hands as it crumbled around his fingers. There was so much he would never know. It was *The Canterbury Tales* incident all over again.

This is not what I wanted, he thought.

Ha! That's a lie, replied a voice in his head that was not his own. Yulric slammed a door in his mind. *Hard.* Hard enough that from the other side of his mental barriers, he could just make out the sound of Catherine's thoughts saying, *Ow!*

Stay out of my head, woman, Yulric thought.

Fine, replied Catherine. Her consciousness departed, leaving only a lingering *be careful.*

"Pah," Yulric snorted. "Careful."

"What was that?" asked Arru as the vampires re-formed around him.

"Let us go," Yulric said, retrieving his ax from the ground.

Nothing could stand in their way. Not a hundred vampires. Not the cast of *Phantom.* And certainly not The Doctor Lord Talby. They were invincible. They were power. They were proper vampires. And, as the collection of Old Ones pushed through the double doors, they all had the same thought.

Everything is going according to plan.

Chapter 33

The Doctor Lord Talby looked up from the end of a long conference room table. "Ah, be with you in a moment," he said in Latin. He turned back to the lawyer standing next to him. "What's next?"

"Sign there," the man instructed pointing at a piece of paper. The Doctor did. "And on the next page, you need to initial—"

Where he needed to initial, they did not learn, for at that moment, Yulric's ax separated the man's head from his body. The body fell with a thump. The head remained balanced on the blade of the ax, which was now imbedded in the wall.

Talby looked up at the suspended, severed head. "That was uncalled for." He finished signing his papers. "There. Shall we talk surrender?"

The elder vampires laughed.

"You think we should surrender?" Yulric snarled. His body tensed with power and magic as he prepared for the final battle.

"Oh no. I was speaking of my surrender," Talby answered.

"What?" the vampires uttered. They looked from one to another, confused. Their kind did not surrender.

"I am surrendering to you. Unconditionally." The Doctor smiled pleasantly. He picked up the papers on his desk. "That's what these are. I have officially signed over all my assets and holdings to you."

"This is a trick," Yulric accused.

"Afraid not," Talby indicated the six chairs around the table. "If you'd like to have a seat, I thought before you killed me, we should go over the details of the *empire* you now command."

In a flash, Yulric was on the good doctor. With one hand, the older Englishman held the younger's head to the table; with the other, he retrieved his ax from the wall. "I think not." Yulric raised his weapon.

Cold, hard fingers wrapped themselves around his wrist. Yulric turned to find Arru firmly holding his arm back. "Let us hear more."

Turning from her to the others, he realized his misstep. In his fury, he hadn't noticed the slight emphasis Talby had put on the word *empire*. And now greed had subtly wormed its way into their minds. Just as the Doctor had undoubtedly intended.

Reluctantly, Yulric released Talby. The Doctor stood, straightening his suit. "Please, have a seat."

They vampires spread out along the table. Yulric took the space on the end opposite Talby. He did not sit.

"Now, before we get started, can I offer you anything to drink? Coffee? Tea?" The Doctor paused strategically. "Blood?"

"Blood," said Cebrian and Tezcatlipoca at the same time. They wheeled their chairs away from each other, as if proximity had betrayed that they had something in common.

"Anyone else?" the Doctor asked. Slowly, more hands were raised.

"Well, in that case . . ." Talby smiled. He pressed a button, and a few seconds later, some excited young people entered through a side door. Seven, to be exact. They were dressed mostly in black, with mostly black hair, and black lipstick, also mostly. There was nothing *mostly* about the amount of eyeliner present.

The leader was a short young woman with curly black hair, slightly more filled out than her companions, who all looked as though Famine had just ridden by. She went straight up to the Doctor and, with a frightened glance at those watching, curtsied.

"My lord," she said, "you asked me to bring my coven?" She shook, obviously unnerved by the collection of horrors the room provided. All manner of thoughts passed through her head, primarily involving the Doctor betraying her and feeding her and the others to these . . . things. To her credit, she almost managed to keep the fear out of her voice.

"Do not worry, Cassandra. You are perfectly safe, I promise you." The girl breathed a sigh of relief at the Doctor's words. "I have afforded you a great honor. For your good service, you and your coven shall be the first to pledge themselves to the elder vampire lords."

"Oh," Cassandra replied. Her eyes fell back upon those sitting at the table, as did the gazes of the other black-haired mortals. There was less fear this time and more awe.

"They have traveled far, from foreign lands, and"—he looked at Yulric—"suburban basements, to be here today."

"My lords," Cassandra said with another curtsey. The members of her coven followed suit, bowing and dipping as necessary.

"And ladies," prompted the Doctor.

For a moment, Cassandra gave the Doctor a look as if to say "Really?" but that moment passed, and she did in fact say, "And ladies."

Then, without prompting, the young people spread themselves out, one for each vampire at the table. "In respect of your wisdom and power," Cassandra recited, "we of the Black Crystal Coven of Orange County offer this gift to you."

Together, in motions that were obviously practiced, all seven of them produced a small crystal goblet and a silver dagger. They raised their blades high into the air, then lightly placed the tips at their elbows and pressed. Blood welled up from the wounds, more so as each of them hit the veins. The goblets were positioned to collect the blood as it flowed down their arms and dripped from their fingers. Once each was filled, the cups were offered to the vampires, who drank. Mostly.

"Is there a problem, my lord?" asked the one blond member of the coven. There was a strong and clearly intentional resemblance to Amanda.

"I can get my own," growled Yulric, even more annoyed. He did not like being mocked.

"Y-yes, my lord," she said with an obsequious little bow.

"I don't suppose you mind if I . . . ?" asked Cebrian. He stretched out his hand, and the girl moved to pass her cup to him. Yulric, out of sheer contrariness, slapped the goblet to the ground. The girl backed away, muffling sobs of fear and disappointment. This, more than anything, caught the vampires' interest. Not only were these mortals willing to give their blood, but they were actually upset if you rejected it.

"You may go, Cassandra," said the Doctor, drinking deeply from her cup as he did so. "See to your wounds. I will buzz if we need any more."

"We live to serve," she said. All of them bowed and slowly walked out of the room, holding their arms.

The Doctor Lord Talby began handing out prepared folders. "Apologies. I wasn't aware of your origins, so this may not be legible to all of you. Copies will, of course, be made available in your respective native languages. Now, if you'll turn to page two, you will find statements outlining both my personal holdings and those of this studio."

"Never mind that," said Adze. He indicated the door through which the humans had exited. "Tell us more about them."

The Doctor smiled. "What would you like to know?"

"Do we get them, as well?" asked Cebrian, licking his lips.

"Naturally," answered the Doctor. "With control of my assets comes control over the vampire community, both mortal and immortal. All those willing to shed their blood for you are yours."

"Willing. *Ha!*" barked the Yu Mei.

"Willing, yes," responded the Doctor. "And you must do your best not to kill them."

"And why should we do that?" responded Arru. The vampires all eyed the Doctor suspiciously, and Yulric could feel their moods shifting back to a quick beheading.

"Well, first of all, because it's a waste of blood. No need to overtax a system that works so well."

Tezcatlipoca glared significantly at Cebrian, who refused to translate this.

"And then, of course, there is the danger to your own lives."

"What danger?" asked Arru.

"From the mortals, of course," the Doctor made a big show of looking around the table in disbelief. "Has he . . . Has he not told you?" He pointed an accusatory finger at Yulric. The others eyed the elder Englishman suspiciously. "The world has changed, my friends—guns, flying machines, horseless carriages. You've seen some of this for yourselves?" The vampires nodded. The Doctor, however, shook his head. "You have not seen the half of it. They can communicate with each other instantaneously from anywhere in the world. They can track each other's whereabouts with machines in the sky. And guns. Guns are everywhere."

Yulric interrupted. "Vampyrs cannot be—"

"Killed by guns?" the Doctor finished for him. His face was stern, but the old vampire could see a smile lurking just beneath the surface. "Well, what about machines that spit flames? What about fire that can melt metal in seconds? What about explosives that can destroy entire cities? Can these kill vampires?"

Silence fell across the room. None of them had ever heard about *this* part of modern life.

"Mortals have devised new and more deadly ways to kill each other," explained the Doctor, "and in doing so, have discovered new and undeadly ways to kill us, as well. We can no longer risk being monsters. People kill monsters.

"Of course, as your humble servant, I can assist you. Be your guide to this brave new world. All I would ask, my lords and ladies, is that until such time as you have no use for me and dispatch me, as is your right, you allow my experiments to continue. After all, what is an empire without an army of minions behind it?"

The word *minions* set off a number of nods. Suddenly, those hopeless dreams of leading an army of vampires didn't seem so hopeless. Had they not slaughtered just such an army, on their way in?

"You've been awfully quiet, Master Bile," Talby said. "Do you approve of this arrangement?"

"No," said Bile. It was a bitter whisper, but the room had become so quiet that the sound grew to fill it.

"Why not, if I may ask?"

"Because," said Yulric. For a moment, that appeared to be all he was going to say. For a moment, that was the only reason he could think of. He knew that the proposition was good. He was being offered power and safety and freedom to do as he pleased. And in exchange for what? Killing? He was not one of these young things who treated blood like a drunkard treats ale. He had once gone a century not drinking blood, simply to win a bet. He knew he should sign the paper. It just . . . felt . . . wrong.

Yulric picked up the forms in front of him. "This is not what a vampyr is," he said and threw them across the table.

"Beauty? Blood? Immortality? Power? If that is not *what a vampire is*, then, please, Master Bile, enlighten me. What is a vampire?"

Yulric didn't have a response for this, except for the ax in his hand. He let the handle fall farther into his grip and readied himself to attack and be slain. But just as he was about to leap forward, an unseen force held him back.

Let it go.

Yulric turned to see Catherine's mental projection tightly grasping his arm.

Those who fight and run away. She raised a set of car keys up to his face.

Yulric looked from the woman only he could see to the vampires, who were all waiting for an excuse to rip off his head.[65] He made a decision. With as much dignity as he could muster, he gave a curt nod of defeat and faded into a fine mist, which leaked out through the cracks in the door, and was gone.

"Well," said The Doctor Lord Talby after a moment of awkward silence, "shall we get down to business? If you would all

---

65. Vampires, as previously noted, deep down, really do not like one another very much.

turn to page one of your packets"—they did—"we'll go over how much each of you are now worth. I'm sorry, Mistress . . . ?"

"Arru."

"Mistress Arru, I have to tell you, you have wonderful bone structure. You know, there have been some remarkable advances of dermal hydration. Perhaps, if you'd like to make an appointment, with the right moisturizer and some glass eyes, I think . . . Say, does anyone else hear a bus horn?"

◆　◆

Yulric Bile emerged from the bus and stepped out onto the rubble that had once been the conference room. The dust was still settling, as were the pieces of plaster and live electric wires. A quick glance around the carnage revealed little evidence of those who had been sitting at the table, other than Arru's spiderlike hand poking above the wreckage and the mangled splat peeking out between the grill of the vehicle and the wall. Closer inspection revealed The Doctor Lord Talby's arm sticking out of it. And Yulric did inspect it. Closely. With a smile on his face.

Yulric turned to leave only to find Tezcatlipoca emerging from the shadows near the bus-sized hole in the wall. The two vampires stared at each other long and hard until the jaguar-headed creature caught sight of the Spaniard's red cloak crushed beneath a tire. The big cat gave an appreciative grin and stepped aside.

"You know that won't kill them?" Tezcatlipoca said in considered but perfect Latin.

"No," Yulric replied in Nahuatl as he passed, "but it hurts like hell."

Chapter 34

Once more, Yulric Bile, the elder vampire of ancient myth and terrifying legend, sat on the couch flipping through channels. With equal unconcern, he moved from a show about good-looking doctors who sleep with each other to one about good-looking lawyers who sleep with each other to another about good-looking police who sleep with each other. From there, he journeyed down the rabbit hole of reality TV, passing by the lives of self-proclaimed famous people, dangerous occupations, and ghost hunts wherein absolutely nothing happened. He decided to stop on the wrestling program where large-muscled men and women beat each other with chairs. It reminded him of his childhood.

"You know it's fake," said the small boy seated beside him.

"Yes," growled the vampire, remembering the conversation distinctly. The boy had taken particular relish in Yulric's angry disbelief, just as he took relish in reminding the vampire of that fact now. If Yulric Bile hadn't been feeling especially good, he'd have brained the child where he sat. At least, that's what he told himself.

The doorbell rang. Neither boy nor vampire moved from his position on the couch. It rang again. From upstairs, frantic footsteps made their way across the ceiling, down the stairs, and to the front door.

"Don't worry. I'll get it," said a harassed-sounding Amanda. She was currently half-dressed, which meant fully clothed but without makeup. The bob-cut black wig she'd put on was askew, and she quickly adjusted it before opening the door.

"Amanda," said the equally attractive black-wig-wearing blonde on the other side.

"Nora," Amanda greeted her friend with a little hug. "Come upstairs. I'm almost ready." She began to run up the steps. "Oh, could you grab my boots? They're in the closet."

"Sure thing," Nora called back. She opened the closet and paused. "Amanda!"

"Yeah."

"There's an old woman in your closet."

The quick pitter-patter of stocking feet running down-stairs could be heard. "She lives across the street." Amanda appeared in the entranceway to the living room. "What is Mrs. Havenaugh doing in the closet?"

"We needed her penmanship," muttered Simon quietly.

"What was that?" barked Amanda.

"He said they needed her penmanship," Nora tattled.

Yulric struck the boy upside the head for forgetting there was more than one person with extraordinary hearing present.

"Unenthrall her," said Amanda, now addressing the ancient vampire.

"At the commercial break," he muttered.

"Now!" Amanda repeated. She may not have been a vampire, but people who raise children develop their own super-hearing for sarcasm and passive aggression.

Yulric grumbled as he got up to release Mrs. Havenaugh from the closet. After the confused old woman apologized for wandering into the wrong house and left, he returned to the couch, where he and Simon proceeded to keep up appearances.

Fifteen minutes later, there was a knock but not at the door.

Knock, knock.

Yulric did not get up.

Knock, knock.

Yulric still did not get up.

Knock, knock. Knock, knock. Knock, knock. I can do this all night. Knock, knock.

Fine! Yulric stamped his way to the door, flung it open, and went back to his seat.

"Nice to see you, too." Catherine giggled.

"Catherine, is that you?" called Amanda from upstairs.

"Yes, hi," Catherine replied with a shout.

"Sorry, I didn't hear you knock," Nora apologized.

"Don't worry about it," Catherine told her.

"We'll be down in a sec, k?" Amanda said.

"No rush," Catherine answered. She entered the living room and sat down on the other side of Yulric. The vampire very pointedly did not acknowledge her presence, which in ancient-Saxon vampire translated to *hello.*

"Hello, Simon," greeted Catherine, talking across Yulric, who was very stiffly not looking anywhere but at the images of men in underwear jumping off ladders onto one another.

"Miss Dorset," Simon responded without looking up.

"What are you reading?" she asked, angling herself to glance at the open book on his lap.

The boy blocked the pages from view with his shoulder and arm. "Nothing."

"Okay," she said with a smile. She silently began watching TV.

So . . . wrestling, she thought.

Yes, Yulric replied, hoping that maybe if he responded she would be sated and go away.

Wow, this takes me back to my childhood, she said mentally. Yulric could not tell if she were being truthful or teasing. Likely both.

Who are you rooting for? she asked.

The villain, he answered shortly.

I think they call them heels, she corrected him.

I do not call them that, he spat.

Well, to each their own. She shrugged. The two sat in mental silence. Somewhere outside their heads, they registered the sound of Simon flipping pages in his booklet.

Who do you root for if two villains fight? she asked.

Whoever is the most devious, he answered, careful not to smile. Those were indeed his favorite matches.

Catherine drummed her fingers on the little blue handbag that matched the midnight-blue dress she was wearing. *What do you think of those characters that the fans seem to love, no matter how villainous they act?*

Yulric turned his head and looked at her. Her mouth, lightly coated in lipstick, pursed seriously, though the edges twitched upward ever so slightly.

Yulric turned back to the television and made a point to change the channel. *I despise them most of all.*

She gave him a playful nudge with her shoulder. He pretended she did not nor ever had existed, which made her laugh.

Two sets of footsteps descended the stairs, and a pair of nearly identical, black-haired beauties entered the room in matching backless long black gowns. Together, they looked like a movie starlet from the twenties and her image in a mirror.

"Catherine!" said Amanda in greeting. Catherine stood and they hugged. "You really shouldn't be sitting. You'll wrinkle your dress."

"Oh, like anyone's going to be looking at me with you two nearby. Hello, Nora."

"Catherine. You look well," said Nora.

"Don't I?" Catherine gave a playful twirl. "I nearly fit into myself again."

"Okay?" Nora agreed, not quite understanding the intricacies of how mind images and comatose bodies worked.

"We should get going. Nora can't be late for her own party," said Amanda with a look at her phone.

"Nonsense," Nora corrected her. "It's my party, which means it doesn't really start until I get there."

"Are you sure you don't want to come?" Amanda asked Yulric. "You'd be one of the first to see the preview for *Nights of Nora.*"

"Are *they* going to be there?" he asked, making sure to put plenty of extra bile on the word *they*.

"Arru and Adze," added Nora. "They're a thing now."

"Really?" Amanda exclaimed. "That's sweet. And horrifying."

"Isn't it?" Nora agreed.

"I will stay," Yulric said, flipping briefly to some atrocious program that filmed those with mental illnesses and then away to a sporting event with rules he did not understand, other than it involved a ball and running. "Someone needs to watch the boy."

Amanda's attention shot to Simon. He didn't quite hide his books in time.

"What are you looking at?" she asked him.

"Nothing," he replied. It was said with a complete lack of fear or guilt. He could have fooled a lie detector, but Amanda knew her brother.

"Give them," she ordered, her hand outstretched.

Simon pulled two items out from behind the couch cushions. One was an encyclopedia of ancient weaponry, the other a blacksmith catalogue he'd picked up at the Renaissance fair a few months prior.

She grabbed the latter from him and put it in her bag. "I thought I took this away from you already." She'd caught him trying to order things with her credit card. If he hadn't needed to call the blacksmith personally to put in special size requirements, she wouldn't have found out until, in both senses, the mail had arrived.

Simon shrugged in a noncommittal way that did nothing to reveal whether this was the same catalogue from before, which he'd stolen back, or one of several that he'd picked up and was hiding somewhere.

She turned on Yulric. "And this is how you are going to watch him?"

Yulric flipped the channel. "You would not have noticed had I not spoken."

Two sets of Linske eyes shot daggers at the vampire; one because he'd been betrayed, the other because what he'd said was true.

"I'll be back in the morning," she said with an undertone that read *to search your room.*

"Okay," Simon replied, not quite hiding his own subtext of *I have until then to hide them better.*

"See ya, short stuff," Nora said to Simon, kneeling down and giving him a kiss on the cheek. He hissed and squirmed more than a vampire confronted with a cross dipped in garlic.

Yulric could not help thinking that if he were truly so indifferent to girls, he would not care so much. Typical Puritan.

Nora and Amanda sashayed their way to the door, though Amanda stopped at the threshold of the living room to look back. The eight-year-old and the vampire, the perfect pair, each ideally suited to babysit the other. She knew her brother would not allow the ancient one to leave his sight, lest he rampage and ravage. And she knew the vampire would not allow anyone or anything harm her brother, lest he lose the chance to do it himself. It wasn't what she'd intended. It wasn't what she'd wanted. But it was what she had, and she could live with that. Emphasis on *live*.

Then again, her brother had said, "*We* needed her penmanship."

"You two behave yourselves," she called back, suddenly very worried.

"Yes, Amanda," intoned Simon in that singsong way of all children responding to authority.

Yulric grunted, which could either be recognition of what she'd said or a reaction to the alien-history show he'd found. With a final suspicious glance, Amanda headed for the waiting limo.

Catherine, too, hung back a moment, just long enough to wink before joining the others. It might have been nothing—a speck of dust, an eyelash, some misguided sign of affection. But then, why had she winked Yulric's eye?

"She knows," said the vampire.

"Will she tell?" posed Simon.

"No," Yulric replied.

"Well then," said the boy, hopping down from the couch. "Let's get to work."

Chapter 35

The full moon loomed large and orange on the horizon as its light hit an attractive figure standing outside the Pink House. The mysterious individual was slight, of average height and below-average weight, though possessing all the proper bulges that men's fitness magazines said it should.[66] Its clothes were perfectly tailored originals, which accentuated the wearer's physique, especially in the absence of a shirt. Red hair hung like wilting spikes, perfectly coifed and gelled to keep it in place through hurricane winds and all but the most intense lovemaking.

Vermillion took two notes out of the pocket of his sleeveless trench coat. One was tearstained and, to his acute vampire senses, reeked of loneliness and despair. It was addressed *To Rusty* in a hand he vaguely recalled belonging to that fat girl he'd known in his old life. She must have slipped it into his

---

66. Including that one.

pocket as he'd passed her at the club. He didn't even bother crumpling it as he threw it away.

The second note was an invitation he'd received in the mail. Pink ink on pink paper in a clear, looping penmanship, which undoubtedly belonged to a woman, had lured him away from his usual haunts with an enclosed picture and plenty of *x*'s and *o*'s. It was all topped off with a light mist of Chanel, which promised rather than requested a very pleasurable evening.

Vermillion inspected his shirtless torso in the moonlight. Bulging pecs and well-lined abs glowed impressively as he flexed them, though he could not help but rub a little more glitter lotion on, just to be sure. Then, in a graceful, athletic motion, he leapt up onto the second-story balcony and passed through the open glass doors.

He was slightly disappointed that the blonde he'd come to see was not lying in wait for him, half-naked beneath the satin sheets of the bed. However, once he spied the trail of pink rose petals leading out of the bedroom, he got over it. He followed them down to the first floor, through the living room and kitchen, and toward the basement, where he could tell they were joined by a multitude of white, scented candles. With one last check of hair and breath, he slowly and sensually descended into the cellar.

"What the . . . ? Who are you?" Vermillion cried in surprise when he reached the bottom.

"Simon," replied the little boy, pointing a crossbow at his sparkling chest.

Above Vermillion, the door slammed shut. A pair of steady footsteps followed his own path down the stairs. A pale corpse of a man appeared on the landing, an ancient battle-ax in his hand.

"Shall we begin?" Simon proposed.

As he approached the now-panicking Vermillion, a cruel, broken-toothed smile spread across Yulric Bile's face. In a world where vampires were heroes, he had finally found a way to be a monster again.

Acknowledgments

First and foremost, I need to thank my parents again for all their love and support, despite my continued insistence on impossible careers with no financial stability.

Thank you to the two women who were waiting in line ahead of me and discussing this thing called *Twilight*. You don't know who you are, and I sure as hell don't know who you are, but you started this.

Thank you to all those who read drafts and gave notes along the way: Clayton, Scott, Lindsey, and David. You monsters made me cut out so many jokes in the name of making this "better." I hope you're happy.

This book was destined to languish in the dreaded "writer's drawer" until that glorious day Tom and Veronica came on my iPod and told me the *Sword and Laser* was holding a book contest. So thank you both; this is your fault as well.

Thanks go out to my coworker Nicole for saying, "Yeah, you should enter that contest."

Thanks again to my friend Lindsey for saying, "No, she's right. Enter that contest, already."

Thank you, Adam, for being the first person with authority who showed actual enthusiasm about this project. You made me consider that I might actually have a chance.

Thank you, Inkshares, for (a) holding this contest, (b) putting out my book, and (c) existing.

Thank you, Avalon, for being my guide to the mysterious world of publishing.

Thank you to the team at Girl Friday Productions: Devon for keeping me in the loop and on schedule; my developmental editor, Lindsay, for challenging me to try little things like world building and "making sense"; my copyeditor, Jerri Gallagher, for having to contend with my love of commas and the adverbial clause; and all the others who spent their precious time on this earth working on a silly book about vampires.

Thank you to anyone I'm forgetting to thank. I'm sure there are many of you, and I'm sorry. Please don't hate me.

Finally, thank you, everyone who bought this book, both during the Inkshares contest and after. Without you, this would not exist. I hope you enjoyed it. If not, well, I'm sure there's something good on TV.

About the Author

Jim McDoniel is a writer of weird, funny things. A graduate of Minneapolis's Brave New Workshop and Chicago's Second City conservatory programs, he has spent several years writing mad science and molepeople for the sci-fi audio drama *Our Fair City*. This is his first novel.

List of Patrons

This book was made possible in part by the following grand patrons who preordered the book on Inkshares.com. Thank you.

Adam Gomolin
Alex Rosen
Barbara Melbourne
Barbara Pasmore
Bethany Martin
Catherine McDoniel
Chris Vanspeybroeck
Dan Donahue
Dann Tincher
David Thies
David Rheinstrom
Ele Matelan
George G. McDoniel
George M. McDoniel
Gabrielle Vanspeybroeck
Jeffrey Johnston

Joel Kolander
Kate McDoniel
Kylie Picco
Lawrence McDoniel
Lindsey M. Dorsey
Margaret McDoniel
Tammy Schaefer
Meghan McDoniel
Melissa Kittok
Randy Linn
Lyn Burke
Cheryl Donahue
Richard Simpson
Sandra Seeley
Thaddeus Woodman
Vernon Stackhouse

Inkshares

Sword & Laser is a science fiction and fantasy-themed book club, video show, and podcast that gathers together a strong online community of passionate readers to discuss and enjoy books of both genres.

Listen in or join the conversation at swordandlaser.com.